THREE QUICK AND FIVE DEAD

Gladys Maude Winifred Mitchell – or 'The Great Gladys' as Philip Larkin called her – was born in 1901, in Cowley in Oxfordshire. She graduated in history from University College London and in 1921 began her long career as a teacher. She studied the works of Sigmund Freud and attributed her interest in witchcraft to the influence of her friend, the detective novelist Helen Simpson.

Her first novel, *Speedy Death*, was published in 1929 and introduced readers to Beatrice Adela Lestrange Bradley, the heroine of a further sixty six crime novels. She wrote at least one novel a year throughout her career and was an early member of the Detection Club, alongside Agatha Christie, G.K Chesterton and Dorothy Sayers. In 1961 she retired from teaching and, from her home in Dorset, continued to write, receiving the Crime Writers' Association Silver Dagger in 1976. Gladys Mitchell died in 1983.

T0315614

VINTAGE MURDER MYSTERIES

With the sign of a human skull upon its
back and a melancholy shriek emitted when
disturbed, the Death's Head Hawkmoth has
for centuries been a bringer of doom and an
omen of death - which is why we chose it as
the emblem for our Vintage Murder Mysteries.

Some say that its appearance in King George III's
bedchamber pushed him into madness.
Others believe that should its wings extinguish
a candle by night, those nearby will be cursed
with blindness. Indeed its very name, *Acherontia
atropos*, delves into the most sinister realms of
Greek mythology: Acheron, the River of Pain in
the underworld, and Atropos, the Fate charged
with severing the thread of life.

The perfect companion, then, for our Vintage
Murder Mysteries sleuths, for whom sinister
occurrences are never far away and murder
is always just around the corner …

GLADYS MITCHELL

Three Quick and
Five Dead

VINTAGE BOOKS
London

Published by Vintage 2014

2 4 6 8 10 9 7 5 3 1

Copyright © The Executors of the Estate of Gladys Mitchell 1968

Gladys Mitchell has asserted her right under the Copyright, Designs
and Patents Act 1988 to be identified as the author of this work

This book is sold subject to the condition that it shall not,
by way of trade or otherwise, be lent, resold, hired out,
or otherwise circulated without the publisher's prior
consent in any form of binding or cover other than that
in which it is published and without a similar condition,
including this condition, being imposed
on the subsequent purchaser

First published in Great Britain by
Michael Joseph Ltd in 1968

Vintage
Random House, 20 Vauxhall Bridge Road,
London SW1V 2SA

www.vintage-books.co.uk

Addresses for companies within The Random House Group Limited
can be found at: www.randomhouse.co.uk/offices.htm

The Random House Group Limited Reg. No. 954009

A CIP catalogue record for this book
is available from the British Library

ISBN 9780099584025

The Random House Group Limited supports The Forest Stewardship
Council® (FSC®), the leading international forest-certification organisation.
Our books carrying the FSC label are printed on FSC®-certified paper.
FSC is the only forest-certification scheme supported by the leading
environmental organisations, including Greenpeace. Our
paper procurement policy can be found at
www.randomhouse.co.uk/environment

Printed and bound in Great Britain by Clays Ltd, St Ives plc

CHAPTER ONE

Under the Greenwood Tree

'She made no sound, no word she said –
Lowlands away my John!
And then I knew my love was dead –
My Lowlands away!'

---

(1)

It was the middle of the third week in November. There had been a sharply-glittering ground-frost in the early morning, followed by a clear and windless day, but by four o'clock a bluish, thin mist was beginning to fill the valley and blot out all but the tops of the trees.

At the Stone House just outside the village of Wandles Parva on the edge of the New Forest, Henri the chef and George the chauffeur were playing draughts. At the opposite end of the huge kitchen table, Zena, the kitchenmaid, was exercising her one and only art, that of cutting, at incredible speed, the paper-thin slices of bread and butter which accompanied her employer's cups of tea, while Henri's wife was making a pile of sandwiches, some of potted meat and others of cucumber, for the sturdier appetite of her employer's secretary.

The employer and the secretary were in the library. Dame Beatrice was reading; Laura Gavin was writing a letter to her husband. The curtains were drawn, the log fire had been replenished, the lights were switched on and the atmosphere was homely and restful. Laura finished her letter, looked it over, addressed and stamped it and said,

'I'll just about catch the post if I take this now. I'd rather like Gavin to get it in the morning. Hope he can manage the week-end.'

'Yes, indeed. Shall you take Fergus to the post-box with you?'

'Yes, he can do with a run.'

9

The Irish wolfhound, hearing his name, raised his noble and unkempt head from Dame Beatrice's bony knee. Laura had bought him; she also fed him, groomed him and took him out for exercise, but it was for Dame Beatrice, who seldom so much as spoke to him, that he had conceived a supreme and totally irrational affection. On her he had doted, from his first entrance into the Stone House, with an intensity of devotion which (as Laura pointed out) would have been excessive in a priestess of Isis confronted by the goddess in person.

The dog nominally belonged to Laura's son Hamish. A change of Staff at his preparatory school had seen the introduction of a young woman to teach biology, and it had been at her suggestion that the headmaster had agreed, with some reluctance, to allow the boys to keep their pets at school. Hamish had secured a long week-end from school in order that his mother might take him to Crufts. He would lose face, he maintained, if he turned up at the beginning of the summer term without a pet, and his choice of pet was a dog.

'You've got your pony,' Laura pointed out, 'and you keep him at the riding stables near the school.'

'But not *in* the school, mamma.'

Full of misgivings which proved to be fully justified, Laura had taken him to the dog show of his choice. Fergus was the result. The headmaster, gazing at the Gargantuan offering with horror, issued a kindly-expressed but unarguable veto, and Fergus was banished to the Stone House, where, as Assistant Commissioner Robert Gavin pointed out to his disconsolate son, he would be in the proud position of guarding the place against marauders and the women from attack.

'Although what he'll probably do,' said Laura privily to Dame Beatrice, 'is to take any intruders by the sleeve and lead them to all the stuff that's best worth pinching. What's more,' she added, 'at his present rate of progress, he'll eat us out of house and home in a fortnight.'

(2)

To reach the post-office from the Stone House involved following a country road alongside a stretch of common and then crossing a shallow watersplash by means of a wooden footbridge. The ground rose fairly steeply, after this, to the main village street with its shops. Beyond these lay the railway station and, about a mile further on, the golf-links.

When she had crossed the watersplash, Laura slipped the lead on to the dog's collar and, in obedience to her long strides, he padded along at her side until they reached the post-office. She kept him on the lead until they had passed the level-crossing and were in a winding lane. This brought them alongside the common again, this time on its south instead of its west side. Here she set the great hound free.

They had passed some old cottages and a small guest-house when Fergus became uneasy. He stopped and gave a whimpering sound which Laura had not heard from him before.

'Come on,' she said. 'It's not dark enough for you to be seeing ghosts.' The sun had set, and the mist and the purple twilight were an invitation and a reminder to her to get indoors to a lighted room, a log fire and her tea, but the dog remained immovable. Laura dropped a hand to his collar and could feel that he was quivering. 'Whatever is the matter?' she asked. For answer, Fergus backed away from her restraining fingers and, before she knew what was happening, he had given a howl and had set off across the common, following a glimmering path which led ultimately to some woods.

Laura called to him, ordering him to come back, but the great hound loped on, and she lost sight of him in the misty twilight. She took the same path and began to run, shouting his name, but the darkness was closing in, so she gave up the hopeless chase and retraced her steps, feeling sure that the dog would return in his own good time. She was, however, surprised that he should have turned disobedient to her voice, for, although he was only half-trained, he was extremely docile.

'You've been a long time,' said Dame Beatrice mildly, when Laura returned to the library.

'Our lunatic hound felt the call of the wild and galloped off across the common. I went after him for a bit, but I lost him in the murk. I expect he'll come home when he's hungry.'

This was not the case. Six o'clock, his feeding time, came, but there was still no sign of his return, and at half-past six, when Dame Beatrice was about to go up to change for dinner, Celestine's threatened hysteria caused Henri to send Zena to the library to ask whether somebody should go out in search of the dog.

'George said he'd be very pleased to try and find the doggie, mum, and has got a torch in the car like a young searchlight, he says, mum, to shine him on his way.'

'No, no,' said Dame Beatrice. 'George is to have his supper. The dog will come to no harm.'

'I'll go out there myself after dinner,' said Laura, 'and give vent to a couple of yells. I wonder what came over him? He can't have been chasing rabbits. I say! You don't think he would worry the Forest ponies? I thought I heard some about.'

Dinnertime came, and the after-dinner coffee, but the dog had not come back. Laura finished her coffee and went upstairs to change into slacks. Her bedroom window overlooked the common and, obeying a sudden thought, before she went downstairs she took a previously unused dog-whistle out of a drawer and, with a superstitious thrill as she remembered a frightening episode in *Ghost Stories of an Antiquary*, she opened the window and blew the high-pitched pipe. Then she picked up an electric torch and went downstairs. She found George waiting respectfully in the hall.

'Madam's orders, madam,' he replied in response to Laura's question, 'and we are requested not to proceed to any great distance beyond the house, as madam thinks the mist may be getting thicker.'

'Which it is,' said Laura, when the front door was open and the mist swirled in against the light from the hall. 'Our torches are not going to make a lot of impression on this.'

They went as far as the beginning of the path across the common, then Laura stopped. She took the dog-whistle from her raincoat pocket and blew again, then she stood still and they waited and listened, but there was nothing but the cold, wet mist and the darkness. She blew once more and they waited for a response which did not come.

(3)

Laura needed very little sleep. Once before midnight, and twice between two o'clock and six, she crept downstairs and blew the dog-whistle again. At half-past seven, just after sunrise, she dressed, slipped out of the house and took the path across the common. The ground was damp but the mist was dispersing in the face of a light wind. She crossed a culvert over a ditch and then the path climbed to a slight eminence. Here she stopped and looked about her. On either side stretched the common, but in front of her, a mile or more away, there was a considerable wood.

The only evidences of life upon the common, so far as her keen eyes could make out, were half a dozen ponies and a donkey. Of the dog there was no sign. Laura, taking advantage of the long, gradual, downward slope which lay before her, made at a round pace, half-walking, half-running, for the woods. Between them and the common ran the pretty little Lymington River, crossed here by a broad plank bridge. She stopped to look at the clear brown water and then blew the whistle again and entered the woods.

On one side of the broad path which formed a clearing there was a fenced enclosure barred off by a gate. The Forestry Commission's lorries had churned up a muddy road on the other side of the fence. Laura leaned on the gate and listened, then made up her mind to try the enclosure before she explored the open woodland.

The foresters' lorry-track was so soft and deep with mud that she left it almost at once for an ill-defined path on higher ground which marched with the boundary fence. Here she was constantly impeded by trailing blackberry stems and, at the frequent dips in the path, she had to find a way round pools too wide to step across or jump over. There was about a mile and a half of the enclosure. At the far end was a cattle grid, then another bridge over the river, a stretch of grass interspersed with oaks and, beyond all this, the main Bournemouth road which by-passed the village and went over the level-crossing.

Laura looked at her watch. By this time breakfast would be on the table and she was hungry. She had no mind to footslog it into the village and over the watersplash to reach home, so she pushed her way back along the path by which she had come. Unwilling to give up the hunt until she had made every attempt to find the dog, she fastened the gate of the enclosure behind her and took the broad path through the woods, stopping occasionally to call, whistle and listen.

Giant beeches, with, here and there, a mighty oak, bordered the path on her left; the wooden fencing of the enclosure and a shallow, mossy ditch were on her right. Behind the great trees, however, there was a tangle of brushwood and thorn, and, beyond this, a further wilderness of gorse and waist-high, dead, brown bracken.

The broad path ended, as Laura had known it would, in a vast pond, shallow, but with treacherously muddy fringes. Here she had to turn back. Without hope, before she did so she called the dog by name, repeating it several times. Then she stood still and listened, for, from some distance away, she thought she had heard a despairing howl.

She called again and was answered. Certain that, roughly at least, she had located the sound, she ran back along the path, repeating the call, and then, tripping over the roots of a beech-tree in her haste, she plunged in among the undergrowth along a narrow track which suddenly opened up among the gorse and bracken.

Her heart missed a beat as she saw a foot, with a woman's shoe on it, sticking out from behind a gorse bush. At the same moment Fergus sidled up to her and licked her hand.

(4)

Laura ran all the way back to the Stone House and precipitated herself into the morning-room where Dame Beatrice was seated at breakfast.

'Will you please ring up the police?' she gasped. 'The big boys, not the village cop. I'm too breathless to talk to them myself. Tell them to come here at once. It's urgent.'

Dame Beatrice asked no questions, but went immediately to the telephone in the hall. After a very short time she returned and poured Laura a cup of coffee.

'They'll be here as soon as they can, but they have some distance to come,' she said, 'so you have time for breakfast before you need talk to the Superintendent.'

'Not sure that I want any breakfast.' Laura had recovered her breath. She drank the coffee and passed her cup for more. 'It's the German girl. I think she's been murdered. I'll have to lead the police to the spot. It might take them ages to find it on their own. Fergus is guarding the body and won't come away.'

'I will accompany them and disengage the dog. I should not wish him to bite a policeman. Now please have some breakfast. We may have a long morning before us and nothing is to be gained by feeling faint from hunger. No, don't tell me anything more until you have eaten.'

Laura contrived to grin, and Dame Beatrice, motioning her to sit still, went to the sideboard to serve her. Laura discovered that, in spite of shock, she was still hungry.

'I suppose you'd like to hear the details now,' she said, pushing aside an empty plate and helping herself to marmalade. 'Well, here's what happened.'

'You think it is the German girl from whose mother you bought Fergus?' Dame Beatrice enquired when she had heard the tale. 'And you think that when the girl realised she was in danger, she blew the dog-whistle which you say is on a cord around her neck?'

'Well, *something* caused Fergus to vanish into the mist last night. It looked to me as though somebody had tightened the cord, too. There's a deep red mark on her neck.'

'That would have induced unconsciousness, no doubt. I suppose you are perfectly certain she was dead?'

'Good gracious, yes. No doubt about it at all. You'll know what I mean when you see her.'

This came about in due course. At Laura's suggestion, since it would mean shortening by at least a mile the walking-distance between the Stone House and the body, she drove her own small car, with Dame Beatrice as passenger, and led the police car, containing a superintendent, a sergeant and a uniformed constable, through the village and along the main road until they left the two cars on a wide stretch of grass at a stone bridge and followed the path through the wicket-gate which marked the boundary of the enclosure.

At the other side of the enclosure Laura led the way confidently through the woods to the spot where she had come upon the body. The dog was still on guard. Dame Beatrice went up to him, while the Superintendent halted his men and Laura stood back.

'Come, Fergus,' said Dame Beatrice. 'You're a good dog and you must be hungry.' She held up a string bag she had brought with her. 'Come along with me. It's all right now.' The dog pricked his ears and looked into her face. 'Good boy. It's all right now,' she repeated encouragingly. The great hound sighed and slowly got to his feet. She led him away from the body and along the path until they came to the river. On the bridge she spread out the food, patted him, and stood beside him. The dog looked up at her again, then, trusting her soothing voice, he ate voraciously, then padded to the edge of the stream. When he had finished drinking, she said to him firmly, 'Stay'. Then she returned to the others.

'Perhaps you'd take a look at her, ma'am,' said the Superintendent, who had worked with Dame Beatrice before, 'and let me have an opinion as to time of death, then Gunter can stay here until we get back with our own doctor and the photographer. We'll need a stretcher to move her when they've done their stuff. Can't get an ambulance up here.'

Dame Beatrice looked at her watch and then knelt beside the body. The time was a quarter to eleven.

(5)

'But it doesn't make sense,' said Laura, when she and Dame Beatrice were in her little car and on the way home with Fergus lying along the back seat.

'What doesn't make sense, child?'

'The time of death. You say that poor Miss Schumann has been dead for at least twenty-four hours, so why would Fergus have answered her whistle only about seventeen hours before I found her body?'

'The answer would be obvious if we could take *rigor mortis*

as an infallible guide, but that, as you heard me remark to
the Superintendent, we cannot.'

'But would even a tricky thing such as *rigor* be as much as
seven or more hours out?'

'It is unlikely, certainly. The conditions were normal,
although I doubt whether she was killed in those woods. There
were no signs of a struggle. It would be most interesting to
find out how the dog managed to locate the body.'

'The only thing which would have made Fergus leave me,
and go careering off like that, was that somebody he knew
even better than he knew me must have called him. He couldn't
have heard a voice, otherwise I would have heard it, too –
you've said yourself that my hearing is pretty acute – therefore
he must have answered a dog-whistle, a sound he can hear,
but I, like most other adults, can't. Even so, a dog-whistle
only carries for between three and four hundred yards, or so
Mrs Schumann told me when I bought Fergus, and the body
was a good two miles from the edge of the common where
Fergus left me.'

'Of course, we have no proof that Fergus heard a dog-whistle
at all, have we?'

'No, and I don't believe Fergus would have answered any old
whistle, any more than he answered mine this morning. Mrs
Schumann had a special call for her dogs. She told me so. She
wouldn't teach it to me because she said it would be best to
train Fergus to answer my own personal note which, so far,
I haven't invented. So what about that?'

'If you will pursue your present line of argument, you will
come to a conclusion. Whether that conclusion is correct, only
time, of course, will show. By the way, when the police have
done the necessary things with the body, the Superintendent
will want a word with you.'

'As many as he likes – not that I can help him very much.
You don't suppose Mrs Schumann murdered her daughter and
then whistled up Fergus, do you?'

The Superintendent arrived at the Stone House at half-past
two. He and Laura were old friends. He knew of her husband's
position at Scotland Yard and he was honorary uncle to her son
Hamish.

'Before I take a statement from you, Mrs Gavin,' he said, 'I suppose I'd better warn you that you may be wanted at the inquest. This death is so clearly a case of murder that I don't suppose anything but identification and the medical evidence will be taken, but, as you found the body, there might be something . . .'

'Right. I should have attended the inquest in any case.'

'Yes, so I supposed. Now, perhaps I could have your account of how you came to find this Miss Schumann. You knew her, I gather?'

'Oh, yes, in a way. I bought my dog from her mother last April. I did not know her before that, and that is all I had to do with her. As I told you, she lived with her mother over at Leveret Copse, on the other side of those woods. Mrs Schumann breeds Irish wolfhounds and clumber spaniels. She exhibited at Crufts this year. That's how I got the address.'

'We've been to see Mrs Schumann to break the news and get her to identify the body. She's terribly cut up, of course. This daughter was one of twins. The other is a son and, according to his mother, not much good. She poured out quite a lot, but, naturally, she was in such an upset state that we shan't take official notice of what she said until after the inquest. By then we shall have made more enquiries. Now, what can you tell me about your discovery of the body?'

Laura gave him her account of this, and the reason for her early-morning walk.

'Interesting about the dog running off like that,' he commented, when she had told her tale. 'You assume he was obeying a signal that he recognised?'

'I'm sure he was, but there's a mystery attached to that. I thought Miss Schumann must have whistled him up when she found she was being attacked, but, if she has been dead as long as Dame Beatrice thinks, she couldn't have whistled up the dog at something after four last evening, which is when Fergus left me and went galloping off across the common.'

'How far does a dog-whistle carry?'

'That's another point. Not more than three to four hundred yards. Fergus couldn't possibly have heard it from where the body was found. I worked that out. But, if he didn't get the message, what could have made him go careering off like that?'

'It's a bit of a mystery, Mrs Gavin. The likeliest thing is that he went off for some other reason, and not because he had heard the whistle.'

'Well, whatever it was, it led him to find the body and mount guard over it.'

'You say you bought him in April. How old is he?'

'One year and a bit. Of course, I intended to buy a tiny puppy. It was for Hamish to show off at school. But the puppies were too young to be weaned, and Hamish refused to wait and, in any case, had fallen heavily for Fergus and implored me to buy him. Mrs Schumann was quite keen to sell, and accepted my offer of a lower price than the dog was worth because her daughter had had a great disappointment over him. It appeared that she'd picked Fergus out, bought him from her mother and reared him herself. She intended, when he was fully trained, to give him as a birthday present to her fiancé, but the fiancé wouldn't have him and they had a row and she was left with the dog, and, I've no doubt, was pretty sick about it.'

'So there was a fiancé, was there? And a quarrel about the dog? That might prove interesting. I don't suppose you've met the young man?'

'She did not mention his name. I don't even know whether he is an Englishman . . .'

'Ah, yes. The Schumanns were naturalised, but were of German origin. Mrs Schumann has given us the family history. When you found the body you probably spotted something rather interesting which might also prove useful to us. Skewered over the heart by a thin steel knitting-needle was a piece of paper. The bushes had kept it pretty dry in spite of the mist, and on it you may have read: *In Memoriam 325.*'

'Yes, I saw it, of course. One couldn't miss it,' said Laura. 'Could it tie up with the Nazis, do you think? Revenge for a death in a concentration camp – something of that sort?'

'It's possible. I don't want to worry Mrs Schumann more than I can help until she's had time to recover from the shock, but, of course, I'll have to question her again. She told me a good deal, none of it very useful, but I may be able to get something more when she's had time to think things over.'

(6)

The medical evidence given at the inquest was straightforward and uncompromising. The girl, whose age was given as twenty-four, had been garrotted by a piece of stout cord which would certainly have rendered her unconscious, and death had been made certain by manual strangulation, the murderer having used his right hand and having gripped his already unconscious victim from the front. There were no fingernail scratches, but there were a series of small bruises on the victim's throat, and there was the impression of a thumb on the right side of her neck, high up and under the lower jaw over the cornu of the thyroid. The jury had no doubt about returning a verdict of murder. That it was by person or persons unknown went without the necessity of a formal statement, but the jury added it, all the same.

(7)

Assistant-Commissioner Robert Gavin had taken week-end leave, but had returned to London on the day before the inquest. He was sufficiently intrigued by the murder of Karen Schumann, however, to come down again to the Stone House on the following Friday. He and Laura had a bedroom and a sitting-room of their own there, and a flat in Dame Beatrice's Kensington home, for both of which he insisted on paying rent. He would have preferred, with masculine independence, to have had a place of his own, but Laura, good-naturedly obedient to most of his wishes, had remained obstinately non-co-operative over this one, her place (as she had pointed out very firmly when she agreed to marry) being with Dame Beatrice, whose company she preferred, she added relentlessly, to that of anybody else on earth, and Gavin, who, in his silent, undemonstrative way, adored her, had given in, wisely realising that she meant exactly what she said. Fortunately, his own admiration for Dame Beatrice was boundless and it was certainly comforting to know that his headstrong, comely, imaginative wife was in her care and, while so situated, would do as Dame Beatrice told her, and not get into too much mischief.

On the Friday following the inquest, therefore, he was again at the Stone House and at a quarter to five was taking tea in the library with the ladies.

'No more news, I suppose?' he asked. 'What happened to the girl's mother?'

'She seems to have found herself a lodger, a Spanish girl who is at a south-west Redbrick, but wants to be in the country on Saturdays and Sundays and for the Christmas vacation,' said Laura. 'She speaks four languages, including German and English. It seems an ideal arrangement. With the money she pays, and a little money the daughter left, and the cash for the dog-breeding, Mrs Schumann thinks she will be able to manage quite nicely, so that's a blessing.'

'And how is Phillips getting on?' asked Gavin.

'I do not think the Superintendent's enquiries are leading anywhere at present,' said Dame Beatrice.

'Oh, well, it's early days yet,' said Gavin. He fondled the dog's rough head. 'Why can't you talk?' he asked him. '*Did* somebody whistle you up that night?'

'If so, the man must have been on horseback and led the dog on,' said Laura. 'The body was a good two miles from where Fergus left me, and the whistle doesn't carry more than, at the very most, about one-eighth of that distance.'

'A horseman moving forward and enticing the dog to follow him all the time, while he himself kept a few hundred yards ahead?' said Gavin thoughtfully. 'A bike would have been just as good, and a great deal quieter. You can hear a galloping horse quite a long way off.'

'I did hear the sound of hooves, but I thought it was the Forest ponies. They're always about on the common.'

'Have you suggested this theory of yours to the Superintendent? It's quite a likely one. I certainly think he should pay considerable attention to the fact that the dog went belting off like that. After all, Fergus is a sober sort of fellow, aren't you?' he added, putting his hand under the dog's chin and looking into his eyes. 'The thing is, *if* this is what happened, was the horseman or cyclist the murderer? If so, why did he want to lead the dog to the body? It seems a lunatic sort of proceeding. Was the girl pregnant, by the way?'

'No,' said Dame Beatrice, 'nor was it the usual pattern of a sex crime.'

'No Jack the Ripper stuff?'

'There had been no attempt at anything but manual strangulation preceded by the tightening of a ligature – in this case, a stout cord attached to a dog-whistle – which must have induced unconsciousness.'

'Dog-whistles do seem to insist on presenting themselves, don't they? Any other unusual features?'

'Yes, indeed,' said Laura. 'Fastened to the body by a very thin steel knitting-needle was a bit of paper marked *In Memoriam 325.*'

'Well, that means Phillips has something to go on, at any rate.'

'The bit of paper had been taken from one of those very ordinary unlined writing tablets that you buy with envelopes to match, and, although probably there will be fingerprints on it, they won't match with any on record, I wouldn't mind betting. As for the number 325, well, it probably means nothing except to the murderer,' said Laura.

'It must have meant something to the victim, too, and that might indicate that it means something to somebody else – her mother, maybe. Is there any chance of my having a word with her, I wonder? I'll mention it to Phillips, of course. It's his case, not mine.'

'Superintendent Phillips will be delighted to hear from you, I am certain of that,' said Dame Beatrice, 'and Mrs Schumann will be more than willing to help in any way she can.'

Both these statements appeared to be true. Gavin drove to the police station and was received with a welcoming smile and given a comfortable chair in Superintendent Phillips' office.

'Good of you to come, sir,' said Phillips. 'I haven't much doubt that we shall call in the Yard, and I've suggested to the Chief Constable that it ought to be sooner rather than later.'

'If you've decided on it, then I agree that the sooner the

better,' said Gavin. 'But why? You've handled cases of murder before this. What seems to be the trouble?'

'Well, sir, it seems to me that we need to know a lot more than we do about the poor young woman's background. It seems to me that the motive for the crime must lie somewhere in her past.'

'Interesting that you should think so. What I wondered was whether you'd have any objection to my having a word with the mother. I don't want to interfere, of course.'

'Only too glad, sir. She's quite co-operative and seems to be getting over the shock all right, but, unless you can get more help from her than we've been able to do, I doubt whether you'll feel justified in spending your time on her. There's only one thing, sir. This kind of crime is apt to be one of a series, so I hope we catch the joker good and quick!'

'One of a series?'

'The complete absence of motive worries me, sir.'

(8)

Mrs Schumann was a fair-skinned, well-scrubbed woman of about forty-five to fifty. To make Gavin's questioning appear to be less formal than it actually was, Dame Beatrice invited her to lunch at the Stone House, a bidding which she accepted with pathetic and touching gratitude.

'So kind, so kind,' she said. Dame Beatrice introduced Gavin first as Laura's husband, and then, in fairness, informed the visitor of his position at Scotland Yard, but added that he was not directly concerned with the local police investigation.

Mrs Schumann appeared apprehensive at first, but Gavin's charm and good looks soon overcame her suspicions, and the talk, during lunch, was on various subjects of general interest. After lunch, however, Mrs Schumann herself introduced the subject which Gavin had been wondering how to approach. She asked Dame Beatrice whether it would be necessary for her to attend the resumed inquest.

Dame Beatrice passed the question across to Gavin who replied that he thought it probable that she would be wanted as a witness.

'So I shall be required to answer questions?'

'Not difficult questions,' he assured her.

'Such as? . . . You see, I am anxious with the police, even after all these many years of safety. We had to leave Germany soon after the Nazis began to gain power.'

'But you're not Jewish, are you?'

'Oh, no, but my husband was a man of liberal views, a scholar, a pastor, and one of the first, I think, to realise what was coming. So, while it was possible, we left our country. My husband died five years ago. I am glad he did not live long enough to know what has happened to my Karen.'

There was silence for some moments. Dame Beatrice thought it kinder to her guest not to allow it to go on too long.

'You were wondering what kind of questions would be asked you at the resumed inquest,' she said. 'Well, one of the things they may want to know is whether your daughter had any men friends apart from her fiancé.'

'Karen was a good girl, a very good girl. She made friends, men and women friends, at the University, of course, but they are scattered now. She wrote to some of them, I believe, but since she has become engaged to Edward she has not any men friends. It was not at the University that she met him. He is of a serious mind and would not care for her friends, perhaps. Students – well, you know of them, some serious, some light-hearted, but all without much money.'

'And has her fiancé much money?' asked Gavin.

'Oh, no, nothing but his salary from the school where he and Karen were teachers. Karen taught German and French, Edward teaches history and something he calls R.K.'

'Religious Knowledge,' said Laura. 'They used to call it Scripture in my young days; Divinity, if you wanted to sound up-stage.'

'I see. He taught this R.K., he said, from the historical point of view, but, as I did not know what it was, this meant nothing to me. Well, Karen came down from the University and took this teaching post, and Edward was one of the senior masters. Soon, between him and Karen, there was an under-standing which turned into an engagement, but Edward did not wish to marry until they had saved money for a house. My husband, you see, brought very little out of Germany, and also left us almost nothing when he died.'

'You say that – er – Edward—'

'Mr James.'

'That Mr James was one of the senior masters,' said Gavin. 'Does that mean he was older than your daughter?'

'Oh, yes. It gave me a little anxiety, that. He was the same age, almost, as myself. Karen was only twenty-three when they became engaged, and I asked myself what would happen when Karen was forty-three and Edward sixty-three, and so on.'

'Twenty years is not a serious difference in age, if the parties are compatible,' observed Dame Beatrice.

'You think that? You may be right. But what I asked myself is how to find this compatibility. Karen was fun-loving, fond of dogs, liking to dance and go to parties. Edward is serious, learned, does not wish to love dogs, does not like to dance, thinks parties a great waste of time and money. He is ambitious. Karen had no ambition, either for him or for herself. I was anxious about them.'

'Yes,' said Gavin, 'but, after all, there must have been something. I mean, what do you think attracted your daughter to him in the first place?'

'He is interested in the things her father was interested in. Karen loved her father very dearly. His every wish was her law, always, always.'

'You think, then, that she substituted Mr James for her father?' asked Dame Beatrice. 'It is likely enough. I have met such situations many times in the course of my work. But, if she found satisfaction in this substitution, I do not see why you were anxious.'

'I felt she was not awakened, my little Karen. I thought that, some day, perhaps sooner, perhaps later, she would realise that a father-figure is not a lover-figure. You understand me?'

'Perfectly.'

'And you agree?'

'With some reservations, yes, I do, especially when, as in this case, there is some conflict in tastes and outlook. Did you ever speak of these things to your daughter? Did you talk matters over with her and offer her any advice or give her any warnings?'

'Oh, yes, but you could not move Karen once she had made up her mind, so me, I made the best of things, and hoped in my heart that she would be very happy. Edward is a good man. That I know.'

'Did your daughter mind when you sold Fergus to me?' asked Laura, struck by an aspect of the matter which had not occurred to her before.

'Mind? How so?' Mrs Schumann sounded surprised.

'Well, I understand he was your daughter's dog. Hadn't she bought him from you and trained him?'

'Oh, that! When she found that Edward did not want him, she gave me permission, well, she almost begged me to sell him. I gave her the money you paid me, of course.' She looked down at the huge dog, who was asleep in front of the fire, and stirred him caressingly with the toe of her shoe. Fergus raised his noble head, banged the floor politely with his tail, and went to sleep again. 'He is a good dog. He found my Karen in time, before her body was too long above the ground. He knew where to find her. He guarded her. He is a very good dog. He wanted her to be found quickly.'

'Yes,' said Gavin, 'that's a point which I find of very great interest. How could he have known where she was?'

'They have instinct, these hounds.'

'Enough to lead them more than two miles from home to find a body which nobody but the killer knew was there?' He spoke with what Laura reproachfully thought of as brutal directness.

'It is mysterious, that,' agreed Mrs Schumann. 'But what do we know of animal instinct?'

'That it is held by some psychiatrists not to exist,' said Dame Beatrice. 'They believe that behaviour pattern, not instinct, is a more suitable and exact term to employ. So you cannot offer any explanation of Fergus' conduct in leaving Laura's side and bounding away some two miles to where your daughter's body lay?'

Mrs Schumann shook her head.

'He was very fond of my Karen,' she said. 'More than that I cannot explain. But now, please, the inquest. What more will they want me to tell them?'

'Possibly whether your daughter had enemies and whether you knew of any recent quarrel between your daughter and her fiancé.'

'Two only, all the time they knew one another, and both quarrels so stupid, and not recent, either. One I think Mrs Gavin knows about. I told her when she bought Fergus for her son.'

'Oh,' said Laura, 'you mean when your daughter wanted to give her fiancé the dog, and he refused to accept it?'

'Yes, that was the second quarrel. Karen was deeply hurt and disappointed when Edward would not take the dog. She had been training Fergus very carefully and keeping him a secret, and she could not understand that Edward did not want him. She was hurt, and the hurt made her angry. Edward was not very kind or tactful, either. He said that he did not "have time to look after a wretched dog". He was needing all his evenings and week-ends to study for his further degree. He had his B.A. but he had set his heart on obtaining, ultimately, his doctorate in divinity. There was what one calls in English a flare-up.'

'And the first quarrel?' asked Dame Beatrice. 'You mentioned there were two.'

'Ah, that first quarrel! So unnecessary and so ridiculous, I thought. Karen came home one Friday evening and said to me: "I have had a big row with Edward. What do you think he called me? He called me his misguided little Aryan! What do you think of that, mother? His misguided little ARYAN! As though I have ever made any distinction between Germans like yourself" – she was born in England and claimed to be English, you see – "and Germans who are already Jews!" Oh, she was at boiling-point, my little Karen. Of course, she got over it later. Edward had meant it as a joke, he said, not to offend, and he apologised.'

'Why misguided, I wonder?' said Dame Beatrice. 'And why Aryan? It is not a word that Englishmen would often use.'

'Is it not?' said Mrs Schumann. 'I asked Karen what had occasioned him to taunt her, and she said they had been arguing about religion.'

'A bold thing to attempt when one of the protagonists is a student of theology,' commented Dame Beatrice, 'but it might account for his having referred to your daughter as misguided. I suppose you know of no enemies she may have made? Was there anyone on the school staff, for instance, whom she had offended in any way?'

'I know of none. Karen was good-natured and friendly. Whenever I went to functions at the school she seemed to be quite well-liked.'

'When did you speak to her last?' asked Gavin. 'Did she live at home?'

'Yes and no. By that I mean the school, it was too far for her to go day by day, so she and two other young teachers – women, of course – shared a flat, and Karen came home after school closed on Fridays and returned to the flat on Sunday evenings. Then, of course, she was with me at holiday times, so my house was her home.'

'Yes, I see. So the last time you saw her was on a Sunday?' said Gavin.

'Until I was taken to identify . . .'

'Yes, yes, of course.'

'It makes me sad now to think that I might have seen her again before – before—'

'Please don't distress yourself, Mrs Schumann. I am only asking a question which is almost certain to be put to you at the next enquiry,' said Gavin hastily.

'I know. I am sorry. You see, there was a day's holiday given to the school, following the annual Speech Day. A half-holiday was normal, but there was also another half-day due, so the teachers decided to have the two put together to make a whole day, and Karen telephoned to ask whether I would be at home, but on that day I was going over to Ringwood with my dog Monty to give service to a thoroughbred clumber bitch. It was all arranged, and the bitch was on heat since ten days, so I could not break the contract. If I had not gone, I ask myself, day and night, whether I might not have saved my

Karen's life, for it was on that day, so I understand from the doctors, that she must have died.'

'I wouldn't worry about that,' said Gavin. 'Whoever killed your daughter would have done so, sooner or later, anyway. It was no unpremeditated action, you know. The message left on the body proves that. It was a deliberately planned murder. You can't explain the message, I suppose?'

'The very kind policeman, Superintendent Phillips, asked me that. It means nothing to me, nothing, nothing at all.'

(9)

'So there's a fiancé,' said Gavin, 'and he's at the same school as the dead girl, and they had a holiday on the day she was killed, and they'd had quarrels. Well, he'd be the man for my money, if I were in charge of the case. I think I could bear to take a look at him. I'm going to find out from Phillips when it will be convenient for us to have another little chat, and at the same time I'll get him to introduce me to the school. I wish you'd come with us, Dame B., so that we can compare notes afterwards.'

The headmaster received them in a reserved although courteous manner, but, understandably, was not at all happy about the unwelcome publicity given to his school by the murder of one of his staff.

'Of course you must see Mr James if you wish,' he said stiffly, when Gavin had produced his credentials and had introduced Dame Beatrice (quite truthfully) as a psychiatrist attached to the Home Office, 'but I feel sure that he has already given all the help he can, and he is in a sad state about the whole dreadful business, as you may imagine.'

'I quite realise that, but I'd be glad of a word with him,' said Gavin. The headmaster rang through to his secretary and a few minutes later there was a tap on the door and a tall, middle-aged man wearing pince-nez and a sober, dark grey suit came in and inclined his head with rather affected courtesy towards his headmaster. He then stared in hostile fashion at the visitors. When the headmaster, having performed the introductions, had gone out, Edward James said coldly,

'I presume I may sit down.' He took a chair. Gavin looked him over.

'I expect you're tired of being questioned,' he said, with a sympathetic smile, 'but I've talked to Superintendent Phillips here, and there are just one or two points which Dame Beatrice and I would like to touch on.'

'I don't know anything more than I've already told the police,' said James, even more coldly than before.

'I am not sure that what we would like you to tell us has any bearing on what you have told the police,' said Dame Beatrice.

'For instance?' He raised supercilious eyebrows.

'For instance, why did you once call your fiancée a misguided little Aryan?'

'I have no recollection of having called her any such thing.'

'No, it was some time ago, I believe. However, according to her mother, Miss Schumann took exception to the phrase.'

'Did she? I don't remember anything about it.'

'Why did you refuse her present of an Irish wolfhound?'

'The obvious reason. I didn't want the dog.'

'She must have thought you did, surely?'

'I suppose that, knowing she and her mother bred the things, I felt it incumbent upon me to show interest. Her mother, I ought to warn you, has never approved of me as her daughter's prospective husband, so I think you would be well-advised to treat any statements she makes about me – derogatory statements are what I mean, of course – with very great caution.'

'We are accustomed to treat all statements made to us with very great caution, Mr James, until we are able to get them checked and confirmed,' said Gavin.

'Oh, yes, of course. I beg your pardon. You will realise that I have been through a difficult time.'

'Quite so. Can you ride a horse?' asked Dame Beatrice.

'A horse? No. I have never taken riding lessons.'

'A bicycle, of course?'

'I imagine most people can ride a bicycle. I sold mine years ago.'

'You teach history, I believe, and something which is called R.K., and is connected with the Scriptures.'

'Quite so. I am hoping to take a degree in theology. As to history, well, I have to follow the school syllabus, of course, but my special interests lie in the events and trends of the sixteenth century.'

'Ah, yes, the Reformation and the emergence of the Puritans. So a date in the fourth century, for instance, would mean little to you?' suggested Dame Beatrice.

'355 to 363 would suggest the reign of the Emperor Julian the Apostate, would it not?' replied James.

'Ah, yes. He, I suppose, would occur to you, as would the sixteenth century you mention, in connection with your theological studies, as well as with history. But you may feel that we are wandering from the point. Now I am sure that you have given Superintendent Phillips a fully satisfactory account of yourself for the time in question. What I did not ascertain from him is whether you know how Miss Schumann spent that day.'

'Oh, he asked me that, and I told him I did not know. On the previous afternoon we had had an Open Day followed by the prize-giving, and the principal speaker asked, as we had anticipated, that there should be a half-holiday on the following day. As it happened, we were also due for a half-day in honour of a pupil who had saved a child from drowning, but *that* came in the middle of G.C.E. so the headmaster had put it off and we asked to have it added to the prize-giving half-day. I myself spent the day in the school library, but I have no idea what Miss Schumann did. The girls who shared a flat with her might know.'

'Thank you very much indeed, Mr James,' said Dame Beatrice, 'for your co-operation. Perhaps...' she looked at Gavin, who shook his head to indicate that he had no further questions to ask... 'perhaps we should now take leave of the headmaster.'

James left them. Gavin looked at Phillips and raised his eyebrows. Phillips shrugged.

'Not much gets past *his* guard, I'd say,' he remarked.

'What was all that about dates in history?' asked Gavin.

'A shot in the dark,' Dame Beatrice replied.

'That missed its mark?'

'There are more artful dodgers than have found fame in literature, dear child.'

Phillips looked gratified.

'Just what strikes *me* about that smooth alec,' he said. 'He can bear watching, I reckon.'

Dame Beatrice said,

'His response to a question he could hardly have been expecting was prompt, and very much to the point.'

'Well, I suspect him,' said Phillips sturdily, 'but I can't get any further forward. He answers all questions smoothly and even promptly, as you say, otherwise he claims that he doesn't know or can't remember. He's even got an alibi of sorts.'

'Oh, yes. He claims that he spent the day in the school library. Can that be confirmed?' asked Gavin.

'No, sir. I tried the head caretaker, but he, the boilerman and all the women cleaners had the day off as well. As you probably know, sir, as soon as the school closes of an afternoon, the women cleaners come in, but, as the school was not in session that day, no cleaning took place and the boilers were stoked last thing on the prize-giving afternoon – the school uses coke – and then were let die down, according to the official orders applying on such occasions and on school holidays and at the week-ends. All the head caretaker knows is that Mr James went to him as soon as the day's holiday was decided on and told him he would be working in the library that day, probably all day long, and so he would want it left unlocked, so that he could get in.'

'How soon, I wonder, *was* the holiday decided on?' asked Laura. 'I thought the school governors and the Ministry's Inspectors had to be given a fair amount of notice if the school was to be closed for any reason.'

'It seems the teachers were able to take the half-day extra – the one asked for at the prize-giving – for granted. It was a long-established custom. So they were able to give due notice all right, because they had the other half-day coming to them anyway.'

'Why should James have had to ask to have the library left unlocked? I should have thought all keys would be hung up on little marked pegs in the secretary's room or in the Staff Common Room,' said Laura, 'so that they were handy.'

'I wouldn't know that, Mrs Gavin. I'll make a note of it. It adds a further bit to my suspicions of James. It makes it look as though he wanted to bolster up his alibi by mentioning it to the caretaker. It's an old trick and doesn't always work. However, it may be that the caretaker himself keeps the school keys and locks up the staffroom and the secretary's office.'

'He's bound to have a set of keys, of course,' said Laura, 'and if the secretary's room, or wherever the staff's set of keys is kept, was locked, as, of course, it might well be – yes, yes, it's my nasty, suspicious mind running away with me.'

'It's a point, all the same, Mrs Gavin,' said Phillips weightily. 'What was to stop him just hanging on to the library key from the day before? That would have been the sensible thing to do. Then he need not have bothered the caretaker at all.'

'I suppose you've had a word with the two girls who shared the flat with Miss Schumann?' said Gavin.

'I have, sir, but they weren't much help. They took a bus-ride into Bournemouth, had a slap-up lunch and went to the big cinema near the Lansdowne with a couple of fellows they know who teach at the art school. They have no idea what Miss Schumann was planning to do.'

'It's a bit odd she telephoned her mother to ask whether Mrs Schumann was going to be at home that day,' said Laura. Phillips cocked an eye at her.

'How do you mean, Mrs Gavin?'

'Miss Schumann went home every week-end. She took an interest in her mother's job. She *must* have known that her mother was due to go over to Ringwood with that champion clumber to give a service. It's big money when you've got a good dog at stud. Her mother is bound to have told her about the contract, so why phone her to confirm the arrangements? To make sure the house was going to be empty, do you think?'

'So that she and James could have the day to themselves there?' asked the Superintendent. 'It's a thought. And, of course, she wasn't killed where you found her. We're certain of that. On the other hand, knowing the other two girls were going to be out, she could equally well have invited the boy-friend to the flat, couldn't she?'

'Ah, but there might have been prying eyes there – the other flat-dwellers, you know – whereas her mother's place is a detached cottage with lots of garden all round it and no company but the dogs and puppies.'

'And there he could have killed her, and nobody the wiser? Something in that. But then he'd have had to get the body to those woods, and the difficulty there is that there's no access from the main road except for that small wicket-gate. The main gate the woodmen's lorries use is on the woodland side, you'll remember, not so very far from where she was found. He couldn't have brought a car in from the main Bournemouth Road.'

'How do the lorries manage, then? They must get into the enclosure somehow, and that means there must be a way round,' said Gavin.

'Yes, there is,' said Dame Beatrice. 'They use the old gravel road which skirts the common and comes out about three miles away from my house. If a car of almost any size, from the largest to the smallest, took that way, it could get into the woods and almost opposite the spot where the girl was found. Of course, if there are no traces of a car having been parked there . . .'

'Yes, well, we had a good look at that gravel road, ma'am, but the autumn rains have made the rut-marks so soft and deep that there's not much hope of tracing any individual wheelmarks. Anyway, James doesn't own a car. Of course, he may have used Mrs Schumann's, I suppose.'

'Not if Mrs Schumann had taken her prize dog over to Ringwood in it,' Gavin pointed out.

'I think Miss Schumann must also have had a car,' said Dame Beatrice. 'It would be a most tiresome cross-country journey by rail from the school to her home, and would involve a very long walk after she had left the train.'

'So it might have been simplicity itself for Miss Schumann to have picked James up somewhere near the school and driven him to her mother's house,' said the Superintendent. 'Well, well, well! So, if we can break this school-library alibi of his, we shall really be going places! '

'Keep on plugging away,' said Gavin, grinning. 'I shall watch your progress with considerable interest. Seriously, though, Phillips, I've a feeling you've pin-pointed your man all right. It's a question of proof now. The only thing that bothers me is the apparent absence of motive. Surely the two quarrels we've heard about were not of sufficient importance to lead to murder? They seem to be old hat, anyway. Do you think the girl was pestering for marriage, but that James wanted to oil out? Could he have preferred murder to a breach-of-promise case?'

'I'm not sure a woman teacher would bring a breach-of-promise case,' protested Laura. 'Think how some of the beastlier kids and their horrible mums would react! I mean, however much you might vengefully soak the man for his dough, you must still look a pretty average fool if you let him walk out on you. Personally, placed in such a position, I should emigrate to New Zealand.'

'No, you wouldn't,' said her husband. 'You'd throw the defaulting bloke into the nearest pond and then jump on his stomach. But, to proceed, there's one other possibility I've just thought up. Don't I remember we were told that Miss Schumann had a brother?'

'Yes, named Otto,' said Laura. 'His mother doesn't seem to have a good word to say for him.'

'No, she hasn't. She mentioned him to me,' said Phillips. 'Always dunning her and his sister for money, or so Mrs Schumann says.'

'Have you tailed him?' asked Gavin. 'A known bad hat is always worth a second glance, I feel.'

'He's a merchant seaman, sir. Second officer on a biggish ship which picks up cargo anywhere between Spitzbergen and the Canaries. Calls regularly at Poole and Southampton. There doesn't seem any reason to think he's mixed up in any way with his sister's death. He certainly couldn't have been her murderer. He was at sea. We've checked that very carefully.'

(10)

'So that is the verdict of us all,' said Laura, when they had left the Superintendent at his office and were on their way back to the Stone House. 'I feel it's a bit premature, considering that we haven't a shred of proof.'

'I know,' said her husband. 'All the same, I can't help feeling, as I told him, that Phillips has got the right pig by the ear. As I see it, it's one of the classic cases of a lovers' quarrel followed by a manual strangulation – a routine set-up and all according to the formbook.'

'I agree that Edward James is an immediate and obvious suspect,' said Dame Beatrice, 'but I should be far happier about your suspicions of him if the young woman had been pregnant.'

'She may have *told* him she was,' said Laura. 'That trick is well known if a girl is trying to blackmail a man into marrying her when he doesn't really want to, or if he isn't in too much of a hurry to put up the banns. In this case, if James intended to get his doctorate before he married, the girl would have had to wait a jolly long time, and that means she might have been prepared to try pretty rough methods to hurry things up a bit. After all, he isn't exactly young enough to have all his life before him.'

'There's another aspect to that, though,' said Gavin. 'James might have known that a story about a baby on the way could not possibly be true. As a theological student – and, I should be inclined to guess, a pretty cold fish at that! – he may be the most virtuous and abstemious of men, in which case he'd have known she was simply telling the tale.'

'But suppose she had told him that she was pregnant by another man,' pursued Laura. '*That* would have put the cat among the pigeons all right.'

'My dear girl, do stop using that famous imagination of yours! These are but wild surmises. No. If I may put forward a less picturesque point of view, my guess would be that if James is guilty – and remember that we have absolutely nothing to go on in supposing this, and are probably being disgracefully unfair to the chap – but *if* he is guilty, then I do agree that he and the girl must have had some far more serious row

than the two quarrels the mother knows about. Either that, or
he simply tired of his engagement and couldn't face breaking it
off. Some fellows would sooner murder a woman than have
her weep on them.'

'A good thing I'm not given to shedding tears, then!' retorted
his wife. 'It seemed to me that you spoke those trenchant
words with a wealth of sinister meaning behind them.'

'I shall go to see Mrs Schumann again,' said Dame Beatrice.
'Another heart-to-heart talk with her seems indicated. She *must*
know more about this than she has told us.'

(11)

For a reason known to herself but kept from Laura, Dame
Beatrice did not ring up Mrs Schumann, but descended upon
her, accompanied by Laura and Fergus, at three o'clock of a
cold, cloudy, windy afternoon in December. They found her
in one of the outhouses where she kennelled her dogs. It stood
at one end of their exercise-paddock and was a reasonably
roomy building and, although weatherproof, it was dilapidated
and somewhat ramshackle in appearance. A man was with
her. They were in animated discussion until Mrs Schumann
was aware of the visitors.

'I'm so sorry,' said Dame Beatrice, insincerely. 'I am afraid
we come at an unfortunate time.'

'No, no, my dear friend, not at all. You have brought Mrs
Gavin's dog, I see. How nice. You want me to look him
over, perhaps?'

'Oh, no, I don't think so. He seems in good health.'

'His spirits are high?'

'Well, he's a quiet dog, but he seems quite happy with us.'

'Leave him with me, and please to go inside. It is cold for
you to stand about here. The back door is open, if you will be
so good. Please to make yourselves at home. Mrs Gavin
knows the way. She has been here before.'

As it was very chilly in the garden, Laura took Dame
Beatrice into the cottage. The back door led into a scullery
which opened into the kitchen. On the kitchen table were
several printed folders. Laura glanced at them in passing. Dame

Beatrice gave them closer attention. They were from firms which specialised in properly constructed kennel ranges.

Beyond the kitchen a passage led to the front door, and a couple of rooms opened off this passage. Laura tried the first of these, but it was locked. The second opened into a small sitting-room smelling strongly of dog.

'I wonder what's hidden in Bluebeard's Chamber?' said Laura lightly. 'It wasn't locked when Hamish and I bought the dog.' She walked to the window and looked out. The view was of a tangle of bushes, a large paddock of unkempt grass and a half-dozen pine trees. Beyond the fence was the Forest. The cottage was a lonely one and a possible inference was that in some part of it or its grounds Karen Schumann had been murdered. 'I wonder where it happened?' Laura went on. 'In that locked room, do you think?'

'We do not know for certain that this is where the murder took place,' remonstrated Dame Beatrice. 'We know only that it was not where the body was found. The room is locked, I expect, because it was the domain of the master of the house and has been kept sacrosanct since his death.'

'Oh, no, I don't think that's the reason, because I remember we were given tea in there. It was smothered in books from floor to ceiling. I had a look at them while Mrs Schumann was getting tea. A pretty mixed bag they were, as regards publication dates, but mostly they were hardly up my street – commentaries on the scriptures, sermons and such – all, or nearly all, in German. I imagine that they belonged to the husband, as you say. He was some kind of parson, wasn't he?'

'Mrs Schumann referred to him as a scholar and a pastor.'

'Wonder how long she'll be?'

They were not kept waiting. Mrs Schumann came in and apologised for leaving them alone.

'A man I needed to see. In early spring I re-house my dogs. Expensive, but what? The old sheds, they almost fall down. Besides, nobody will buy my puppies if the place looks so bad. Bad housing, bad dogs, they think. Dame Beatrice, you are a psychiatrist. You believe I am right?'

'Yes, I think most people are influenced by their surroundings,' Dame Beatrice agreed. 'But, tell me, do you not keep a kennel-maid?'

'No, no, I manage. My Karen helped me at week-ends, in holidays, and so on. Otherwise I manage. My husband did not help, but I did not mind, and now that he is dead, Karen also, the more I have to occupy me the better.'

'I understand that very well.'

'Edward tells me you have been to see him. Did you find him helpful? I fear not.'

'No, we did not find him helpful, although I am sure he did his best. We wondered whether he could help us to reconstruct the manner in which your daughter spent that day. The school was on holiday . . .'

'Yes, I told you.'

'You also told us that your daughter telephoned to find out whether you would be at home.'

'So. And Edward? He was not with Karen. He spent the day with his work.'

'Studying in the school library, it seems.'

'It would be like that, yes. Sometimes I think he paid too little attention to my Karen. It is not a good plan to neglect a young woman. She went out with her friends, perhaps?'

'If you mean the two young women with whom she shared a flat, Superintendent Phillips has been to see them. It appears that Karen did not go out with them, and gave them little indication of the way in which she proposed to spend her day.'

'If only she had been with them, or with Edward or with me, this terrible thing would not have happened!'

'Who can tell? You cannot suggest any reason why your daughter should have telephoned you?'

'It is simple, is it not? To find out whether I should be at home, but, as I told you, I could not be at home that day. Perhaps you think I should have broken my engagement with my client? But that is not the way to do business.'

'Of course it is not. Neither is it the way in which I think you should have acted. All I meant was that I should have thought your daughter would have known that you had this engagement, and therefore would not be at home that day.'

'I cannot remember whether I told her of it or not. I think

most likely I did not, as I would not have expected her to be on holiday that day, and therefore my engagements would not concern her.'

'I see.' There was a pause, and then Mrs Schumann said,

'One thing I do not understand. The doctor at the inquest says that my Karen died not later than at midday.'

'I came to the same conclusion myself when I first saw the body. I would have put it even earlier than the doctor did, but, of course, it is not possible to make an exact estimate.'

'But at what time in the morning, then, did she leave her flat?'

'The police, no doubt, have worked that out, but their findings may not tally with the evidence of the two young women who lived there.'

'You do not know this? – what the police have worked out?'

'I have not asked.'

'But, to arrive in those woods, only a few miles from where you live, she must have set out as soon as it was light. Why would she wish to start so early? She was a girl who loved her bed. Often and often she has said to me that she looked forward to Saturdays and Sundays because she had no need to get up early to go to school. As for the holidays, well, I would be half-way through my morning before she would come downstairs.'

There was another pause. Mrs Schumann gave the impression that she was waiting for a remark from Dame Beatrice, but, although the latter realised this, she remained silent, and it was Laura who spoke next.

'As it was only an extra day, I expect Karen wanted to make the most of it,' she said, 'and perhaps there wasn't much peace with the other two bustling about and getting ready to go off to Bournemouth.'

'She had her own room. She could shut herself away from them,' said Mrs Schumann. There was another pause, and then, in a brisk tone, she added, 'And now, my good friends, you have come for a purpose. *Is* there any news?'

'No, I am afraid not. Our purpose is to ask you to answer even more questions, if you will,' Dame Beatrice replied.

'But of course! Ask me anything you want. I will do anything which will help to find out this madman who has killed my Karen.'

'A madman? Do you mean that literally, I wonder?'

'I think so, yes. She was so kind, so peaceable – who but a madman would harm her? Ask your questions. I will answer everything.'

'The first question I was going to ask will be irrelevant if your guess is correct and the guilty person is insane.'

'Ask, all the same.'

'Well, can you – have you thought of any possible explanation of the note which was found on the body?'

'I see it always before my eyes. *In Memoriam 325.* So strange. But to me it means nothing at all.'

'Nor to me. You were shown it, were you?'

'By the kind Superintendent, yes. He asked, as you have done, for any explanation I could offer. Was my daughter born in March of nineteen twenty-five? I say no, how could she be when at death she was barely twenty-four? Had I relations who sent people to concentration camps, maybe? I am indignant. I say no, not possible. Have I copy of Tennyson's poems? I say no. I ask why. and I learn that the title of a very long poem is *In Memoriam* by Alfred, Lord Tennyson. English lords are strangely named. Why not, I asked the kind Superintendent, Lord Alfred Tennyson? He does not know.'

Dame Beatrice explained the difference between Alfred, Lord Tennyson and Lord Alfred Tennyson and then asked, somewhat abruptly,

'What did you think of your daughter's engagement to Mr Edward James? – apart, I mean, from the difference in their ages?'

'I thought only that it was likely to be a long one. I was sorry. I wanted Karen to marry soon, but I was afraid that, with Edward's ambitions and his cold nature, she might have to wait until she was more than thirty, and then Edward would be more than fifty.'

'Did she herself contemplate a long engagement?'

'I hardly know. If I mentioned it she would change the subject and, after all, her engagement to Edward was by her choice, not mine.'

'But, apart from the difference in their ages and the fact that it looked like being a long engagement, you saw no reason to disapprove of it?'

'No. Why should I disapprove?'

'Why, indeed? You mentioned your son the last time we talked to you. Did *he* approve of his sister's engagement?'

'Only to try to borrow money from Edward. As I told you, Otto is not a good boy.'

'Does he come to see you between voyages? We heard that he is a merchant seaman.'

'Sometimes he comes, more often not. He wastes his pay as soon as he lands and then – off again.'

'Did the brother and sister get on well together?'

'As I said before, Otto is not a good boy. However, I believe he was fond of Karen in his way.'

'When I asked you what you thought of your daughter's engagement, you did not sound particularly enthusiastic about it. Won't you tell me what you *really* think of Mr James?'

'I do not care for him much, but he was Karen's choice, not mine. I have no reason to dislike him, but I think he is a cold man, calculating, ambitious – so unlike my dear husband.'

'And yet, when we saw you last, I thought you compared the two. Mrs Schumann, I am about to ask you a difficult and perhaps a painful question.'

'Nothing matters now.'

'Well, you mentioned two quarrels between Mr James and your daughter. Have you ever wondered whether perhaps there were other disagreements about which your daughter did not confide in you?'

'You mean that the police suspect Edward? Oh, but that is nonsense! Edward is a most religious man.'

'How often did Mr James visit your daughter here at weekends?'

'How often? Oh, one in three or four. He needed his weekends for study. Karen understood that. I did not mind. It was better to have her to myself.'

'A very discouraging interview, don't you think?' asked Laura, when she and Dame Beatrice were on their way home. 'I noticed that you took little part in it.'

'Thought I'd better keep out, in case I said the wrong thing. It's clear she has no suspicions of Edward James, though, isn't it? One thing – you didn't let on, I noticed, that we don't believe Karen was killed where she was found. Is it a police secret?'

'The Superintendent did not say so, but perhaps the fewer who know the better.'

'Mightn't it have stimulated Mrs Schumann to tell us a bit more if you'd told her? While she thinks Karen was killed in those woods she's naturally flummoxed. She can't understand her having travelled so far in the time at her disposal.'

'There is something in what you say. What I want to know now is how Mrs Schumann herself spent the day.'

'But we know that, don't we? She took her dog – oh, look here, surely you don't suspect *her* of killing her daughter? I believe I asked you that some days ago.'

'I would like to know from what hour, and for how long, the house was empty that day. I also want to know at what time Miss Schumann left her lodgings that morning and whether she used the car we suspect (but do not know for certain) she possessed. You see the point, of course?'

'I think so. You believe that Karen Schumann was up to something, and that, if we knew what it was, we might make a guess as to why she had to be killed. But surely you were on the ball when you suggested that Karen and Edward James may have had a more serious row than the two Mrs Schumann mentioned. That being so, it's very likely that the couple planned to meet at the cottage, knowing that Mrs Schumann would be out, in order to get things settled privately, where nobody would disturb them. My guess is that, instead of a reconciliation taking place, there was a further bust-up, and James – perhaps without really intending to – did for Karen by choking her with the dog-whistle cord and then, not being sure whether she was quite dead, finished off matters by strangling her.'

'It is a tenable hypothesis. How do you account for the comparatively early hour at which this would have taken place?'

'Oh, that's simple. Karen knew the time when her mother was leaving the cottage with the clumber spaniel, but had no idea of when to expect her back, so she played it safe, as she thought, and arranged to get there well before lunch-time.'

(12)

The next interview was with Phillips.

'So you got nothing new from Mrs Schumann,' he said. 'I've had another talk with her, too, and I'm sure she's told us everything she knows. I've done my best to jog her memory, but I can't get anything more, and I'm pretty certain there's nothing more to get. The only extra bit of information she supplied doesn't help at all, so far as I can see. I asked her for the address of the house to which she took her stud dog. It's in Ringwood. I went there, and confirmed with the people that the service was given, and seems to have been successful.'

'At what time did Mrs Schumann get there?' Dame Beatrice enquired.

'As near as they could remember, at about a quarter past twelve. The dog was eager, the bitch willing, so matters did not take long, and Mrs Schumann stayed to lunch and drove herself and the dog away again at half-past two or thereabouts.'

'So she would have left her cottage . . .'

'Roughly speaking, at eleven forty-five, and would have got back to it at about three.'

'So her daughter must have been dead before she left her cottage.'

'I suppose so,' said Phillips, staring. 'Surely, ma'am, you're not suggesting . . .'

'I am not suggesting anything, Superintendent. I was merely passing a remark.'

'Well, they say a nod is as good as a wink to a blind horse, ma'am, but I really don't think we need to nod *or* to wink in *that* direction.'

'Of course not,' said Dame Beatrice meekly. 'Have you traced the telephone call which was said by Mrs Schumann to have come from her daughter to inform her of the day's holiday and to ask whether she would be at home?'

'Oh, yes, the call has been checked. It was made from the school. The school secretary made it at Miss Schumann's request, but, of course, she did not stay in the room to over-hear what was said.'

'Is the school telephone in the secretary's room, then?'

'The one the staff use, yes, ma'am. There is an extension to the headmaster's study, of course, and another to the care-taker's house.'

'One would think Miss Schumann would have put her own call through. What was the object of getting the secretary to do it, I wonder?'

'There was a reason for that, ma'am. The secretary now does all the ringing up, whether it's school business or staff private calls. It seems that the teachers are supposed to pay for private calls, but last year there was such a discrepancy between the telephone account and the money in the kitty – the headmaster and the secretary keep a careful record of all their own calls – that the head decided that staff using the telephone were neglecting to brass up, so now the secretary does all the ring-ing up, keeps a list of staff calls and charges them up each month when the teachers get paid.

'An admirable system.'

'I've also had another go at the young ladies, Miss Tompkins and Miss O'Reilly, both teachers at the school, and with whom Miss Schumann shared the flat. They can't add anything use-ful, either. They simply repeated what they had told me before. Miss Schumann was up earlier than they were, and had told them previously that she was going to spend the day with her mother. That must have been a lie, of course. She must have known that her mother was going to be out.'

'In other words, she meant to spend the day in some way that Edward James – if his story about spending the day study-ing is true – wasn't supposed to hear about at second hand,' said Laura. 'That sounds to me like a clandestine assignation.'

'Quite so, Mrs Gavin. But, if there *was* a man involved, we haven't found hide or hair of him yet. As for James's alibi, well, Dame Beatrice might like to have a word with the school caretaker. Mansfield is his name. He's not much good to us, though, I'm afraid. As the school was closed, he had a long lie-in and wasn't breakfasting until ten, so if James claims to have been in the school library from nine o'clock onwards,

Mansfield isn't any good as a witness either for or against him.'

'I see no point, at present, in contacting the caretaker,' said Dame Beatrice, 'but I shall speak to the two young women and should be grateful for Mr James's address. At what time did he return there on the day of the murder, I wonder?'

'He went back for his tea at five. He had told his landlady that, as there would be no school dinner that day, he would get some lunch in the town. There are only two places where he could have done that. One is a pub which does snacks at the bar but no set lunch; the other is the Rosebud Café. I've made enquiries at both, but with no useful result. The pub is always three deep round the bar counter at midday, so they're not prepared to swear to anybody, and although they agree they *might* have noticed someone who wasn't one of their regulars, they don't remember anybody in particular. The café is in the same boat – always full for lunch, and two out of their three waitresses are newcomers. I even tried the local fish and chip place, but you can guess what the answer was there! Queues all down the street from a quarter to twelve until two o'clock! They couldn't swear to anybody.'

'Well, we'd better get weaving,' said Laura, when she and Dame Beatrice were on their way home, 'and the best of British luck to us, say I! '

This pious wish lived up to its ironic nature. The visits produced nothing helpful whatsoever, and Edward James was left with an alibi which he was unable to prove and which the Superintendent was equally unable to break. Miss Schumann had possessed her own car and had been alone when she took it out of the lock-up on the morning in question. It had not been returned, and was later found abandoned, after a police search, among other parked cars on the edge of Rhinefield, just outside Brockenhurst.

'From there,' said Laura disgustedly, 'all the murderer had to do was to walk to Brockenhurst Station.'

'A description of Edward James was given at the ticket office there, and to the porters, but with no result. His landlady said he was wearing the dark suit in which he habitually went to school, but she did not actually see him leave the house because she was having her own breakfast when she heard him close the front door, so, of course, he could have changed his clothes before he went out,' said Dame Beatrice.

'Taking a chance, wasn't he?'

'No. The Superintendent found out that the landlady always has breakfast in the back room basement, so she never sees Mr James leave the house when he goes to school.'

'So we're no further forward. Oh, well, it will soon be Christmas. Hamish breaks up at school tomorrow, and Gavin says he can take a few days' leave. If you can spare me, I think I'll take them both to see my parents. What did you think of doing?'

'I am still considering which of three invitations I shall accept, so make your plans. What does Hamish want for Christmas?'

'To have Fergus to sleep in his room.'

'Fergus,' said Dame Beatrice, 'knows the murderer.'

Laura looked startled.

'He's actually seen him, you think?'

'I am sure of it.'

Laura shook her head.

'As always, you speak in riddles,' she said, 'and yet I can see that you're serious. Anyway, *may* Hamish have Fergus in his bedroom while he's here?'

'Why not? Will Hamish wear a kilt, if you're going to Scotland?'

'He hasn't got one.'

'He is tall for his age, and of pleasing build. He would set one off, I think. It shall be my Christmas present to him if he would like that.'

'I should think he'd adore it, and he's just about the right colouring to wear the Menzies white and red. You'll have to spring him a *sgian-dubh* to stick in his stocking, and a crest brooch for his bonnet. Great gosh! He'll be insufferable! I can just see him swanking around!'

CHAPTER TWO

Blow, Blow, Thou Winter Wind

'Farewell and adieu, all you fine Spanish ladies,
Farewell and adieu to you, ladies of Spain,
For we've received orders for to sail to old England,
But we hope in a short time to see you again.'

---

(1)

'Well, I'm damned! He's done it again!' said Gavin. He and
his wife had spent Christmas and Hogmanay with Laura's
people, and then, leaving their son with his maternal grand-
parents, they had gone on to Skye to spend the last few days
of Gavin's leave together and without encumbrances.

They were staying in a small hotel on the north-east coast
of the island and so were avoiding the seasonable snow which
had fallen heavily on the mainland mountains. From the windows of the lounge, and from their bedroom, the prospect was
of a sweeping bay with two small islands, a long promontory
which sheltered the hotel and, beyond the promontory, the
misty, snow-covered mountains of Wester Ross.

Here and there, on the green uplands which surrounded the
bay, were the white houses of the crofters which had succeeded
the ancient dwellings, stone-built, thatched, the roofs weighted
down with stones, in which, less than two generations ago, their
ancestors had lived.

Behind the hotel, on the opposite side of the rough and
narrow road which came north from Kyleakin, Sligachan and
Portree, and which followed the coast from Staffin and
Flodigarry round to Uig and southward, rose mountainous
cliffs of bare and stratified rock. To the south was the extraordinary formation called the Quiraing. To the north, at the
turn of the road, Duntulm Castle, the ruined stronghold of
the MacDonalds of Skye, was perched on its tremendous head-
land.

Gavin had not brought his car. They had hired transport in Kyleakin and would return to the ferry by the same means. They had walked, keeping to the roads, (for the mountain mists were treacherous), they had eaten, they had lazed and they had gone to bed early and risen late. It was an ideal existence, from their point of view, and Gavin's exclamation had cut into a silence of repletion after breakfast on the fourth morning of their stay.

'Done what again? And who has?' asked Laura. Her husband handed her the newspaper, now several days old, which the manager of the hotel had offered him and which he was perusing more for courtesy's sake than because he wanted to read stale news.

'This strangler of young women,' he said. Laura read the paragraph he pointed out, and then re-read it before she handed the paper back.

'It's what Phillips was afraid of,' she said. 'Do we have to go back straight away?'

'I see no reason why we should. It isn't anything to do with us officially. Wonder whether Dame B. knows about it?'

'Doubtful, I think. She never reads the newspapers at Christmas time, and, anyway, she isn't at home. She went to spend Christmas with Carey Lestrange on his pig-farm in Oxfordshire. The paper doesn't tell us much, does it?'

'It tells us quite enough. The same district, the same kind of death, the same verdict at the inquest.'

'Another foreign girl, too.'

'Ah, well, Miss Schumann claimed to be English. Both her parents were naturalised.'

'I think I'll telephone Mrs Croc.'

'Why? She won't thank you for interrupting her holiday. Time enough for her to take action when you're both back at the Stone House. What about hiring a car and taking a run to Dunvegan this morning?'

'In this rain? Not worth it. I'd rather take a walk and get really wet.'

'You have strange tastes.'

'They are what endeared you to me when we met. No, stop scrapping! Remember I'm the mother of your son!'

'Talking of which, it sometimes seems to me that we've rather put all our eggs into one basket. What do you think?'

'Please yourself. But I don't admire your description of our child.'

'Got your marriage lines to back up your opinion, too, haven't you? Anyway, I'm not sure Hamish would approve of a baby sister.'

'Why sister? I'd be just as likely to have another boy.'

'Ah, no,' said Gavin, 'Shakespeare knew the answer to that one. "Make thee another self, for love of me, That beauty still may live in thine or thee." '

Laura stared at him.

'So you really mean it,' she said.

(2)

Dame Beatrice had been back in the Stone House for less than two hours when she received a frenzied telephone call.

'Oh, my dear friend, it is I, Karla Schumann. I am in dreadful trouble. Please may I come to see you? I am so sorry, but I am so desperate.'

'Of course you must come,' said Dame Beatrice. 'What about lunch tomorrow?'

'I am distracted!' announced Mrs Schumann, as soon as she was shown in on the following morning. 'First my Karen and now that wicked Otto! Perhaps you have heard?'

'No. I've been away since just before Christmas and have not seen a newspaper or listened to any of the broadcast programmes except for the Queen's speech. Let us have lunch first, and then you shall tell me all about it.'

'I am not anxious for food,' said Mrs Schumann. She did some sort of justice, however, to the meal prepared by Dame Beatrice's French chef and, as soon as coffee had been brought in and there would be no further interruptions, she told her story.

'Where to begin? I tell you I am distracted! I cannot think. I do not know where to turn. Help me! Please help me! '

'What has happened to Otto? Why do you call him wicked?'

'Nothing happens to him yet. I think he has murdered Maria Mercedes Machrado.'

'Your lodger? The student from the University?'

'*Ja, ja!* I will tell you. You know already that I have this young girl at week-ends and for the College vacation at Christmas. Well, she seems a very nice girl, quiet, modest, anxious to give no trouble, but soon I am finding her not so nice. All I ask of her is to make her bed and be a little tidy, that is all – no dusting, no polishing of furniture, no floors – and to be indoors on Fridays and Saturdays by ten o'clock. That is all I ask, and also, if she have boy-friends to call, that they shall please to be out of the house by ten o'clock, when I like to go to bed. Not unreasonable, I think?'

Dame Beatrice doubted whether the modern young would think it not unreasonable, but she made no comment.

'Well, at first, the first two week-ends, all is as I wish. Nobody could be nicer, quieter, more considerate. I am very happy – well, as happy as I can be without my Karen. Then comes the end of the term – a concert, a dance and so on. Maria asks whether I will mind, for once, some late hours. Well, I am not so pleased, but I remember that Karen also keeps some late hours on these occasions, so I say to Maria, "But how will you get home so late? I cannot come and meet you at the station, and it is a long walk in the dark for you, and it may be raining." '

'You did not think of meeting her with your car?'

'No. I do not care to drive at night in case there may be ponies on the roads. Not all the Forest is fenced. This she understood. She shrugged her shoulders and said that she would be brought back after the dance and that I need not worry and must leave the front door unbolted. She had, of course, a key, in case I should be out at any time during Saturdays, so that she would be free to come in and go out as she pleased. That was an arrangement from the beginning.'

'And you agreed to leave the front door unbolted?'

'I was not very happy to do it. Karen's death has made me

very nervous. However, I agreed, and asked Maria please to come in very quietly, as I am a light sleeper and would not wish to be awakened. Well, if she is to be escorted home, I tell myself that there is nothing for me to worry about, but I ask her how late she expects to be. She says she does not know. It is her first term at the University and she has no idea how long are the College functions.

'Well, she returns, as usual, to College on the Sunday, and I continue to tell myself that there is nothing to worry about, but I find myself worrying, all the same, so on the following Thursday I telephone the number I have been given in case Maria is taken ill at week-end and will not attend lectures, and I ask about the function on Saturday and at what time it will be over. They reply that I am making a muddle. There is no function on the Saturday because all the students went down already on the Tuesday.'

'Dear, dear!' said Dame Beatrice, feeling that some comment was expected. 'How very disconcerting for you!'

'What to do, I ask myself. I am *in loco parentis* to this naughty, deceitful girl. How shall I act for the best?'

'Ring up her College landlady and ask what is going on, I imagine.'

'Exactly so. That is what I do.' There was a pause. Dame Beatrice ended it.

'And?' she asked. Mrs Schumann clasped her hands together and groaned histrionically.

'The landlady says that on Tuesday a ship's officer calls for Maria and says he is my son and that he will take her home, as he has shore leave for Christmas.'

'So *that* is how Otto comes into the picture! But how did he know where to find her?'

'Ah, that! When he finds out about Karen he is given leave of compassion to come and see me. It was after the inquest and after the funeral, of course, but he has heard nothing until the ship docked at Poole. I will say for him that, for once, he comes straight home, not even waiting to get drunk, and is very sympathetic and kind. That is on the Friday, when Maria comes to me the same evening also.'

'I see. That is how they met.'

'Well, as my duty to her, I take Maria aside and warn her, because I see that she likes him. "Otto," I say to her, "is not good with women." '

'*To* women,' said Dame Beatrice, in automatic correction.

'Please?'

Dame Beatrice apologised and then explained.

'How did Miss Machrado take your warning?' she added.

'Maria shrugged it away and said she was well able to manage her men.'

'Dear me! How very advanced and adult that sounds, does it not?'

'So. I say to her, "You are a very silly little girl, and do not know what you are saying". But will she listen to me? No. All of two Saturdays and Sundays they go out together, where I do not know, but Otto takes my car – without permission, of course – and on the Sunday evenings he takes her back to her lodgings in it. I say to him, "You will not get back until the little hours of the morning, and I shall not leave the door without bolts". He says to me, "Then I sleep with Maria at her digs". I think perhaps he will do so, because I know him to be a wicked naughty boy, so I pretend I make a joke and I say that of course I do not bolt the door, and I give him my key so that he can let himself in, but I do not sleep until I hear him come back, and that is at half-past three.'

'How long was he able to stay with you?'

'Two weeks, as I tell you, so he sees Maria two week-ends, and then comes Monday, when he says he must go back to his ship. But, of course, he does not go back to his ship. He goes to Southampton, but not to any ship, not there, not at Poole. He sleeps all the time with Maria at her lodgings, so I find out now, and makes trouble for her so she is with child. Then I think she makes trouble for him also, to marry her, but, instead, I think he kills her, for she is dead of being choked, just like my Karen. So what am I to do? I am a mother. I cannot go to the police and tell them that my son is a murderer.'

'Of course you cannot. Have they questioned Otto?'

'Yes, oh, yes. Me also. Both of us. Otto denies, and I – how am I to say to them that he is lying?'

'It will not be necessary. They will conduct the inquiry along their own lines and find out the truth. There is no reason for you to incriminate your son. No mother could be expected to do that. What kind of questions have they asked you?'

'How long Maria has been coming to me, and why. What kind of young girl. How long has she known my son. Did I allow men friends to the house. Nothing difficult to answer, except that I have this dreadful feeling that Otto has killed her, but, of course, I am not saying so.'

'Do not dream of saying so. You must let me find out more about all this. When did the police question you?'

'On Wednesday of last week. I telephoned you as soon as they had gone, but your servant said that you were not here, and told me that you would return yesterday, so then I telephone you again and you are so kind to say "Come".'

'Where is Otto now?'

'With his ship.'

'Why are you so anxious, then? Clearly the police do not suspect him, or they would never have allowed him to go to sea again. Apart from the fact that Maria was to bear a child, what makes you think he killed her?'

'He is wicked.'

Dame Beatrice began to think that he took after his mother. She said: 'But even wicked people do not necessarily kill others. I want you to put such thoughts of Otto right out of your head. Is anybody staying with you at present?'

'My sister from Germany, for a few days.'

'Good. I shall inform myself fully of the matter, and then I will talk to you again.'

Laura and Gavin returned to the Stone House after Gavin had called on Phillips.

'Yes,' said Gavin, in answer to Dame Beatrice's question, 'it isn't Scotland Yard's pigeon yet, although I'm pretty certain it soon will be, but I'm now pretty fully informed about this second death. It's rather interesting. To begin with, the girl was another foreigner, a Spaniard, as, of course, you know; then the method of the murder was exactly the same as in the other case, a tightened ligature to produce unconsciousness, followed by a right-handed manual strangulation; thirdly, there is this connection with the Schumann household, and, lastly, there was a similar message pinned to the body with a precisely similar knitting-needle – size eighteen, I am told. The only difference was in the digits which followed the message. The whole thing read: *In Memoriam 380.* In spite of all these similarities, however, the police are treating with caution the theory that the job may have been done by Karen Schumann's murderer. Unfortunately, a lot of detail leaked out in that first case, and it's more than possible that some other lunatic got an idea from this and decided to try the same method.'

'In that case,' said Laura, 'wouldn't he have used the same set of figures? Why 380 instead of 325?'

'Yes, that might be a point, of course. Incidentally, the message on Karen Schumann's body was *not* reported in the papers. Anyway, owing to the similarities, Phillips and his chaps are working on this second case too, but I don't suppose he'll have any objection if you pump him.'

Superintendent Phillips, far from having any objection, called at the Stone House on the day following Gavin's departure.

'The Assistant Commissioner told me you'd had a visit from Mrs Schumann, Dame Beatrice,' he said, 'and were interested in this second case that's cropped up. We've got a feeling – although, of course, being his mother, she hasn't said so to us – that she thinks her son knows something about it. I wonder whether she's got anything definite to go on?'

'To the best of my knowledge she has not. She merely writes him off as a wicked boy who has seduced this girl. What did you make of him?'

'Lively young spark. Big, fair, good-looking. Womaniser, obviously. I liked him.'

'And you do not suspect him of the murder?'

'We know how to get hold of him if we need him,' said the Superintendent evasively. 'Personally,' he went on, coming into the open, 'although my colleagues are keeping in mind the idea that this may be a copy-cat crime, I myself am convinced that we're looking for the same man as killed Miss Schumann, and as that couldn't possibly have been her brother, because we checked that he was at sea at the time, I'm inclined to think that we can write young Otto off.'

'If only we could find out what those numbers mean!' said Laura.

'Or if they mean anything at all, Mrs Gavin. I still think we're looking for a maniac. I thought so when we began our investigation of the first murder, whether James did it or not. I only hope we don't get a run of them. If I'm right, and he isn't picked up soon, there's no knowing how far this kind of lad is likely to go. Remember the Ripper and Landru and Neill Cream?'

'What had Otto to say for himself?' asked Dame Beatrice.

'Said that Miss Machrado wasn't the first girl he'd put in the family way, and probably wouldn't be the last. Said that she knew her way around and the risk she was taking. Said that he had never had the slightest intention of marrying her, as he wasn't the marrying kind, and had made this clear from the first. Said that she had told him that her religious denomination was not in favour of the pill. A fair lot of cheek, of course, but I took to him, and I can't see him as a murderer. He's a Don Juan and a Casanova and what have you, but that sort don't kill their women, they simply love 'em and leave 'em.'

'Where and when was the body found?'

'Soldiers on exercises found it by some gorse bushes at the side of one of the tank tracks on Bere Heath. It must have been placed there the night before, that's to say on the night or evening of January fifth. There were winter manoeuvres the day before, and if it had been there at that time it must certainly have been spotted, and . . .'

'It wasn't?'

'That's it.'

'That gives us another point of resemblance to the first murder, then.'

'You mean the impossibility of sorting out any recognisable car tracks? Quite so. The tanks had made such a mess of the heath that any tracks anything else might have left were indistinguishable. Oh, yes, the fellow may be a madman, but there's certainly method in his madness.'

'How long had she been dead?'

'According to the evidence at the inquest – which will have to be resumed, of course, when we've anything more to go on – less than twelve hours. What's more, there had been no attempt to conceal the body. It had simply been dumped.'

'And Otto? When did he rejoin his ship?'

'Three days ago. We picked him up, of course, and gave him a pretty good going-over, you may be sure, but we got nothing except, as I told you, a lot of cheeky answers. When he docks again – they're only toddling round the Dutch ports, so it won't be all that long – I'll pull him in for further questioning, and you can have a go at him, if you like, and see what you make of him.'

'Did he seem upset in any way by the girl's death?'

'Well, he said that if he caught the bastard who did it he'd make him wish he'd never been born. He also said that he and the girl had had a flaming row and that she had thrown him out on his ear a couple of days before the murder.'

'Hardly the statement a guilty man would be likely to make. It could hardly be more damaging.'

'Just so. He has an alibi, too, of sorts.'

'The same sort as Edward James' library one?'

'Just as difficult to prove or disprove. Claims that after the girl kicked him out of her digs he got drunk, had his pocket picked and slept rough in a stable-loft just outside Lyndhurst. Got up at the first grey of the dawn and toddled off. We gave the forensic boys the clothes he said he'd slept in, but he'd been to his mother's place before we collected him, and she'd given the suit a thorough brushing and pressing. There weren't even any turn-ups to the trousers to give the back-room boys a bit of help.'

'So you had to let him go? Did you question the girl's landlady?'

'Yes. The landlady's evidence was that he and the girl had had this toss-up and she'd given him the air, and that he certainly hadn't been back to her digs. That seemed to be as much as she knew. After Otto Schumann had gone, the land-lady kicked the girl out as well, and (though, according to Mrs

Schumann, she had not been near her) she said she was going back to the cottage for a day or two.'

'By the way, the landlady seems to have been a party, at first, to the goings-on between Otto Schumann and Maria,' said Laura. 'Does she admit as much? Of course, I know things are a lot slacker now than they were when I was at College. All the same . . .'

'Ah, well, there, you see, Mrs Gavin, you may be maligning the landlady. It seems that Miss Machrado was all ways round a little bit of a beauty. She had told the landlady from the very beginning that she was married and that her husband was a sailor and might be coming to see her, and that he would, of course, share her room. I should say, although it seems unkind to mention it now that she's dead, she had it coming to her, all right.'

'Interesting,' said Dame Beatrice. 'I look forward to meeting Otto Schumann.'

(3)

This meeting took place some ten days later.

'Well, Herr Schumann?' said Dame Beatrice with her crocodile grin.

'*Mister*, if you don't mind,' said Otto. 'Born and bred in the briar patch, you know.'

'Yes, I do know. But Señorita Maria Mercedes Machrado was not similarly born and bred, I believe.'

'That little tart! She wasn't a Spanish-born Spaniard either. Came from South America or somewhere.

'Really? On one of your ships?'

'Hell! How did you know that?'

'It was an inspired guess, I admit.'

'How many of those do you average to the minute?'

'The usual "sixty seconds' worth of distance run". Look here, Mr Otto, you could help us, I think. You had quarrelled with the girl. You've admitted that. What was it all about?'

'God knows, I don't.'

'She was with child.'

'So she said, and, of course, she may have been.'

'Was the quarrel . . . ?'

'About that? No. Besides, I don't admit it was my doing. It might have been, of course, but I don't see how she could have known she was pregnant if it *was* my kid. It takes a few weeks, surely, to make certain.'

'I take your point, and I do not believe that you killed her. Who did? You must have some idea.'

'I haven't. I know what you're thinking, though.'

'Indeed?'

'Well, it's more than a bit obvious, isn't it? Some bloke killed my sister, and the same bloke killed Maria. Personally, I think the king rat James is indicated.'

'On what do you base this assumption?'

'It's just a hunch. I deeply distrust that godly guy.'

'Have you any idea of what the notices on the bodies stand for? I believe the police have mentioned them to you.'

'Sound like car numbers to me.'

'*In Memoriam*?'

'Blokes and girls do get killed on rallies and in motor-smashes, don't they? – so *in memoriam* would be quite appropriate.'

'Unfortunately, that is true. Car numbers would also include some letters of the alphabet, though, would they not?'

'Might be part of this *In Memoriam* bit, don't you think? Karen could drive a car and had had a smash or two, I believe.'

'And Maria?'

'Well, she couldn't drive, so far as I know. I always took her out in Ma's little bus.'

'Did you ever receive the impression that she was afraid of anybody?'

'No. She was quite a girl, in her way. Cap over the windmill type. *You* know.'

'A professional, would you say?'

'Not really. Just a type which was bound to run into trouble, that's all.'

'And you ran her into it – or so she seems to have thought.'

'She didn't commit suicide, you know.'

'According to the medical evidence, that is indisputable.'

'What do you want me to tell you?'

'Nothing which might incriminate you, of course. If you would give me a plain, unvarnished tale of how you came to meet the girl, and of what followed from the meeting, it might help.'

'Help who? Me?'

'That is possible, although that was not the thought in my mind.'

'I suppose you mean you want to help serve the ends of justice, then, but if the rozzers really suspect me I doubt whether I'd still be at large, you know. Whose side are you on, by the way?'

'I rarely take sides. In this case I am on the side of two dead girls.'

'Fair enough. Me too. Maria wasn't a bad bit of homework in her way, and if I'd been Karen's full brother instead of only half...'

'I understood that you were twins.'

'That's Ma's bit of cover-up. I'm illegit. I think. That's why she hates me. Hadn't you rumbled? I did, years ago.'

'I have gathered that you are not her favourite child, yes. She has made no secret of that fact.'

'What has she said about me?'

'That you are wicked.'

'And a murderer? Does she say I'm a murderer?'

Dame Beatrice saw no reason to reply to this last query. She said, as she took out a small notebook,

'You are going to tell me about your first meeting with Señorita Machrado, are you not?'

'And of all that followed from it, I suppose you mean. I've no objection. I've nothing to hide. We carry a limited number of passengers on my ship. They eat at the captain's table. We don't carry a stewardess, so we don't take unaccompanied ladies. Maria came on board as another passenger's wife, which, of course, she wasn't, but they asked for, and got, separate cabins because she complained her husband snored and kept her awake at nights. Our first officer, a bloke named Lilley, opined that they weren't married, and, when I got to know Maria, she told me that the chap was her uncle and a widower, so he already had a passport made out for himself and wife.

I don't know how they got over the photograph difficulty, but I suppose it was easy enough to substitute hers for that of the dead wife. There was nothing fishy about their relationship. I imagine they had come with us because we charge only about half the fare you'd pay on a liner. Anyway, I found Maria a sporting sort of kid, but, of course, you don't, on our ship, play any games with women except shuffleboard when our old man's got his eye on you, so I didn't have much fun until we docked, and then not a lot, because Maria had to report to the University.'

'Ah, yes, of course.'

'Her uncle had a headwaiter's job ready for him in London, so he soon buzzed off, but before he left he found Maria some digs and saw her settled in. Well, I had a few days while the ship turned round, and I promised to look her up next time I was in the neighbourhood, and I did, and we had our bit of fun, and that was that.'

'When was this next time?'

'Mid-October, when we docked at Southampton. As usual, I didn't go home. I whooped it up a bit with some of the boys after I'd seen Maria, and then I went to London for a day or two, and forgot all about her until I went back to the ship and found a letter from her. Well, we weren't sailing until the second tide, so I sneaked a couple of hours off and went to see her, but, of course, I couldn't stop, so we had a drink with her landlady and then I had to get back to the ship.'

'How did your mother get to know her?'

'I haven't a clue. You could have knocked me down with the usual feather when I went home after I heard of Karen's death and found Maria there.'

Dame Beatrice looked sceptical.

'You haven't a clue?' she asked. 'But how could your mother have met Miss Machrado except through you?'

Her sharp black eyes sought his blue ones and held them for a moment; then Otto laughed uneasily, dropped his eyes and stared at his large hands.

'So, far from meeting Señorita Machrado for the first time at your mother's cottage, and only a comparatively short while

before she was murdered, you had actually known her for
several months. Is that it?'

Otto raised his eyes again for a moment.

'You don't have to believe everything I tell you,' he said.
'I like pulling people's legs.'

'Well, that being settled, how much of your story is
true?'

'Not much of it. Didn't it ring true?'

'It was a reasonable sort of tale. It could have been true.'

'Well, it wasn't. The truth is that I met her at my mother's
cottage after I heard about Karen. Does that sound more
likely?'

'Just as likely as the other.'

'Well, I can leave you to sort it out, then, can't I? What
right have you to come here asking me questions, anyway?
You're not the police?'

'No, I am consultant psychiatrist to the Home Office.'

This calm statement appeared to alarm Otto.

'Here, I'm not a madman!' he exclaimed.

'Then you may not be the person the police are looking for,'
said Dame Beatrice.

'That's what I mean! It must be a madman, mustn't it?'
His cocky, slightly insolent attitude had changed to one of
seriousness and fear.

'How often did you ask your mother and your sister and
your sister's fiancé for money?'

'Ask them for money? I never did. Oh, I know what you
mean, but half of what she got – only she swore she didn't
get it – was mine by rights, you know.'

'Half of what who got?'

'Karen. She had a big win on Ernie. I only heard about it
by accident. My father bought us a few Ernie Bonds not
very long before he died, and one of them came up last year.
I was in a pub with some of the chaps from the *Carmilla* one
night. One of them was the purser. He was looking at the
paper and he said some people had all the luck, and pointed
to the figures where they give the winning numbers. I took out
my pocket-book where I'd jotted down our numbers, Karen's
and mine, and gave a bit of a laugh and said I didn't suppose

I'd clicked, but, by God, I had! I got home as soon as I could and asked for my share, but there wasn't any share. Karen said she had claimed, but the paper had misprinted a figure or something, and ours was not a winning bond after all. I couldn't do anything more about it then, because my ship sailed the next day and we were away for six months after that.'

'And you did nothing more about the prize money?'

'What was the use?'

'But you really think your sister had it?'

'Oh, I know she had it, but I think my mother persuaded her to include me out. Probably softened it up to Karen by saying I'd only drink it or spend it on girls.'

'Did she leave you anything in her will?'

'Karen? I shouldn't think so. I haven't bothered to find out. We never got on. Both of them always hated me. What do I care? It's always been the same as long as I can remember. Everything for Karen, nothing for me. For her a decent education, college, clothes, spoiling – the lot. For me, grudging, kicks, hard words, until I got sick of it all and ran away to sea.'

'And are now second officer.'

'Yes. I worked up. I've got my father's brains.'

'And are alive, while your sister is dead.'

'Yes. It's an odd world.'

'And you *are* Karen's twin, in spite of what you said.'

'Yes, and born in lawful wedlock, as they say.'

'I advise you not to try to pull the wool over the Superintendent's eyes when he questions you. You said that you quarrelled with Señorita Machrado. Keeping now to a bald and, I hope, a convincing narrative, will you tell me what the quarrel was about?'

'Oh, just what you might expect,' said Otto, raising his eyes again. 'She was a proper little gold-digger, of course, and she dug a bit too deep. I spent as much of my pay on her as I could afford, but she wanted more. I couldn't give it her, so she tried to blackmail me by threatening to tell my mother of our goings-on. I countered that by telling her that she was welcome to do it. I had nothing to lose. Then she went for me with a knife and I knocked it out of her hand and smacked her face, and so we parted, but I never expected things to end like this.'

'When did you hear of her death?'

'Read about it in the London papers. We had some re-fitting to do, so I snaffled a day's leave and went up to Town.'

'Alone?'

'Well, I was alone when I started.'

Dame Beatrice left it at that.

'So what did you make of the saucy sailor?' asked Laura.

'Rather a childish person in some respects, and, I would say, a psychopath. He spun me a rigmarole and then complained that his mother hates him . . .'

'Well, that seems to be true enough.'

'. . . and that he suspects his sister cheated him out of some money which was paid out on a premium bond which they held in common. He seems fond of female society, and I imagine that his alibi depends on the word of a prostitute he seems to have picked up in London after he parted from Señorita Machrado.'

'But whose word, for or against, is not likely to be accepted by the police. Still, they haven't arrested Otto, have they? That's something in his favour. After all, there would be nothing to stop him jumping his ship in foreign parts and going to ground on the Continent.'

'The police have little inclination to trouble themselves over-much about him. They are convinced that the same man killed both girls. That man cannot have been Otto Schumann. His alibi for the murder of his sister is unbreakable.'

'You and the Superintendent seem certain that the murders were committed by a man.'

'One goes partly by the nature of the crimes and partly by the size of the hand which did the strangling. The marks on the victims' necks . . .'

Laura spread out a shapely palm.

'My own hands are pretty large,' she said, thoughtfully.

'Not large enough for that to which we refer.'

'I suppose you've noticed Mrs Schumann's hands? And

both girls were domiciled with her when things happened to them.'

'I do not lose sight of that fact, but I ought to point out that neither of the girls was actually *living* in Mrs Schumann's cottage when the murders were committed.'

'It doesn't look as though James had any reason for committing the second one, though, does it? We don't even know that he knew the Spanish girl.'

'Superintendent Phillips will establish whether he did or whether he did not, and the handwriting experts will give their opinion, no doubt, as to whether the notices found on the bodies were by the same hand.'

'Handwriting experts are not infallible, and the notices were in Roman capitals. We may be doing James the most frightful injustice. After all, why *do* we suspect him? Just because he can't prove his alibi?'

'That cannot be our only reason, surely?'

'Then it must be a case of "I do not like thee, Doctor Fell", mustn't it?'

'There are worse reasons for suspecting people of murder, although, perhaps, not many,' said Dame Beatrice. 'And, of course, Edward James *could* have been acquainted with the Spanish girl. We know that he visited Mrs Schumann at least once – and it may have been several times – after her daughter's death.'

(4)

'A psychopath, you say?' said Phillips. 'Oh, dear! That makes you think a bit, doesn't it? I'd say nothing was more likely than that he'd murdered this Spanish girl – a proper little tart she was, by all accounts – except that nothing will shake my opinion that the two crimes were committed by the same person, and that person definitely could not have been Schumann. I've taken too many corroborative statements to the effect that he was at sea when his sister was killed to believe that he could have had anything to do with her death. But – a psychopath! Sort of lad who might do anything, including imitating a murder he'd read about. Would you go along with that, Dame Beatrice?'

'Not altogether, and for what seems to me a sufficient reason. The second murder seems to have been as carefully planned as the first, yet Otto Schumann knew nothing about his sister's death until his ship docked and that was some time after it had occurred. How much is actually known, by the way, (apart from what may have been surmised), about this second death?'

'Damn-all, if you'll excuse the expression, Dame Beatrice. We know where the body was found, and we know that Mrs Schumann wrote to the girl's other digs telling her she need not come back to the cottage. We found the letter among Miss Machrado's things. That's about the lot. She came from Bilbao, and we've been in touch with her family, but they can tell us nothing that helps us in any way.'

'Otto Schumann claimed that she was a South American. What does her College landlady have to say about her now?'

'Oh, that she was every kind of a little trollop and that she had kicked her out of the digs.'

'She discovered, then, that the girl and Otto Schumann were not married?'

'She turned her out on the strength of the row they had. Apparently Miss Machrado pursued Schumann to the front door and part-way down the street, screaming abuse at him in Spanish. After she was turned away from the digs we haven't been able to trace her movements.'

'Nor those of Edward James?'

'Well, there, of course, we've had to be rather careful because, so far, there's no actual evidence that he had any more than the most casual and passing acquaintance with the girl. He spent Christmas with friends in Kent – his parents are dead – but he left there the day after Boxing Day. He went to see Mrs Schumann – that's how we know as much as we do – and then, so far as she can tell us, he spent the rest of the school vacation in London so that he could use the British Museum and the London libraries for his studies.'

'But Mrs Schumann doesn't know his London address?'

'She says he talked about finding a cheap hotel, but she doesn't know where he was going to look for one. She doesn't know London at all well, it seems. Anyway, of one thing, so she told us, she is certain. He did not meet Miss Machrado on

his last visit to the cottage, although Mrs Schumann admits
she told him about the girl's goings on and of how they parted
brass-rags because of the girl's association with Otto and the
lies she'd told about the College end-of-term arrangements. She
also admits that James had met the girl once or twice at her
place before all the scandal blew up. There's not much help
to be got out of that, though, Dame Beatrice, and, if he was
working hard in London, James wouldn't have had the *time*
to plan this second murder, let alone carry it out.'

'If he killed Miss Schumann, he had "learned the ropes", so
to speak, though, hadn't he?' said Laura.

'But if he had only the slightest acquaintance with the girl
Machrado – and it's difficult to see that it could have been
more than that, Mrs Gavin – why on earth should he murder
her? He's not a maniac.'

'But young Otto is a psychopath!' said Laura.

'Makes you think a bit, that does,' agreed the Superintendent.
'Different from the way I found him at first. I'll need to take
a closer look at him.'

'And when you do, you might also ponder on Mr Rucastle,'
said Dame Beatrice.

'Sherlock Holmes' methods? I doubt whether I'd find them
very useful, ma'am,' said Phillips.

(5)

'Well,' said Laura, 'now that Scotland Yard has been called
in, the whole business is out of our hands, I suppose, and has
ceased to be a purely local matter.'

'Yes. It might be interesting, however, from a purely
academic point of view, to note the differences, as well as the
similarities, between the two cases.'

'The differences? Well, let's see now. First of all, we know
that one body was found within easy walking distance of this
house, the other a good many miles away on Bere Heath. The
first was found by me – or by Fergus, if you like – the second
by members of the Tank Corps. Karen Schumann was a virgin,
Maria Machrado was pregnant. Edward James was engaged
to Karen, but, so far as we've been told, he knew very little

about Maria, and that mostly by hearsay, and the police can't prove anything different. Karen was killed towards the end of November, when her school had a free day, Maria early in the New Year, during her College vacation.'

'Which was during the school holidays, too.'

'Yes, I hadn't forgotten that, but we still can't find any connection between James and this second murder, can we? My last point of difference is that Karen was of German descent, Maria was a Spaniard.'

'I thought we had decided to treat that as a similarity, since neither was of English ancestry. Incidentally, you left one of the points of difference at the half-way mark. Edward James was engaged to Karen and knew of Maria chiefly by hearsay, but it seems that Otto Schumann must have known both girls very well indeed. On the other hand, there is no doubt that it would have been impossible for him to have killed his sister. There is no escaping the fact that he was on his ship, and not even in port, at the time of Karen Schumann's death.'

'Then it seems to me that we are faced with a copycat murder.'

'A theory which we have already rejected.'

The C.I.D. Inspector from Scotland Yard did not reject it, however, and news came from Phillips that Otto Schumann was, in the classic phrase, assisting the police in their enquiries into the death of Maria Machrado.

'Their view,' said Phillips, 'is that Schumann copied the methods of his sister's murderer, and there's no doubt he can't produce any sort of alibi for the time when Muchrado was killed. He says that after they had the row about money, and had parted, he went to London on the spree. He doesn't seem to remember much of what he did up there and, as he was under the influence most of the time, he can't give himself much help.'

'What is the evidence against him?'

'That he and Machrado had had this row – he admits it, and, of course, her landlady's description of it has lost nothing in the telling – and that Maria was pregnant. They don't believe him when he says she didn't expect him to marry her, and, naturally, any other boy-friends she may have had are not in a hurry to come forward for fear of being implicated. He's not yet remanded in custody, but, although they are continuing investigations, I'm certain the Yard believe they've got the right man.'

'What is their attitude towards the murder of Karen Schumann, then?'

'They regard that as *my* pigeon. They were called in to investigate the death of Machrado, and, as they've convinced themselves that the murders are not connected, that's that, in their view. I can't say I blame them, although I'm certain they're mistaken. Of course, they've unearthed a lot of information which I hadn't got hold of, including evidence that Schumann could be violent and had slugged a couple of Dutch sailors ashore in a pub and half-killed a Lascar seaman on his own ship. Added to that, his mother has admitted that she was physically afraid of him in some of his moods, and *that* hasn't done his case much good, as you may imagine.'

'But you yourself retain an open mind?'

'Not altogether an open mind, ma'am. I still think the same man killed both girls, and as that man can't have been Schumann, well, that's where I stand, and, following my hunch, I'm still tailing James.'

Laura telephoned her husband.

'Oh, there's method in our madness,' Gavin replied. 'The case can't possibly come to trial for several weeks. Meanwhile, if Phillips is right – and, like most Hampshiremen, although he may be slow, he is apt to be very sure – our joker will try again, and, when he does, I should think we'll get him.'

'Of course, Otto Schumann's such a liar.'

'Yes, just the type – pathological, as Dame B. points out – to be the sort of person who commits a string of murders, and he's known to be violent, of course. The magistrates have now remanded him in custody, but that doesn't necessarily mean that he'll be brought to trial. They'll still go on looking. Phillips is positive Otto is not our man, and he's quite a hard-headed old cuss and not a bad psychologist, in his way. Incidentally, you know we've been certain all the time that Schumann couldn't have killed his sister? Well, but for an odd coincidence, he could have done. I'll tell you all about it when I see you.'

But it was Phillips who came with the next bit of news. Scotland Yard's case against Otto was stronger, and his own case against James was weaker, than he had thought. Not quite all of the first story with which Otto had amused himself by recounting to Dame Beatrice was untrue. The London C.I.D., with far greater resources than those vouchsafed to a police officer in the provinces, had unearthed some interesting facts about it.

It had occurred to minds sharper, more suspicious and more astute than Phillips' admittedly rather slow intelligence, that as Bilbao, Maria Machrado's home town, was also a sea-port of considerable importance, Otto's ship might well have called there to pick up cargo. Not only did this prove to be the case, but it was also established that the uxorious Otto not only knew the girl, but that she had indeed come to England on his ship, although not with the uncle he had postulated. Further, a reluctant and tearful Mrs Schumann had been persuaded to admit that it was Otto who had sent the girl to her as soon as he had learned of his sister's death.

'And I am thinking at first,' moaned Mrs Schumann, 'that my wicked boy has had a change of heart and is sorry for his mother in her loneliness, and sends me this young girl to comfort me, so that I shall have somebody with me at week-ends and for College vacations, as before.'

'And when did you change your mind?' asked the patient, gentle voice of Detective-Inspector Maisry of Scotland Yard.

'When, of course, he takes pleasure of the girl, and takes her out in my car, and all the rest. And when I warn the girl against him she laughs in my face and asks me what I expect. She tells me she is pregnant by Otto on board the ship, and that he will have to marry her, although he says not, and that he would rather kill her than marry her.'

These fell words being repeated to Otto by Maisry, he denied them, which made no difference whatever to Maisry's conviction that Mrs Schumann had been telling the truth. Then Maisry investigated Otto's statement that he had got drunk, been robbed, had slept in a hayloft and had foot-slogged it back to his ship. It proved to be an altogether highly-coloured account of what had actually happened.

'It seems, ma'am,' said Phillips, recounting to Dame Beatrice the story he had had from Maisry, 'that after Miss Machrado had threatened him with a knife, and after she had run half-way down the street after him – he having taken the knife away and smacked her face – all this is vouched for by the landlady – he went on a drinking spree with some of his friends and then those who were sober enough got the drunks, including Otto, back to the lodging house where they were staying while they were ashore.'

'And after that?'

'He went back to his ship on the following day.'

'What about his story that his mother brushed and pressed his clothes?'

'Quite false. You were right when you called him a psychopath, ma'am. He's a pathological liar. Seems incapable of telling a straight story. *Must* enlarge and embroider.'

'Some of that might show a misplaced sense of humour, of course.'

'The police don't appreciate misplaced senses of humour, ma'am.'

'Who does, except the humourist himself? But if, after he had recovered from the results of this drinking bout, he returned to his ship, what reason have you for suspecting him of killing Miss Machrado?'

'I don't suspect him, ma'am – although I well might, if there was the slightest chance that he could have strangled his sister – it's Maisry who insisted on pulling him in. He went back to his ship, yes, but Maisry has unearthed one of the men-students at the College who alleges that Miss Machrado came to his digs and told him that her landlady had kicked her out, that she had nowhere to go, that she was pregnant by Schumann, and begged him to help her. Well, the poor young chap wasn't prepared to do anything much, but he suggested that she should go to Schumann and threaten to report him to his captain if he did not marry her. This, the student asserts, she decided to do. She went to the ship in his company because she claimed, probably rightly, that *he* might be allowed on board, but that *she* would not. To sum up, the student's story is that he persuaded Otto to come ashore and speak to the girl, and that the two of them strolled off together.'

'And does Otto agree that this happened?'

'Yes, so far. Then his famous inventive powers came into play again. He told Maisry that he persuaded the girl to throw herself on his mother's mercy, and that he gave her a note to take to his mother, acknowledging that the coming child was his, and begging her to take the girl in because he proposed to marry her on his next leave.'

'And Mrs Schumann?'

'Denies that either the girl or her son's note ever came anywhere near her.'

'So Detective-Inspector Maisry has plumped for Otto, but you yourself are still on the trail of Edward James?'

'I'm not happy about Schumann, ma'am. I still think both murders were committed by James, or, if not by him, at least by the same hand.'

'If not by him? You are wavering in your opinion that he is our murderer?'

'Not altogether. The only thing is that James really *did* spend his Christmas holiday in London, and went every day it was open to the London Library. That I proved, but it doesn't take into account how he spent his evenings. He gave me the address of the boarding-house where he stayed, but I couldn't get much help there. James was not often in of an evening, and claimed that he did a round of theatres and cinemas. I asked him to show me the theatre programmes as a bit of a check, but he says he never kept them – always left them behind at the theatre. He could certainly give me a pretty good idea of what the plays and films were about, but, of course, an educated man like him could have memorised all the main points from newspaper reports or from what other people had told him.'

'Were you able to convince yourself that Mr James and Miss Machrado had met at least once at Mrs Schumann's cottage?'

'Oh, yes, he doesn't deny that, but says it *was* only once, although Mrs Schumann thinks it may have been twice.'

'Well,' said Gavin, meeting Dame Beatrice at her house in Kensington, 'I've an open mind about who killed Karen Schumann, but I don't think there's much room for doubt about who killed Maria Machrado.'

'When you spoke to Laura over the telephone you made the intriguing suggestion that, but for an odd coincidence, Otto would have been in a position to kill his sister. To what circumstances did you refer?'

'That he was almost sacked for setting about and half-killing a Lascar seaman. The shipping company took a dim view and threatened to sack him there and then, but his skipper stood by him and claimed that the man was insufferably lazy and had also given lip and refused to obey orders, so, reluctantly, (the captain told me), the directors gave way, issued a stern warning to Otto that the sort of conduct which obtained in a whaler in the sixties of last century would certainly not be tolerated in any ship of theirs, and allowed him to make the next voyage. As it chanced, it was during the next voyage that his sister was murdered, and, of course, he had a fool-proof motive for killing her – only he didn't.'

'You mean the money she refused to give him, don't you? But he still would not have obtained possession of it. She left everything to her mother.'

'Who may possibly have killed Maria Machrado, but who cannot, surely, be suspected of having killed her own daughter. I can't think why the idea ever crossed our minds, can you?'

Dame Beatrice wagged her head, but made no reply.

CHAPTER THREE

Done to Death by ...

'Her lips were red, her eyes were brown,
Mark well what I do say!
Her lips were red, her eyes were brown,
And her hair was black and it hung right down ...
I'll go no more a-roving with you, fair maid.'

---

(1)

Dame Beatrice briefed her son, Sir Ferdinand Lestrange, Q.C., for the defence in case Otto should be brought to trial. He did not expect to obtain an acquittal, he told his mother. He did not think there was the slightest chance of one, for the prosecution had a strong case. However, he thought he might be able to confuse the issue sufficiently to cause the jury to disagree, and so get the trial – if it came to that – referred to the next sessions.

'You never know, with juries,' he said. 'Ten to one they couldn't care less if a man with a foreign name murders a girl with a foreign name. On the other hand, the English always fall over backwards to protect other nationals, so we must wait and see what happens.'

'You yourself believe that Otto Schumann is guilty, then?' Dame Beatrice asked.

Ferdinand smiled.

'I am a cautious man, as you know,' he replied, 'but if I were prosecuting I would back myself to secure a conviction. The evidence is all there. A record of violence, although, I admit, he has never been gaoled for it, (and, of course, the prosecution couldn't use it), a whirlwind love affair (if you call it that) with this nymph, a quarrel about money and a pregnancy. What more could you ask for?'

'And, of course, her Tutor at the College was forthright on the subject of Machrado's dilettante attitude towards attendance at lectures, and this, I thought, you might be able to use to great advantage,' said Laura.

'Not altogether with the Tutor's approval, I imagine. She will not intend to indicate what I hope to persuade the jury that she *does* indicate – namely, that the girl was a thoroughly bad lot and cut lectures wholesale so that she could pick up men. As for Schumann's acts of violence, well, if I had been prosecuting I should make sure the jury "heard about them", if you know what I mean. After all, objections may be sustained, but, all the same, the objectionable statement has been made, and, however much the jury may be told to disregard it, in actual fact it's very difficult for them to put it out of their minds. However, I'm not prosecuting.'

Gavin laughed.

'How to win your cases without actually cheating!' he said. 'I wish you luck, but my chaps are pretty thorough and are convinced they've got the man who killed Maria Machrado.'

'Phillips still doesn't think so,' said Laura.

(2)

Edward James set down an armful of exercise books on the Common Room window-ledge, walked across the room and began to tidy his locker. He had never been a popular member of the staff at the Old Bridge Comprehensive School, and after some awkwardly-expressed condolences on the death of his fiancée the others had left him more solitary than ever. It was not with any intention of being unkind or heartless that this attitude was maintained, but simply that the murder of one of their number had shocked them very deeply and had set apart the person most nearly affected by it.

James was not, and never had been, actively disliked, but he was an enigma, a self-centred, silent, pre-occupied man intent only upon his own advancement. It was known that almost all his free time was spent upon study and research for his doctorate, but, as he had no close friends, nobody knew what progress he made or how high his hopes were of success.

He was a capable teacher in the sense that boys and girls did the work he set and gave him their attention in class partly because his exposition was clear and sound and his preparation of his lessons was thorough, and partly because, in their hearts, they were rather in awe of the solitary man, but his nickname was Sunny Jim which, to those versed in the ironic overtones of the young, was comment enough on what they thought of him. He took part in no out-of-school activities on the plea of having no time to spare for these, but his real reason was that he did not care for young people, had no sympathy wtih their adolescent strivings and ideals, and merely regarded them as being useful to him since, without them, he would have been obliged to find some other way of earning a living. As it was, the short school day (since he saw no reason to add to it voluntarily) and the long school holidays suited his ambitious purpose and caused him to be contented with his lot, if not enthralled by it.

He was not alone in the Common Room. With him were the Miss Tompkins and the Miss O'Reilly with whom his fiancée had shared a flat. Miss Tompkins had a free period; Miss O'Reilly was on visiting rounds to extort subscriptions from her colleagues for a wedding present for a member of staff who was getting married during the Easter holidays. Her mission (although, according to the time-table, she should have been in class) was excusable on two counts. One was that to ask for subscriptions in the Common Room during break or in the dinner-hour would be embarrassing if the giftee happened to be present, and the other was that subscriptions, even at the minimal half-a-crown a head, were undoubtedly unpopular, and a united body of opinion could, and probably would, veto altogether the proposed giving of a wedding-present or else whittle the subscription down to a heartbreaking bob a nob. In front of an eager, lynx-eyed, lip-reading class, however, the dunned were helpless and usually paid up without demur.

'Well, I've seen everybody except you two and the Lord of Titipu,' announced Miss O'Reilly, referring in this facetious way to her headmaster, who was somewhat of a martinet, 'so half-a-crown each, please.'

'I'd make it five bob if that little drip was leaving,' said Miss Tompkins, 'but, as it is, we shall have to put up with her until the first baby is well on the way, I suppose.'

'Thanks. I'll tick you off on my list. Everybody has coughed up except Jane, who was taking P.E. and had left her purse in her locker, and Fanny, who, as usual, swore she hadn't any change. Oh, thanks, Edward. What are you going to do for the holidays? Swot?'

'Oh, yes,' replied James. 'I shall be doing research, as usual.'

'In London?'

'Of course, yes. Where else?'

'I thought you might be following in the steps of Saint Paul, or going to Rome or something. First-hand material, you know.'

'Oh, no. It wouldn't help me.' He turned his back on her and continued to tidy his locker.

(3)

Laura read the letter twice before she laid it down. Observing that her employer was still involved with her own correspondence, she said nothing, but began upon a plate of gammon and eggs. At the toast and marmalade stage she noted that Dame Beatrice had put aside the last of her letters and was prepared for conversation.

'Anything there for me to deal with?' Laura enquired.

'I think not. I shall have to stay here in the Kensington house for a week or two. Doctor Fairson has his son from New Zealand staying with them, and, although he doesn't say so, I feel certain that he would be glad to give up the clinic for a bit and enjoy his son's company, and Miss Gibson is too young and inexperienced to be left in full charge.'

'Right. I'll stay here with you.'

'But Hamish will be coming home for his Easter holiday. It would be better for him in Hampshire than in London.'

'Yes, but he won't be coming yet. That's what my letter is about. As Easter is so ridiculously early this year – why they don't fix it I can't think – the headmaster isn't going to close the school until the middle of April. Parents can have their boys home for the Easter week-end if they like, but there will be full religious observance of the festival at school and a school outing (weather permitting) on Easter Monday. If it's wet, the boys will be taken to the pictures. Fair enough, I think? That means I don't have to put up with him for another three weeks. Incidentally, Gavin says he ought to have a baby sister. What do *you* think?'

'What are you going to call her?'

Laura first stared at her employer and then laughed.

'Eiladh,' she said. 'That's if and when. There's nothing on the horizon at present.'

'Hamish, I am sure, will approve.'

'I'm not so sure. There's always something attractive in being the only pebble on the beach. I can just imagine his disgust if I present him with a brother.'

'If I know Hamish, he will become guardian angel to a baby of either sex.'

'Yes, you do know Hamish. I wish I did,' said Laura.

They made a flying visit to the Stone House on the Wednesday before Good Friday, and, back in London, received, *via* the newspapers of the following Tuesday, the first news of the third murder.

(4)

Shane and Agnes Clancy had moved into their new bungalow in May, 1964. They were a young and pleasant couple and had been married for less than two years. Shane was a bank clerk and, until the first baby was expected, Agnes had held the post of secretary at a school in the small town of Milton Cliffs, some ten miles from the Stone House at Wandles Parva.

When Agnes was five months with child, Shane was promoted from his post at the local bank, where most of the staff at his wife's school had their accounts, to a much larger branch in Southampton.

'We shall have to move, I'm afraid,' he said, at the end of a month. 'I can't go on doing a forty-mile journey twice a day every day. It's beginning to get a bit much. A pity, now we've got the garden going so nicely.' He looked with regret at the well-tended lawn and the flower-beds, at the small lily-pond he had installed and at the crazy-paving round it. 'Promotion is all very fine, but there *are* disadvantages.'

'Could we put off moving until after the baby comes?'

'We must. You're in no shape to cope with a big operation like moving.'

' "Shape" is about right, but please don't mention operations.'

'In any case,' said Shane, dropping a kiss on the crown of her head, 'we've still got to find somewhere, and that's going to take a bit of time. Besides, I've got to sell before I can buy.'

'Shall we have to live in Southampton itself? I wouldn't fancy that.'

'Not after this place, no, neither would I.' The bungalow looked out over a valley to green hills beyond. 'I'll have to go into digs for the present, but I can come home on Saturday afternoons and go back early on Monday mornings, so it won't be too bad for a bit.'

'I shall hate being left alone here all the week. Could we afford to have an *au pair* girl?'

'It's the only solution, although if we could find a proper maid it might be more satisfactory.'

'It's an added expense, just when we didn't want one, but I dread the idea of being on my own. It isn't even as if we had any near neighbours.'

'Funny how the chickens come home to roost, isn't it? When we fell for this place it was simply because we *hadn't* any near neighbours.'

The spring and summer passed, the baby was born, but the bungalow had found no purchaser and the Italian maid, whom Shane had found through the kind efforts of one of the bank's customers, stayed on. She proved to be an efficient nursemaid and, what with her keep and her pay and the cost of Shane's digs, Agnes decided that, as soon as the baby was old enough, she herself would look for a job. She obtained a post, again as school secretary, but this time at the Old Bridge Comprehensive School.

When this happened she had had the Italian maid for three years, and a routine was fully established. The following Easter Shane had the long week-end of Good Friday, Easter Saturday, Sunday and Monday, and he and his wife planned to go to Sidmouth, for, now that Agnes was again in full-time employ-ment, money was not as tight as it had been and they had decided upon a little celebration. They took the child with them and left the maid to her own devices, provided that she locked up the bungalow at night and bolted the back door when she went out.

This agreement had been reached at the beginning of Easter week, and, as soon as he could get away from the bank on the Thursday, Shane collected his wife and child in his little car and, having paid the maid her week's wages, off they drove to Sidmouth where, by previous arrangement with the guest-house, they were to be given a late meal.

Left to herself, the maid, a swarthy but handsome woman of thirty, bolted the front and back doors, made certain that all the windows were closed and fastened, made herself a supper of spaghetti and cheese and drank half the bottle of a cheap red wine which was her 'Easter egg' from her employers. Then, having said her prayers, she went to bed. She was nervous at being left alone in the bungalow, which had no near neighbours, and felt safer in bed than anywhere else.

First thing on Good Friday morning she shut the front door behind her, leaving the windows closed and the back door bolted, and tramped on her sturdy peasant legs to Mass. This involved a walk of nearly three miles into the little town where was the nearest Catholic church. She would have borrowed the bicycle on which Mrs Clancy rode to school if she had known how to ride it, but she did not.

After Mass, the priest, a kindly man, arranged for her to go to breakfast with one of his parishioners and she was invited to stay for lunch, an offer she was glad to accept although, on Good Friday, the fare was Spartan. She got back to the bungalow in the late afternoon, taking care that it should be before dark, let herself in with the latchkey which she had been allowed, bolted the door and then nervously explored the small bungalow to make certain that there was nobody lurking. Again she went to bed early, after eating the fish she had cooked for herself. She looked longingly at the wine that was left in the bottle, but decided that it must be kept for Easter Sunday. She did not live to drink it.

On Saturday morning she decided to spring-clean the bungalow, for, when she was in the mood, she was a willing and energetic worker and she felt, too, that to spend the day in toil was a fair enough substitute for making the long journey back and forth to the town to attend another service.

She knocked off at twelve for her lunch – bread and a good handful of sultanas – and then set to again. The caller rang the front-door bell as she was putting the furniture back in position after she had finished polishing the boards which surrounded the carpet in the principal bedroom. It was barely five o'clock and the sun would not set for at least another hour, so she was not alarmed and had no suspicion at all that she was opening the door to her murderer.

Fortunately for Agnes, less so for himself, it was Shane who saw the body when they returned from their short holiday. He turned the key of the front door, leaving his wife to follow with the child, and, finding the bungalow unnaturally silent, he called the maid by name, and then found her dead on the sitting-room floor. She had been garrotted and then strangled. Attached to the body, this time by a large darning-needle, was the legend, in Roman capitals, *The Scholar Gipsy 1155*. A bizarre addition to the scene was a burnt and blackened rag doll lying on a piece of newspaper.

(5)

'You know,' said Laura disgustedly, 'something ought to ring a bell, and it just simply doesn't. This poor woman had no relatives in England except an elderly mother, and there's nobody, so far as the police can find out, who had anything against her. *The Scholar Gipsy*, well, there's only one connection there, and I can't see how it fits in. What on earth connection can a poem by Matthew Arnold have with the death of a maid-of-all-work from Italy?'

'The burnt doll might be a clue either to the mentality of the murderer or to the character of the deceased,' said Dame Beatrice, 'but, until we know which, or whether it is merely a macabre but meaningless addition to an already sufficiently horrid scene, it does not help us.'

'It helps us to the extent that the murderer must be a madman, as Phillips has thought all along,' said Laura, 'and, as madmen are unpredictable, well, that's that.'

'Whether or not the murderer is a madman in terms of the MacNaughton Rules, he certainly seems to have a bias against foreign women, and this particular murder, as you suggest, seems curiously motiveless unless, of course, the woman had an enemy in her own country who has followed her here.'

'The Mafia? Could be, I suppose.'

The police discounted this theory. Searching enquiries had established that the maid, although she was of Italian parentage, had been born in London. She had belonged to no political party, had never been to her parents' country, and did not appear to have an enemy in the world.

'They've called in my chaps again,' said Gavin over the telephone to his wife, 'and the thing, of course, is priority stuff. We may be looking for one killer or we may be looking for two, but it's hardly reasonable to imagine that there are three, and, as the only real suspect, this young Schumann, can't have committed either the first or this third murder, we may be back to square one.'

'What line are the police taking?'

'We've worked out what the movements of this Italian maid must have been, so now they are sorting out all the mental hospitals and any private nursing homes who may have batsy patients, to see whether anyone is missing. We've put out radio and television broadcasts on all networks, and we've got every squad in the country sorting out their own local loony-bins.'

'You're pretty sure the criminal is mentally disturbed, then?'

'Must be. The absence of motive shows that. This last murder makes even less sense than the first two.'

'You know, all the murders have taken place in this part of the country, haven't they? And in each case there has been a connecting link, in a way.'

'You mean the fact that none of the victims was English, and that there were those notices on the bodies?'

'Not only that. Haven't you noticed that, in every case, there has been a sort of tie-up with Mrs Schumann and with James?' said Laura.

'Don't say any more over the phone. I'll come along. Expect me for tea.'

'A tie-up with Mrs Schumann as well as with James?' said Dame Beatrice, when Laura had replaced the receiver.

'As I see it. Mrs Schumann's daughter was engaged to James and is killed. Mrs Schumann's lodger is killed. James is a teacher at the school where this Mrs Clancy was the secretary, and this third dead woman was Mrs Clancy's servant. Don't you think there's a tie-up?'

She put this theory to her husband that same evening.

'Yours is a long shot and, in my view, an unfair one,' said Gavin, when he had listened to her argument. 'There's nothing to connect either Mrs Schumann or James *definitely* with any of these crimes. I admit we looked at him pretty hard over the first one, simply because he was engaged to the girl and there didn't seem to be anybody else in the picture, but, apart from that—'

'They'd had rows, he and Miss Schumann.'

'Oh, but, look here, Laura! Suppose you'd wanted to give me some gosh-awful tie, or a billy-goat or an overcoat trimmed with astrakhan, and we'd had a toss-up because I refused to wear it or accept it, would that mean I'd murder you? And suppose, on another and, actually, a former occasion, I'd called you a misguided little – what shall I say?'

'That I would consider insulting?'

'Yes. Well, never mind what it might be, but, if you took umbrage, *you* might (just conceivably) murder *me*, but it wouldn't make sense if *I* murdered *you*, would it?'

'You did say, though, that, in cases of murder, you always looked hardest at their nearest and dearest, and, in Karen Schumann's case, her nearest and dearest were her mother and James.'

'My dear girl, in the case of Karen Schumann, Phillips looked at the unfortunate Edward James until his eyes nearly fell out of his head. He got nowhere. In the case of Maria Machrado we have no reason to suspect that James so much as knew her. He only seems to have met her twice, at most.'

'He knew that Machrado went there for week-ends and the Christmas vacation.'

'But what could he possibly have against her? My chaps have never even looked at James twice, once we'd got on to this fellow Otto Schumann.'

'Who couldn't have committed this third murder, because he was on remand, awaiting trial, when it happened.'

'I grant you that. I'll go further and tell you a state secret. We're going to let him go. He won't come up for trial.'

'I'm glad you've got that much sense.'

'But, of course, he'll be tailed. No jury will convict him now that it's known he can't have murdered this Italian woman . . .'

'And is hardly likely to have killed his twin sister . . .'

'And we don't want to bring him to a trial where it's a moral certainty he would be acquitted.'

'So you're going to wait for the murderer – and you still really think it's Otto Schumann – to have another go?'

'Well, be reasonable, my love. If he's innocent it's right we should let him go, and if he's guilty we must get him some way or another. He won't be able to get away with a fourth attempt. We shall see to that all right.'

'By the way, you were going to tell me something about Otto Schumann being on his ship at the time of his sister's death.'

'Oh, yes. His guardian angel was working overtime that week, because, if it could be shown that he had had the opportunity to kill his sister, we'd be bound to get him for the murder of Machrado.'

'Yes, I see that, but what did his guardian angel have to do with it?'

'Plenty, according to information received. After we knew about the fuss over that Lascar seaman, my chaps naturally wanted to find out as much about Otto as they could, so as to strengthen their case, so we rounded up the shipping magnates who control that particular line and asked them for a detailed account of the ship's – Schumann's ship's – movements as from the beginning of last November.

'Well, they let us have a copy of her itinerary or schedule, and we thought we were on to something pretty warm, because on November fifteenth she was due in at Poole and was supposed to stay there a week, unloading and loading up again and having something done to the refrigerating plant in one of the holds.'

'A week beginning on the fifteenth, and Karen Schumann was killed on the nineteenth,' said Laura. 'So what happened?'

'Two days out from Las Palmas they got an S.O.S. from a Dutch ship which had started a pretty bad fire, so they were delayed while they helped fight the blaze, then they (and another couple of ships which had picked up the call) had to take off some members of the crew and rush them back to Las Palmas to hospital – burns, you know – so that delayed them another two days and they eventually put in at Poole on the twentieth, the day after the murder of Karen Schumann.'

'And Otto didn't go home that particular time?'

'He didn't have the chance. That's why he had no idea that anything had happened to his sister. There was no shore leave for anybody. The company ditched the refrigerating improvement for the time being, and the ship unloaded and loaded at top speed to make up for the lost time.'

(6)

'If,' said Laura, when she was alone with her employer, 'you delved into Edward James's family history, I wonder what you would find?'

'You are thinking of skeletons in cupboards, no doubt?'

'Something of the kind. I mean, we're agreed, I take it, that these murders are the work of a maniac, so I thought perhaps a study of the antecedents of some of the people who've come into the picture might not be a bad thing. It's obvious that the police are up a gum tree.'

Dame Beatrice refused to identify herself with this opinion.

'The police are taking their own line,' she said, 'and at present I am not prepared to cross it.'

'You don't think Edward James's family tree would be worth investigating, then?'

Dame Beatrice cackled.

'There are certain points in Edward James's favour, it seems to me,' she said.

'Such as? – I mean, I know we've nothing against him that a court of law would consider evidence . . .'

'Quite so. Let us go back to the death of Karen Schumann. I have been studying the notes I made, and there are one or two interesting points which seem to me to emerge. The first of these is Edward James's alibi.'

'A very clever one, I thought. Can't be proved or disproved.'

'A matter of chance. How could he have known that nobody would come to the library while he was (or was not) there? It would have been a most dangerous and unwarrantable assumption.'

'But with the entire teaching staff and domestic staff off duty . . .'

'I am wondering whether the school secretary would have been accorded the full day's holiday.'

'Oh, I see! The school secretary was this Mrs Clancy whose Italian maid has been murdered. You mean Mrs Clancy might be able to give James an alibi?'

'Well, not for the whole day, and possibly not at all. I mentioned her merely to indicate that, if James was lying, but intended to claim his visit to the library as an alibi, he was tempting fortune to a very foolish extent. Again, how could he have known that the contractors for cleaning the school windows might not send their men that day? Or school stock might have been delivered, and a signature required for it. In such a situation, the school would be searched for someone in authority. Boys, knowing the school to be empty, might have come in and have been larking around. The caretaker, or one of the cleaners, might have left something behind in the library and come back to look for it. There are dozens of possibilities which a guilty man would need to consider before producing such an alibi.'

'I see,' said Laura. 'Put like that, your argument does sound plausible. What else have you been working out?'

'Well, so far, in connection with that first death, I wonder whether we have not taken for granted rather too readily that the only person who told us the truth was Mrs Schumann. She said that she had gone to Ringwood that day, and we know for certain that she did, but not until after the time that her

daughter died. She also told us that Karen telephoned to find
out whether she would be at home. At the time we thought
that the telephone message was to make certain that the house
would be empty so that Karen could bring James there, but, of
course, it could equally well have been a genuine enquiry merely
to make sure that her mother would be at home to welcome her
and be able to spend the day with her. You see, we have no
way of proving whether or not Karen Schumann knew that the
stud dog was to be taken over to Ringwood on that particular
day. As a bitch remains on heat for about three weeks, it is
quite probable that she did *not* know.'

'So Mrs Schumann could have replied over the phone that
she *would* be at home, and so enticed Karen to her death, and
then used the Ringwood outing as an alibi. I don't believe a
word of it, you know. It sounds plausible enough, but it
doesn't make sense.'

'Yes, of course it does. So far, there are only three possible
suspects – James, Mrs Schumann and Otto.'

'And, of these, Otto is out of it so far as the deaths of
Karen and of this Italian woman are concerned. Well, what's
the next point? I'm beginning to feel very nervous about all this.'

'The next point concerns the dog-whistle which enticed
Fergus from your side and led him to find the body.'

'Anyone can blow a dog-whistle.'

'But to how many people would it occur to do so, unless
they were accustomed to the procedure? I look at it in this
way. James, we are given to understand, spent only about one
week-end in three or four with his fiancée. If he killed her,
therefore, he had every reason to leave the body to be found
by others and certainly no need to direct attention to it.'

'She'd have been missed at school, and by her mother at the
following week-end.'

'Yes. The school would have given her three days of grace
before a medical certificate was required, and her mother would
hardly have notified the police immediately her daughter did
not appear at the cottage. She would naturally conclude that
some social occasion or school business had intervened.'

'But if – for the sake of argument, mind! – *if* her mother had
killed her?'

'She would have preferred, of course, to have her found by the dog and by you (looking for the dog) than by going to the police to report her missing and perhaps inadvertently making some admission damaging to herself. All this is mere speculation, but there is a practical application which must have occurred to you even sooner than it occurred to me.'

'And that is?'

'That not only does Edward James not care for dogs, but, as human beings (for the most part) cannot detect any sound made by a dog-whistle, the inference is that nobody had ever heard Mrs Schumann's particular call and so nobody could have imitated it in whistling up Fergus and leading him to the body. I have pointed this out to Superintendent Phillips.'

'Wonder what made Fergus chase off like that, then? Still, Karen's wasn't the only death, and the dog wasn't mixed up with any of the others. But, returning to Mrs Schumann, nobody could possibly think that these are a woman's crimes, in spite of what I said about Mrs Schumann's large hands. Besides, there's still the question of motive. You haven't given any reason why Mrs Schumann should have killed her only daughter. She was evidently very fond of her. It's Otto, the son, she hates. Of course, family relationships can be very tricky things, and there's no doubt Mrs Schumann thought James was far too old for Karen. You don't think . . .'

'Stranger things have happened, if I guess your thought correctly. Mrs Schumann is still in the prime of life and must be within a year or two of Edward James's age. Then, of course, there is the five thousand pounds. Phillips has found that that was the handsome sum paid out on the premium bond.'

'Well, yes, I know that some people would do anything for money. But, granted that Mrs Schumann could have had motives for killing Karen, there's really nothing to connect her with the other two deaths. Look, supposing it had been physically possible for Otto to have murdered his sister, wouldn't you suspect him of causing the other two deaths as well?'

'In the case of Maria Machrado, I might suspect him. There seems no reason to suspect anybody in particular of the murder of the Italian maidservant, as you yourself have pointed out.'

'Yet you're convinced that we're not chasing three

murderers. You don't think there can be more than two people responsible for these three deaths, and you're pretty sure the number boils down to only one.'

'What I think is not evidence. We are leaving out of account, of course, the mysterious notices left pinned to the bodies.'

'By the way, what did you mean – it struck me that you had something special in mind – when you said that James answered what must have been an unexpected question without hesitation?'

'It was to do with the numbers which followed the *In Memoriam* notices.'

'Oh, yes, the fourth century *anno Domini*. Obviously it didn't work out. He came across with a couple of dates which, as a theological student and a historian, he was bound to have met with before. You think that cleared him?'

'If it did not, he is a cool customer or a quick thinker, and, of course, he may be both. We really know nothing about him.'

'But you don't *really* think Mrs Schumann is our murderer, do you?'

'It was you who directed my attention to the size of her hands, but I repeat that what I think is not evidence.'

'I'll tell you what!' exclaimed Laura suddenly. 'What's the objection to two murderers in collusion? I kill A, you kill B, and we both kill C just to confuse the issue? Wouldn't that put an end to all our problems?'

'One head is safer than two, when it comes to murder,' said Dame Beatrice, 'but I think you are right about the killing of C. It *was* done to confuse the police, and for no other reason.'

(7)

Dame Beatrice had meant what she said when she had spoken of not crossing the police line, but the murder of the Italian servant was so much more unreasonable than the first two deaths that she thought it would be well within her province in her official capacity to go along and talk to the Clancys.

She mentioned this to Phillips over the telephone and, having obtained their new address from him, she went to their pent-house flat in Southampton at a time when she concluded that Mrs Clancy, at any rate, was likely to have arrived home from school. She presented her credentials and was asked in.

The flat was a two-bedroom affair with a lounge-dining-room and a square kitchen, and was furnished with taste. The child and the dog were sent into the kitchen to play together.

'He understands most things we say,' said Mrs Clancy of her son, 'and I don't want him to hear about poor Lucia. He still misses her. We've told him she had to go home to look after her own little boy, but it doesn't really satisfy him. The only thing about the whole dreadful business which makes me so thankful is that we took him with us. We *had* considered leaving him in her charge, you know, as we were only going away for such a short time. I daren't think what would have happened if he'd been in the bungalow when it – when she—'

'I'm afraid there's not much doubt about what would have happened,' said Dame Beatrice grimly. 'I don't want to bother you with all the questions the police have already asked you,' she went on in a brisker tone, 'but my point of view, owing to the nature of my work, may be different from theirs, so will you be good enough to tell me all you know about Lucia's background before she entered your service?'

'Yes, of course, but it amounts to very little. My husband had to change his job, so we intended to sell our bungalow and live within easier distance of his work, but we couldn't buy until we had got rid of the bungalow, so I stayed on there and he came home at week-ends. It was far from ideal, but better, I suppose, than being married to a sailor. I was pregnant at the time, and naturally didn't want to be left alone, so we set about finding somebody to live in. Well, you know what it's like, trying to get a maid these days when you live in the country and have only a small place and can't afford to pay much. We advertised and we put our name down at employ-ment agencies, but it wasn't a bit of good, and then my husband had a brainwave and mentioned it to one or two of the people at the bank, and one of the customers knew of a charity which helps discharged prisoners, and they sent us Lucia. She'd been in prison for stealing, but they said they thought she meant to go straight if somebody would give her a job and be kind to her.

'When I got to know her, I found out that she'd been made redundant at the factory where she worked, ran through her savings, couldn't pay the rent and was too ignorant and friendless to find out how to get help. The magistrates gave her the lightest sentence they could. I suppose they realised that she wasn't the sort to be a habitual criminal. Anyway, she turned out to be quite a satisfactory worker, and when Derry was born she became genuinely fond of him. I soon knew I could trust her, so, as I knew I would be going back to a job as soon as I felt he was old enough to be left, I kept her on. Who on earth would be wicked enough to want to kill her? She was utterly harmless.'

'Did she get any letters while she was with you?'

'No. She was almost illiterate, you know, and I suppose her friends were the same, although I must say I should be surprised to hear she had any. There was an elderly mother, of course.'

'Acquaintances may be a better term. How many people, so far as you are aware, knew that she was in service at your bungalow?'

'Our relatives, of course, and the people at my husband's work – he's a bank-clerk – and of course I've mentioned her from time to time at my new school since I've gone back to a job, and any friends who came to visit us would have known, but I'm positively certain none of them would have murdered her. It's most likely somebody she knew in prison, don't you think?'

'I might well think so, but for the note left on the body.'

'Then there's a maniac at large in that district! Of course, I couldn't stay on in the bungalow. My nerves wouldn't stand it, so we moved at once and the bungalow is up for sale. I'm thankful for all sorts of reasons that we did move. For one thing, I can get along to school much more easily from here than from the bungalow; for another, John can come home every night, and there's a nursery I can take Derry to, to get him looked after while I'm working, because, of course, I haven't anybody helping me now.'

'How much interest do you find you take in the lives of the teachers at your school?'

'Well, I'm happily married, of course, so I don't exactly pry into other people's affairs,' replied Mrs Clancy, looking slightly surprised by the question. 'How do you mean?'

'Would you, for example, know what religious sects they belong to?'

'Precious few of them belong to any.'

'But there are exceptions?'

'Not that I would know of. The head is C. of E., I believe.'

'No Catholics?'

'Not that I know of.'

'You would not know, I suppose, anything about the late Miss Karen Schumann's views?'

'Oh, well, yes, as it happens, I do know about *her*. She called herself a Lutheran. Her father was apparently a minister before he left Germany. She was of German parentage, you know. But you don't think there is any connection between her death and Lucia's, do you?'

'It is difficult to detect one, certainly, except for some cryptic notices left pinned to the bodies.'

'Then there *is* a madman about! Oh, aren't I thankful we moved! I didn't care much about the idea of a flat in a town at one time, but now it seems so lovely to have other people below me and round about!'

'Has your school library a theological section?'

'There are the usual commentaries and things, but they only occupy a bit of a shelf in the history corner. I hardly ever go into the library unless I have to take a message to anybody who happens to be teaching in there – every class gets a library period a week – and I wouldn't know about there being a theological section except that I had to catalogue the library when the teacher who looks after it was down with flu and we had the County librarian coming. Well, when I say "catalogue it", that isn't exactly true, because, of course, we had a catalogue. What I had to do was to insert the new additions, so that the County librarian could see what to recommend that he should lend us. Part of the library is by purchase, you see, and part is on a long loan from the County.'

'So the number of theological works in the school library would not suffice Mr James for his studies?'

'Oh, our budding Doctor of Divinity! I should think that, years ago, he combed through anything the school had got!'

'Yet he worked in the school library at times, did he not?'

'Oh, yes, but on books he'd borrowed elsewhere.'

'Do you know that for a fact? – that he worked in the school library, but with books he had borrowed?'

'Oh, yes. He and Miss Schumann often used to stay after school and work in there. It was all quite proper, too. My hours are from nine to five, you see, so when my time was up, and the library key hadn't come back to my office, I had to go along and get it from them, so that all the school keys could be locked away. That was part of my job. The two of them were always working. She would mostly be doing her marking and he would be studying and making notes. When I had to interrupt them he never had to put any of his books back on the shelves, because they didn't belong to the school.'

'You wouldn't know whether they came from the public library, I suppose?'

'I expect most of them did, in the early days, but some he borrowed from Miss Schumann's mother. I know that, because one day, when he was slinging them into his bag and arguing his head off about some pope or bishop or something, he dropped one, and she told him to be careful, otherwise her mother wouldn't lend him any more of her father's books. Quite annoyed with him, she was, and, of course, being a man, he didn't like being ticked off in front of me, so he said, "My misguided little something or other . . ."'

'Aryan?'

'That's right – "your father's books are at least being put to some use again". She was mad with him. "Not by being dropped on the floor," she said, "and I'll thank you for not referring to me as a Nazi!" He stared a bit at that, then he gave a nasty little snigger and said, "Oh, were they the fore-runners? I had no idea!" I thought it was time to break it up, so I asked for the key, saw them out, locked up and went home.'

Dame Beatrice had only one more question to ask.

'Does Mr James read German, then?'

'Oh, yes, and speaks it, too. It annoyed some of the others, because he and Miss Schumann used to talk to each other in German in the Common Room. The others thought it was just a bit of show-off, because, of course, Miss Schumann, who was born and brought up over here, could speak perfect English. Anything else I can tell you? I only ask because I don't like leaving Derry too long, although he loves the dog, of course.'

Dame Beatrice said that there was nothing else she wanted to ask. She thanked Mrs Clancy and was invited to come again at any time. She took her leave and went back to the Kensington house, where she found Laura scowling at a piece of graph paper covered with scribbled figures, weird doodles and shorthand symbols. She looked up as Dame Beatrice came in, and pushed the paper away.

'How did you get on?' she asked.

'A glimmer of light is discernable, but, of course, it may be no more than a will o' the wisp. Your own train of thought appears to be of a complicated and unsatisfactory nature – or are you casting spells?'

'I've been trying to work out a problem in progressions, but it won't jell.'

'In progressions?'

'Yes. You see, we've now got three sets of figures to play with, and three nationalities, so I ought to be able to work out the next step, but I can't. Three hundred and twenty-five and three hundred and eighty and eleven hundred and fifty-five don't make any sense at all. Of course, mathematics was never my life's work.'

'There is a number common to all, in one sense.'

'Yes, the fifty-five bit. Three hundred and twenty-five from three hundred and eighty leaves fifty-five, and that comes after the eleven hundred, but I can't get any further.'

'Divide the fifty-five by the eleven, ignoring zero. The result, if you are well versed in the multiplication table, is five.'

'So what?'

'So we may expect two more of these extraordinary murders, making five in all.'

Laura made a face at her.

'All flippancy aside, though,' she said, '*did* you really find out something useful this afternoon?'

'I do not know yet whether what I found out was useful, but it certainly was quite interesting. James was in the habit of working in the school library in his own time, so he may be speaking the truth about the way he spent that day. He borrowed theological treatises from Mrs Schumann's late husband's library, so he may have visited her cottage more often than we were led to suppose.'

'More often than Mrs Schumann admitted, you mean?'

'I think it would be unfair to put it like that. We asked how often he spent the week-end there with his fiancée, I believe. The answer Mrs Schumann gave was no doubt perfectly truthful.'

'She could have added the other bit, though, couldn't she? – that sometimes he went when Karen wasn't there.'

'It may not have occurred to her to do so. Actually, why should it? One more tiny point emerged. You remember Mrs Schumann's telling us of her daughter's indignation when Edward James called her a misguided little Aryan?'

'Yes. It seemed an odd sort of remark to make. We thought so at the time.'

'We did know that they were having a theological discussion, but that remark was concluded in a way that Mrs Schumann did not tell us because I am sure her daughter did not see that it had any significance and therefore, being full of what she regarded as the insult of being called an Aryan, did not think worth repeating.'

'What *was* this significant addition?'

'Mrs Clancy, who was present, said that James sniggered and added, "Oh, were they the forerunners? I had no idea!"'

'Forerunners of what?' asked Laura.

'The Nazis.'

'Doesn't seem a very profound remark to me.'

'It turns on the word Aryan.'

'You speak in riddles, as ever. Tell me more.'

'Oh, no,' said Dame Beatrice. 'You work it out for yourself. Or, rather, you can go to the public library and work it out there. James studied history as well as theology, you know.'

'Is this a genuine assignment?'

'There are more ways than one of spelling Aryan.'

'*Oh*!' exclaimed Laura, enlightened. 'Now I get it! So what I do is to look up – Yes, I see! Of course I see! When do you want me to go?'

'When you like. Of course, even when we have the confirmation which you will acquire, we shall be very little further forward in proving guilt. What I would wish, though, is that we could acquire the power to prevent the murderer from striking again.'

'You think he will?'

'Well, except for (I think) the first one, these murders seem to me motiveless except for the most dreadful motive of all, the lust to kill.'

CHAPTER FOUR

Sigh No More, Ladies

'I says to her "Polly, and how d'ye do?"
To me way-ay, blow the man down.
Says she, "None the better for seeing of you!"
Oh, gimme some time to blow the man down.'

_____

(1)

'We're no further forward,' said Phillips. He looked and sounded exhausted. 'I thought, over the Spanish girl, the C.I.D. had jumped us, and got the man we ought to have got, but it's all gone blue on us again. This third death has got us all hay-wire. There was a possible connection between the first two murders, in a way . . .'

'What was the connection?' asked Dame Beatrice.

'Oh, only that the Schumann family formed a link. James was engaged to the German girl, and Otto Schumann got the Spanish girl into trouble and admits that they had a row. Oh, I agree it's a slender thread,' he added, catching Dame Beatrice's eye, 'but it made me think perhaps something was going to make sense somewhere. This pointless business of the third murder leaves us guessing. There isn't a tie-up anywhere.'

'Except, as a long shot, with the first death.'

'How do you make that out, ma'am?'

'The only suggestion I can make is that there is a tenuous link with the school.'

'You mean that Miss Schumann and James were on the staff – he still is, of course – and this Italian maid was employed by the school secretary? You're right to call it a long shot, I would say.'

'I entirely agree,' Dame Beatrice meekly admitted.

'What we're on to at present,' Phillips went on, 'is checking up on all the foreigners – which includes all the people with foreign names – over a radius of forty miles from Wandles Parva.'

'That means that some of your foreigners live in the sea,' said Laura.

'I'm past making or taking jokes, Mrs Gavin.'

Laura apologised, and Dame Beatrice said,

'I don't envy you your task, Superintendent.'

'It's a routine matter, ma'am, and as dull as most of the sifting-out jobs we do, but it's the only thing we can think of. So far, I reckon we've done about half the area we've marked out, but, of course, this joker may not be a local man at all.'

'Then he's done his homework pretty well,' said Laura. 'I mean, look at the facts. Karen Schumann's body was found almost at the centre of your circle, and Maria Machrado's had been put ten miles or more inside your boundaries. In both cases the murderer must have known that other vehicles, lorries in the one case and tanks in the other, were almost certain to confuse, if not actually obliterate, any tell-tale tracks his car may have left. This Italian woman wasn't taken away by car, but left in the bungalow where she was killed, and that's not so far away, either.'

'I know, Mrs Gavin, and that ought to tell us more than it seems to. Granted it's the same fellow all the time, it looks as though he *had* to move the first two bodies. Why was it safe for him to leave the third one?'

'If we knew that, we should know who he is, I suppose,' said Laura. 'In other words, there was some obvious connection between him and the place or places where the first two murders were committed, but nothing to connect him with the Clancy bungalow.'

'There you are, then! Then there's another fact which ought to be a help to us, but isn't.'

'You mean that each of these deaths has been brought about while some sort of school holiday was in progress, don't you?'

'That's it, Mrs Gavin, but there, again, although two of the murders seem to tie up, they are not the same two. Very few people outside the school would have been able to plan that Karen Schumann was to be killed on an odd day's holiday – one, I mean, that the general public wouldn't know anything about – and Maria Machrado was murdered at a time when most people would be back at work after their Christmas break.

All right, that ought to narrow it. The snag is that *anybody* – just anybody at all – could have planned the murder of Lucia What-Name for Easter Saturday. Even if the doctors hadn't given us the dope about time of death, we could have deduced it easily enough. She went to church on Good Friday – we know that for a fact. Then she must have cooked herself supper because she left a fishy frying-pan in the sink. She hadn't finished putting back the furniture in the bedroom she'd been spring-cleaning when her murderer knocked at the door. We're sure he didn't come on Easter Sunday, (apart from the medical evidence, I mean), because she'd promised the priest she'd go to Mass again on that day and didn't turn up, and also she'd left herself half a bottle of the wine which the Clancys (they said) had given her and, in addition, there was a choice little joint of uncooked chicken they'd left for her in the fridge. There was no sense whatever in that poor creature's death. It just seems as though we're looking for somebody who hates foreigners, and that's why we're checking over this forty-mile radius I mentioned.'

'And warning people?' asked Dame Beatrice.

'Well, it's not our policy to spread alarm, as you're well aware, Dame Beatrice, but, for their own sakes, we've suggested to them that they always have another person with them if they can manage it. It isn't even as if it's Jews or Negroes. We could soon track down the chap and his gang if it was that. It's this promiscuous killing of *any* foreigner, apparently, that's got us up a gum tree.'

An added complication (in Laura's view) and a welcome item of light relief (in the opinion of Dame Beatrice) was supplied by the arrival of Hamish from school three weeks after Easter. He was accompanied by a boy named Cooper and by Cooper's Angora rabbit and his own tiny Yorkshire terrier bitch.

'This is Lindy Lou,' he explained, exhibiting the scrap of a dog. 'Mrs Conelly-Cardew was sorry for me when I had to leave Fergus at home because Mr Conelly-Cardew said he was too big to have at school, so she gave me Lindy for an Easter egg. She gave all of us something for a present, as we weren't to go home, but mine was far the best.'

'Why on earth should she give you a valuable dog like this?' demanded Laura, taking Lindy Lou in her arms and receiving an ecstatic lick from the tiny thoroughbred.

'Oh, she thinks a good deal of me, ' replied her son, with his usual modesty. 'So she ought to, actually. You see, I saved her life – well, I probably did.'

'Some people have all the fun! What happened? Was she drowning in a butt of Malmsey?'

'No. A tramp stopped her, and I happened to be out on Pegasus, so I rode up, and the tramp seemed rather nasty, so I sloshed him with my riding-crop and he staggered back and sat down and Pegasus kicked him on the head, so that was all right, and I dismounted and escorted Mrs Conelly-Cardew back to school and gave myself up.'

'Gave yourself up?'

'Oh, yes. You see, I was out of bounds when I rescued Mrs Conelly-Cardew. Rather a long way out of bounds, actually.'

'I hope the headmaster beat you.'

'Oh, yes, of course he did, but Grandjean looked at my bum through his magnifying glass afterwards, and couldn't see any marks, so that shows Mr Conelly-Cardew's gratitude, doesn't it? I hardly felt the whacking, but, of course, he had to make a gesture. I believe in maintaining discipline, do not you, mamma?'

'I should hardly think *that* was maintaining it,' said Laura. 'You'd better introduce Lindy Lou to Fergus, so that he doesn't think she's something to eat.'

'Is it true Fergus found a dead body? Gosh, I wish I'd been there! Some of the men at school read about it in the paper and were frightfully sick to think that *my* dog had done a wizard thing like that! '

The fourth murder took place on Whit Tuesday, a few days after Hamish, fortunately for Laura's peace of mind, had returned to school.

(2)

Marie-Jeanne Vermier was a French student who had opted to teach English in French schools, and as part of her course had been able to take advantage of a scheme which enabled her to spend the whole of the summer term in England to attend lectures and classes in an extra-mural capacity, and to reciprocate (since she was in receipt of a grant) by giving part of her time to conducting classes in French conversation at an English school while she was over in this country.

The headmaster of the comprehensive school at which James was the history and religious knowledge specialist and Agnes Clancy the school secretary, was not particularly in favour of the scheme. It took children out of their ordinary French lessons once or twice a week, and this was a nuisance because it split classes, since the maximum number of children who could be allotted to the student at any one time was not more than fifteen. Added to this was the vexation of having to alter the time-table in order to incorporate, for one term only, these lessons in French conversation, so that all who were to sit the General Certificate of Education examination might take advantage of what was going on. These alterations were a necessary chore, since Her Majesty's Inspectors of Schools were entitled to insist on them, and although H.M.I.'s are no longer regarded as the autocrats and dictators they once were, but rather as the teachers' friends and advisers, (and sometimes, even, their admirers), their word in some matters is still law.

Marie-Jeanne, therefore, appeared (outwardly self-possessed, inwardly shy and nervous) in the staff Common Room in company with the mistress who had taken Karen Schumann's place the previous term. She was introduced all round, bowed, made her polite and carefully enunciated 'Good morning, how do you do?' and was taken back to the headmaster's room for a further friendly chat and some kindly advice.

He was filled with misgivings, for his G.C.E. boys were not very much younger than Marie-Jeanne, and he asked her whether she would prefer that he did not send them to her classes. Some schools, he knew, relegated their French-conversation students to the first and second year children, but he felt that his G.C.E. groups ought not to be denied something which was calculated to help them in their French Oral examination. Marie-Jeanne said that she would prefer to leave it to him, and it was arranged that she would take mixed groups on a month's trial, 'and then', said the headmaster, 'we can reveiw the situation and see how we stand'.

Fortunately for her, the girls immediately decided to fall for Marie-Jeanne's porcelain prettiness, and therefore protected her whenever they thought she needed protection, which was seldom. To do the boys justice, she was soon regarded by them as beneath their notice and, in any case, the majority of them were far too dignified to stoop to the middle-school practice of 'playing her up'.

Lodgings had been found for her near the school, so she came within the net which the police were casting. Dame Beatrice and Laura were back at the Stone House and had the news of her appointment from Phillips who, because of his local knowledge, was still working on the cases in conjunction with the men from Scotland Yard.

'I'd be happier, ma'am, if a young girl like that, a stranger here, was in the same digs as some of the other women teachers instead of lodging with this Mrs Downton on her own,' he said. 'It's too much of a tie-up, considering what happened to Miss Schumann, to have a good-looking young foreign girl working at the school with nobody really responsible for her safety.'

'You're getting fanciful, Phillips, old soul,' said Laura. 'Who's going to murder a girl who's just come over from France?'

'That's what we don't know, Mrs Gavin. Who'd have thought anybody would murder this last Italian woman? What with the Schumann family and James, I don't feel like taking chances with anybody foreign connected with that school.'

'Well,' said Dame Beatrice, 'bring the child here. I am entirely of your opinion in the matter of not taking chances, and if the girl is in my charge I can guarantee that she will not be molested. George or Laura can drive her to school each day and pick her up each afternoon, and in this house she will be safe.'

'The idea would be grand if she were teaching full time at the school, Dame Beatrice, but one day a week she attends classes at Southampton University and she puts in one morning and one evening a week at a college of languages in Bournemouth, so I'm told by the headmaster. It will be more than can be expected of you and Mrs Gavin to keep the tabs on her all the time, I'm afraid, although I'm obliged to you for the kind suggestion.'

'Nonsense, Superintendent. I will go to the school and obtain a full statement of her commitments from the headmaster, and then we shall see that she is guarded satisfactorily.'

'While it was Karen Schumann and Maria Machrado who were killed, it seemed to make some kind of sense,' said Laura, when Phillips had gone, 'and I would have said that this French kid had no more to fear from the murderer than I have myself, but the unaccountable murder of the Italian maid puts the thing in a different light. It looks – as Phillips himself obviously thinks – that *any* foreign woman is in possible danger.'

So Marie-Jeanne, a little bewildered and slightly put out by her sudden transition to the realms of glory, came to reside at the Stone House. She was given no explanation at first for the change in her lot, but Phillips had his own story for her bereft landlady to the effect that some of the girl's relatives had domiciled themselves near Brockenhurst and had invited Marie-Jeanne to stay with them, and she took up her new quarters immediately.

The arrangement worked extremely well. The girl was always under escort on her journeys to her various assignments, talked English with Dame Beatrice and Laura and French with Henri and Celestine, and was a docile, pleasant addition to the household. Dame Beatrice, however, thought it well, after she had settled down and was obviously happy in her new circumstances, to let her know why she was there, and gave the information in terms which were as little frightening as possible, although it was not possible to make them sound completely reassuring. She felt compelled to enlighten the girl because of an innocent admission which Marie-Jeanne made one evening in the course of conversation. This was almost at the beginning of her stay. Dame Beatrice had asked her how she liked the school.

'Oh,' said Marie-Jeanne, 'but very much! The teachers are so kind, especially Mr James. He speaks French very well, quite as well as the French mistress, who also, of course, is English and takes holidays in France each year and was there in the time of Occupation, so she tells me. But Mr James is more interesting because he has much knowledge of the world and I think is very intelligent. I like the French mistress, for she is intelligent, too, but a woman is not as well-informed as a man, do you think?'

'Oh, golly!' said Laura, later, to her employer. 'So James is on the ball already!'

'He may simply be showing a normal kindly reaction towards the stranger who is within his gates, and little Marie-Jeanne, moreover, is fresh and unspoiled, and really quite charming.'

'But he has the reputation of being withdrawn and unsociable. Why should he suddenly take up with fresh, unspoiled young girls?'

'Perhaps because they *are* fresh and unspoiled, as I say.'

'All the same, you've seen fit to warn her.'

'Not specifically against Edward James. I could hardly do that, at the present stage.'

'She seems to be settling down well enough with us, and her time is pretty fully occupied, what with school and her lectures and her private study and essays, but what's going to happen at Whitsun?'

'According to the time-table with which I was supplied, the school has Whit Monday and the following day as the Whitsun break, the School of Languages has Whit Monday, and her University lectures are not affected, since she attends them on Fridays only. I suggest we take her to London for the weekend and bring her back on the evening of Whit Tuesday. She can miss one session at the School of Languages – she tells me that most of the students intend to stay away from classes on that Tuesday – and she will enjoy a short stay in Town. She will be under our eye the whole of the week-end and will also be out of the danger zone. What is your reaction to my suggestion?'

The programme was carried out to the satisfaction of all concerned, and Marie-Jeanne, who was a nice child, was profuse in thanks and delight. On the Wednesday morning Dame Beatrice greeted Laura with the latest news as soon as George had taken the French girl off to school.

'We may or may not have saved Marie-Jeanne,' she said, when Laura, who had been riding, came down to a late breakfast after a bath and a change of clothes, 'but the death is announced of the senior French mistress. The murder follows the pattern of the others, and the notice on the body, affixed this time by means of an old-fashioned hatpin, reads: *Cathari 1207*.'

'And this is the woman who took Karen Schumann's place at the school,' said Laura. 'Oh, Lord! '

(3)

The name of the senior French mistress was Mrs Castle. Soon after the death of Karen Schumann the two young teachers who had lodged at the same house decided to change their digs. For no reason which they could explain except to one another, they disliked the thought of remaining in rooms which still seemed connected with a girl who had been murdered.

Mrs Castle was recently widowed and had been glad to obtain Karen's vacant post, and it was at her suggestion, because she needed help in paying off the mortgage on a new house, that the two young women should live in with her, share and share alike with regard to food, with the other household necessities and the charwoman's pay, and that they should pay a reasonable rent for their rooms. They were glad to agree, and moved in three weeks before Whitsun, for the headmaster had not been able to find a replacement for Karen Schumann until the beginning of the summer term.

The arrangement worked well. The two girls were each able to have a bed-sitter, there was a common dining-room and Mrs Castle had her own quarters. These consisted of a lounge on the ground floor and the smallest of the three bedrooms. Hers was a modern house, well-appointed and intelligently equipped, and the younger women were more than satisfied with their change of domicile. Christian names, Chris and Terry, (the girls), Thea, (Mrs Castle), were exchanged and used, and all went swimmingly.

In the evenings, after an early supper which the three took turns at cooking, a good deal of school shop was discussed and there was marking and preparation to be done. Chris was the junior history teacher, Terry took R.K. and some of the lower-school French. Thus there was a tie-up with both Mrs Castle and James. The young teachers sometimes went out with their friends from the Art School staff at week-ends, and on Sundays Mrs Castle usually went over to see her parents who lived in Romsey.

These and subsequent facts about the life lived by the three women were elicited later by the police. Meanwhile the days passed and the Whitsun holiday approached. The two girls were to spend Whit Monday with Terry's brother and his wife, who kept a small launch down at Hamworthy. They were to go across to Brownsea Island in it and then perhaps follow the Wareham Channel up to the quay at the town and have tea there before returning to moorings. Mrs Castle was to spend the whole of the week-end, from the Saturday morning until the Tuesday afternoon, with her parents.

As it happened, neither of these plans worked out. Mrs Castle learned that her parents were going for the week-end to her late husband's people who lived in the Midlands. They wanted her to go with them, but she saw little point (she told the others) in spending the short week-end break in a manu-facturing town, so she telephoned her mother more or less to that effect, and promised to visit her parents the week-end after their return.

Upon this, Terry felt impelled to invite her to join the boat-ing party, saying that there was plenty of room in the launch for another person, and that she was certain her brother would not mind. This might or might not have been true, but it was never put to the test since, over the school telephone during the school dinner hour, came a message from the brother's wife to say that the launch was out of commission, and that the couple had changed their plans accordingly, and had arranged to spend the Whitsun week-end in Paris.

'I do think they might have let me know sooner,' grumbled Terry to the other two that evening. 'Now everything's gone phut. What shall we do instead?'

'I suppose I'd better join my parents after all,' said Mrs Castle. 'I haven't any excuse not to, have I? Oh, dear! I really don't want to trail up to Stafford for the week-end, and my in-laws will be there. I suppose they mean well, but they'll do nothing but talk about Stephen and the old days, and that's an awful bore.'

'Well, need you go?' asked Terry. 'You don't have to tell them the boat-trip is off. Let's all think of something quickly. Come on, Chris! Ideas?'

'London?'

'That would do for Monday, I suppose, although we're going on Saturday, don't forget.'

'Oh, I don't call *that* going to London!'

'What do *you* think, Thea?' asked Terry.

'A Bank Holiday in Town?' Mrs Castle sounded doubtful.

'Not London, then. Think again, Chris,' said Terry.

'Well, we could still go to Brownsea. There are public launches from Poole quay.'

'Squashed in among the proletariat?' demanded Terry. 'What a revolting idea!'

'You're very difficult to please. What about a picnic in the New Forest, then?'

This was acceptable to the others, a route was agreed on and picnic viands purchased and put into the refrigerator on Friday evening ready for Monday's outing.

'What made them put off their picnic until the Monday? What happened in London on Saturday afternoon, and what did they do on Sunday?' asked Dame Beatrice, when she received these details from Detective-Inspector Maisry.

'Ah, that's the interesting part of the story,' he replied. 'On Whit Saturday and Whit Monday, as you may know, the British Games are held at the White City stadium. Well, the physical education staff at the school had arranged to take a motor-coach party of boys and girls to London on the Saturday to visit the White City and see the athletics. Well, the idea of a jaunt to London seems to have made a strong appeal to the youngsters, so, instead of a single coach-load which had been envisaged when the plan was first put forward, more than a hundred boys and girls put their names on the list, and three coaches were required if all who wanted to do so could go.

'Well, you probably know about these school outings. If up

to twenty children go, at least one teacher must accompany them; up to forty, two teachers, and so on. For a hundred children, five of the staff were required, which, to all intents and purposes, meant six. The physical education at this particular school is in the hands of one man, a Mr Shorthorne, and one woman, a Miss Huntley, with another girl, Miss Borman, who takes something called Modern Dance. She was perfectly willing to help with the coachloads, but three more volunteers were called for, and the response came from the two young women who were housed with Mrs Castle, and a certain Mr Towsdale, a friend of the P.E. master.'

'But Mrs Castle did not go?'

'No, she did not go. According to the other two, she decided to spend the day in Bournemouth.'

'And she did so?'

'We don't know yet. All we do know is that when the other two returned to the house at about nine o'clock on Whit Saturday night she was not there, and they don't know at what time she came in. She had a key, of course, so they got themselves a bit of supper and turned in early. They concluded that she had gone to the evening performance at the Winter Garden or somewhere.'

'But Mrs Castle did come back to the house that night?'

'Yes, she was there at breakfast, but gave no indication of how she had spent the day and the evening. After breakfast she said she was going to church and, from there, out to lunch. She supplied no details, but they took it for granted that she had met friends in Bournemouth the day before, and had been invited to lunch on Sunday. They never saw her alive again.'

'What happened on Whit Monday, then, if she had not come back to the house?'

'The other two went for their outing.'

'Without trying to find out what had happened to Mrs Castle? Surely they were concerned for her?'

'They say they concluded that she had been asked to stay the night with the friend or friends who had invited her out to lunch, and if you know the sort of easy-going life these unattached professional women lead, it's a perfectly likely story. You see, the majority of them think in terms of boy-friends and subsequent marriage, and there's a sort of gentlemen's agreement – ladies' agreement, I suppose one ought to call it – that they don't muscle in on one another, ask any awkward questions or do anything else to queer one another's pitch. Prostitutes have the same unwritten law, of course – not that I'm making any comparisons, naturally.'

Laura laughed. Dame Beatrice said:

'And then?'

'Well, when she didn't show up at the house on Whit Monday night either, apparently they did feel it was a bit odd, but they did nothing about it until eight o'clock on Tuesday evening, when they rang up the headmaster at his home, but by that time the body had been discovered by a couple of Boy Scouts playing one of those spooring games, or whatever they call them, over by Badbury Rings.'

'Poor kids! ' said Laura. 'How beastly for them! '

'Yes, indeed, Mrs Gavin. Not at all the sort of discovery I'd like my boy to make.'

'Where exactly was this?' Dame Beatrice asked.

'You know that avenue of trees which leads past the Rings and was planted, I believe, by one of the owners of Kingston Lacey, that big house owned by the same Bankes family as own Corfe Castle? Well, between the trees on the left-hand side of the road as you go towards Wimborne Minster, and the big open space where people park their cars, and picnic and play games and so forth, there's a sort of broad pathway with bushes that partly screen it from the road. That's where they found her.'

'And the cause of death?'

'Just like the other three, and, another similarity, the body had been dumped, we think. She didn't die on the spot where these lads found her. The doctor thinks she was killed some-time on Whit Sunday, probably in the afternoon.'

'And any car tracks?'

'Indistinguishable. Any number of cars had passed that way during the Whitsun week-end, of course. The inference is that the body was hidden away and then dumped late on Sunday evening. Whitsun being another school holiday, Phillips has had a go at James again, and we're checking on the movements of the two young women, of course. As I say, I can understand their conduct up to Whit Monday afternoon, but I can't understand why they didn't report Mrs Castle's absence until latish on the Tuesday evening.'

'Just an instinct not to interfere, as I think you indicated,' said Laura.

'Yes, so they told their headmaster. But when she hadn't shown up on Tuesday at eight, and knowing that she'd got several things to get ready before she went to school on the following morning, they decided that something was wrong.'

'And before that time you knew what it was.'

'Yes. These kids found her at just after three on Whit Monday afternoon, but, until the headmaster came forward, we hadn't any means of identifying her.'

'I wonder somebody had not stumbled upon the body earlier in the day. Badbury Rings and their environs are well-frequented,' said Dame Beatrice.

'We've no information. If anybody had found the body earlier, they made no move to let us know.'

'People do hate getting mixed up in anything fishy,' said Laura, 'and on a Bank Holiday, too, when their only object is to enjoy themselves.'

'Not what you'd call good citizenship, Mrs Gavin.'

'No, but my sympathies are with them,' retorted Laura. 'It's not as though there was anything they could do for the woman herself.'

'Well, of course, as I say, we don't know that anybody else *had* stumbled upon the body. It was pretty well screened by the bushes.'

'Was Mrs Castle a big, heavy woman?' asked Dame Beatrice.

'Oh, no, slim and small-boned. Probably weighed less than eight stone. The bushes weren't even broken away.'

'What had Edward James to say for himself? Did he consider that he was being victimised?'

'Oh, Phillips and I interviewed the whole staff, including the headmaster, but, of course, we were chiefly interested in James and the two young women. We also talked to Mrs Castle's neighbours, but there was very little they could tell us.'

What this amounted to was, at that preliminary stage of the enquiry, of negligible help to the police. She was a quiet, pleasant neighbour, went off for week-ends quite often and had once asked whether they would mind if she kept a dog.

'Taking it as it comes,' said Phillips, 'we still don't know where Mrs Castle went on Saturday, or whether she was alone, or with friends, or with whoever murdered her. Maisry thinks the chances are that she went to Bournemouth, as she had stated that such was her intention. There's nothing shady about her past. We've checked pretty carefully, but shall continue with that, of course. However, it seems likely that this is one of the series involving foreigners, and is as motiveless as the other deaths.'

'Mrs Castle wasn't a foreigner,' said Laura.

'She taught a foreign language, Mrs Gavin, and was caught up with the Resistance. Well, we know she went back to her house on Saturday night, because she was at breakfast with the two young women on Sunday morning. It was a latish breakfast, and after it she set out for church. At least, she told them she was going to church, but we don't know which church and the other two don't know which denomination she favoured. We've tried them all, but she doesn't seem to have been a church member and nothing has come of our efforts to trace where she went.'

'Or whether she went to church at all,' said Laura. 'Churches are not so well attended nowadays. You'd think she'd have been spotted if she *had* gone.'

'Ah, but perhaps you're forgetting that it was Whit Sunday, Mrs Gavin. At the big church festivals – Christmas, Easter, Whitsun and, of course, the Harvest Thanksgiving – all churches are much fuller than usual.'

'Christmas, Easter and Harvest Festivals, yes, but I shouldn't have thought Whitsun so much.'

'Oh, yes, the flowers, Mrs Gavin. They are a great attraction, I assure you.'

'So all trace of Mrs Castle vanished after she left the house on Whit Sunday,' said Dame Beatrice. 'I wonder at what time she went out? Presumably, if she went to church, she attended the eleven o'clock morning service.'

'She left her house at half-past ten.'

'On foot or by car?'

'On foot, but, of course, she may have caught a bus. We're still checking on that. There's a bus stop within five minutes' walk of the house, and if she caught the ten-forty she could have been in Romsey, we'll say, for service in the Abbey, at eleven-ten. There is no earlier bus on Sundays except one at eight-fifteen. If she walked, there are five churches in her own town she could have reached before eleven o'clock, and we've called on two vicars, a Catholic priest, a Congregational and a Baptist minister. The Methodist chapel and the Salvation Army headquarters are both so near her house that she would hardly have needed to leave at half-past ten to get to them by eleven, but we are making enquiries, just the same.'

'Still, it's the fact that she didn't go back to the house for lunch, which is the important point, I suppose,' said Laura. 'She must have lunched somewhere.'

'Unless she was killed during the morning, Mrs Gavin, although the doctor thinks the afternoon more likely, but the fact that the body was not reported until Monday afternoon, when the Boy Scouts discovered it, hasn't helped the doctors to fix the precise hour of the death. Then, we don't know where the poor woman's body was hidden before it was dumped, and, as you know, the temperature of the atmosphere can make a considerable difference in determining the time of death, because it affects the onset and disappearance of *rigor mortis*.'

'What have the two young women to say for themselves? — not that there is any reason to suspect them, of course,' said Dame Beatrice.

'They have very little to say. They are upset and horrified, but they knew very little about Mrs Castle. She was merely a colleague and the owner of the house. The three had their breakfast and their other cooked meals together as a general rule, but this was a matter of mutual convenience rather than of individual choice, and accounts for most of the time they spent in one another's company, since, apart from these meal-

times, the young women went each her own way, and Mrs
Castle went hers.'

'How did they say they spent Sunday and Monday? We
know that they went to London with a school party on Saturday, and, in any case, Saturday is not in question, as Mrs
Castle is known to have been alive on Sunday morning. At
least – is there any confirmation of the young women's asser-
tion that she *was* alive on Sunday morning?'

'Oh, yes. A Mrs Reynolds, who lives next door, saw her
leave and, without being prompted, puts the time as round
about half-past ten. As for the young women themselves, they
say that, after Mrs Castle left, they did those bits of washing
which do not get sent to the laundry – small, personal gar-
ments, stockings and so forth – then prepared and cooked lunch
and after lunch went for a stroll in the local park. They came
back to tea, played some gramophone records, switched on the
television, had a snack for supper and went to bed early, as
they had changed their minds about their outing, and intended
to have a long day in London on the morrow instead of
picnicking as they had planned.'

'And they went to London?'

'They went towards it. The roads were very crowded and
by lunch-time they had reached Guildford, where, after having
to wait for some time, they secured a table for lunch. They
did not finish this meal until a quarter past two, and, because
of this, they gave up any idea of going on. Instead, they visited
Guildford Cathedral, which was thronged with sightseers. They
then drove to Dorking, where they had tea at about four
o'clock, and then came back to the house, which they reached
at half-past eight. Some of this is confirmed. They signed the
visitors' book in the Cathedral and are remembered at the
Dorking hotel.'

'And there is nothing in Mrs Castle's past life which would
indicate that she had an enemy or enemies capable of killing
her?'

'No. Her past is an open book. She came of an ordinary
lower middle class family, went to be trained as a teacher,
specialising in French, went to live in France and got caught
up in the Resistance, came home, taught over here for three

years, married, moved with her husband to Hampshire, continued to teach for another couple of years, then, his salary and prospects improving, she gave up her job for five years, but his death made it imperative that she should earn her living again. She has no children.'

'Anything unsatisfactory known about her husband's death?' asked Laura.

'Nothing at all, Mrs Gavin, in the way that I know you mean. He was foolish enough, in spite of warnings, to bathe on an outgoing tide at a noted danger-spot on the North Devon coast and got swept out to sea. We've checked on that. It was a sheer accident caused by his own obstinacy and his disregard of the danger signals which were being flown from the beach.'

'And at the school? Was she popular?'

'She had been there a very short time, as you know, but seems to have been quite an acceptable member of staff, and was kind to this young French girl you have staying with you.'

'And what of Edward James?' asked Dame Beatrice.

'Ah, yes, James. Here the story is not at all satisfactory and we are still trying to check on it. He tells us that on Saturday he went to Oxford to consult a friend on some points in connection with his theological studies. He does not seem to have warned this friend – a certain Mr Halling – to expect him and, not surprisingly on a Saturday afternoon, found that he was out. He says that he then went to Iffley to look at the church, returned to Oxford and had tea at a crowded restaurant near Carfax and then returned to his lodgings where his landlady had left him some cold meat and salad, she herself having gone to Salisbury.

'On Sunday he says that he wrote up some notes for a thesis, went to lunch with another member of the school staff, a certain Mr Such, who confirms this – says they had a snack and a beer in the local – and then that he went in a hired car, driven by himself, to visit Mrs Schumann.'

'Aha!' said Laura. 'The plot thickens!'

'Not so much as you might think, Mrs Gavin. She was out when he got there. We've got her story, and it seems that she'd gone to visit her husband's grave and put some flowers on it.'

'Really?'

'Well, we've found the place where she bought the flowers.'

'On a Sunday?'

'Yes, Mrs Gavin. There's a stall where they sell flowers to the people who are visiting relatives and friends in the cottage hospital. She went to this stall before she visited the grave.'

'And do they remember Mrs Schumann at the cemetery?'

'Who ever remembers anybody?' demanded the Superintendent, with resignation but without bitterness. 'There were certainly flowers on the grave.'

'It doesn't seem as though she was expecting a visitor if she was not at home when James called.'

'When he *says* he called, Mrs Gavin.'

'You suspect him of murdering this Mrs Castle, then?'

'Oh, no, we don't suspect anybody in particular, but Mrs Castle was a teacher at the school, so the school, once again, makes a starting-point, that's all.'

'It's rather peculiar that both Karen Schumann and this Mrs Castle were sharing digs with Miss Tompkins and Miss O'Reilly when they were murdered,' said Laura thoughtfully. 'Added to which, those two girls would have known that Mrs Clancy had an Italian maid. She said she must have mentioned Lucia in the staff Common Room.'

Phillips did not comment on this directly. He said,

'We're up a gum tree. Like the first and third murder, this seems motiveless.'

'I don't think the murder of Karen Schumann was motiveless,' said Laura. 'If only we could get at the reason for her death, I believe the others would fall into line. One thing, again Otto Schumann can't be involved, can he?'

'No, he can't. He's at sea again. There were quite valid reasons for connecting him with the death of Machrado, but with three others deaths under review, deaths in which he can't possibly have had any part, we must consider him at present in the clear.'

'Oh, well, that's something.' The Superintendent took his leave, and Laura added, to Dame Beatrice, 'I wish I could find some way of sticking *my* neck out in the direction of this madman. I don't think he'd find *me* all that easy to throttle.

Could I pretend to be Swedish, or Russian or something? What do you think about James now? Surely he wouldn't have gone over there on the off-chance of finding Mrs Schumann at home?'

'We could ask her whether he was in the habit of paying these informal visits, of course. If he went for the purpose of borrowing books from her husband's theological library, it is possible that he would drop in from time to time without feeling that he must notify her beforehand of his coming.'

'You mean he would suddenly find he could do with some-body's commentary on something or other, and would buzz off to her on the chance that she was in and would lend it to him?'

'It seems a reasonable supposition.'

'What did you make of the last note left on the body?'

'Nothing whatever.'

'I wonder what James did on Whit Monday?'

'If the body was placed in the bushes near Badbury Rings on Sunday night or early on Monday morning, it would scarcely matter what anybody did on Whit Monday, but, as a point of interest, we will find out.' She rang up Phillips a little later in the day.

'On Whit Monday?' he said. 'Well, if he's our man, he's got a first-class alibi for that day, and that's rather interesting, be-cause it would mean that to him the Monday was more im-portant than the Saturday or Sunday. He was at his digs all the morning. This is confirmed by his landlady, who gave him his breakfast at half-past eight, his morning coffee at eleven and his lunch at one-thirty. After lunch he went to Wimborne Minster to look at the chained library there. This is con-firmed by the custodian who recognised the description of the clothes he was wearing – we got this description from his land-lady – and his height and colouring. There were only four other visitors to the chained library in the Minster that after-noon, and the custodian remembers them particularly clearly, as three of them were Australians, a father, mother and little girl. James had tea in Wimborne – there is no confirmation of this, but it hardly matters because, long before tea-time, those Boy Scouts had discovered the body – and then says he went to Shaftesbury and returned to his lodgings at just after eight in the evening.'

'How did he get to Mrs Schumann's cottage on the Sunday?'

'In a hired car, an Austin 1000, whose number, of course, we got from the garage. We have examined it most carefully and there is nothing suspicious about it. He took it out at half-past two and returned it and paid for the hire of it at six. He always hired from the same people. Says it worked out cheaper than running a car of his own, as he lived so near the school that he could walk there.'

'I see. Thank you very much.'

'It doesn't help us, you know.'

'Unless we can show that his story of how he spent Saturday and Sunday is either totally untrue or is false in certain particulars.'

'If it weren't for the fact that he was engaged to Karen Schumann and that, in every case except that of Machrado, there is some sort of connection with the school – although I admit it is very slight indeed in the case of the Italian maid-servant – I'd now be inclined to write him off completely. He seems a steady, conscientious, serious-minded fellow, not at all the type of mass-murderer who is indicated by the present circumstances, and, I would have said, above suspicion, except as aforesaid. I admit I suspected him at first, but that was over the death of Karen Schumann.'

'I think I would like to speak to him again. Can that be arranged? And would you mind?'

'I'd be delighted. I only hope it will lead to something. The line Detective-Inspector Maisry is taking is to research into the background of these women's lives. He's certain there's some connection with their past, but, so far, nothing adds up anywhere.'

'Where will you meet James?' asked Laura, when Phillips had rung off.

'At his lodgings will be the best place. He may be more relaxed and informative there than he was when I saw him in the headmaster's room at the school.'

'He won't be either relaxed *or* informative if he's the murderer.'

'That remains to be seen, does it not?'

What was seen, in the first place, was that James was not prepared to be co-operative. He replied to Dame Beatrice's letter with a curt note to the effect that he was not in need of a psychiatrist and that he was extremely busy. This she countered by ringing him up at the school and inviting him to Saturday lunch at the Stone House, adding that she was including Mrs Schumann in the invitation. James refused, point-blank, to go anywhere near the Stone House, and was abrupt to the point of rudeness.

'A bit suspicious, don't you think?' suggested Laura. 'Anyway, this is where I go to Southampton and do my homework.'

'By which you mean?'

'Didn't you, some time ago, suggest that I try my luck in a public library?'

'It may be a waste of your time, but, if you remember, we thought that the digits printed on the papers pinned to the bodies might be dates.'

'I thought that we'd abandoned that idea, but I'll have a go. If the numbers represent dates, none of them rings a bell in my mind, in spite of the fact that I did history at College. The nearest would be 1140, when the Council of Sens condemned Peter Abelard and a chap named Arnold of Brescia for heresy.'

Dame Beatrice asked sharply,

'*What* did you say?'

Laura gazed at her in astonishment. Then she thumped the arm of her chair. The penny had dropped.

'Arnold of Brescia,' she repeated. 'Matthew Arnold! *The Scholar Gipsy*! I say, do you really think we've got a clue at last?'

'Go to the library and find out,' said Dame Beatrice. 'I cannot see, at the moment, where Arnold of Brescia will lead us, but I deduce, from his name, that he was an Italian, and *The Scholar Gipsy* was the caption found on the body of Lucia, the Italian maid. There *must* be a connection.'

'I'll turn up Arnold in the Encyclopaedia Britannica, then, and see whether I can get a lead.'

'According to our information, James seems to have called

Karen Schumann a misguided little Arian. Was not Arius also a heretic?'

'Yes, of course he was – not that I know anything more than that about him. I'll look him up as well. Have you any other ideas?'

'I wondered whether the word *Cathari*, found on Mrs Castle's body, might be worth looking up.'

'It's a stranger to me, but I'll get on its trail.'

She came back at tea-time on the following day, having set off at half-past nine in the morning.

'I'm a mine of information,' she announced, 'but how it's going to solve our problems I haven't the faintest idea.'

'Did you have any lunch?'

'Yes, ate like a horse at the *Dolphin* and then returned to my studies. I got on swingingly with 325 and 1155, and *Cathari* turned out to be fool-proof. It means that lot we usually hear of as the Albigensians. 380 gave me a lot of trouble, but I tracked it down at last, and it ties up in a way.'

'Excellent. Let us have some tea, and then, when you are refreshed, I must hear the full results of your researches.'

These did not take long to describe.

'Arius doesn't quite fit,' said Laura, 'but the others do. He was a Christian priest in Alexandria and was condemned as a heretic by the Synod of Antioch in A.D. 325 because he believed Christ was not the equal of God, but was more or less an adopted Son and was capable of change and subject to pain, and so was not immortal. Arius was also considered equally unsound on the Third Person of the Trinity and seems to have made himself a pain in the neck to the authorities and, in the end, got himself excommunicated. All the dates are a bit sketchy, I thought, but 325 is as good as any other.'

'Why do you say he does not quite fit?'

'You'll see what I mean when I tell you about the others. In his case it's the nationality which doesn't make sense.'

'What about the Cathari or Albigensians?'

'Not really open to the same objection – at least, not as seriously. They flourished especially in Provence, which ties up, vaguely, with Mrs Castle and the teaching of French. Saint

Bernard didn't like them, and the Dominicans and Franciscans were also anti-Cathari. The movement more or less collapsed in the thirteenth century, but lingered on, here and there, for another couple of hundred years.'

'And the specific date of 1207?'

'That was the beginning of the Crusade against the Cathari. Some put it at 1208, but it's near enough.'

'And Arnold of Brescia?'

'Well, he seems to have had a very rough passage. Pope Innocent the Second condemned him in 1139 and he was banished from Italy – ties in with Lucia, as we noted – and went to France. He seems to have known Abelard, as I said. After the Council of Sens had chewed the fat with both of them, Abelard gave in, but Arnold fled. In 1148 the Pope excommunicated him, and in 1155, the date on Lucia's body, he was hanged in Rome, his body was burned – ties up with the burnt doll – a very unpleasant feature, as I thought at the time – and his ashes were thrown into the Tiber.'

'You say you had difficulty with the 380 date?'

'I certainly did, but I tracked it down at last. Actually, 384 would have been nearer the mark. Anyway, I realised by this time that our murderer must have a bee in his bonnet about heresies in the early and the mediaeval church, so that gave me a pointer and brought me at last to a chap named Priscillian. He was a Spaniard – Maria Machrado, you know – and in 380 he was condemned by the Council of Saragossa, but was later elected bishop of Avila. However, he struck unlucky, and in 384 he was tried for sorcery and immorality and condemned to death. He was, as a matter of fact, the first person to be executed for heresy.'

'I see what you mean about Arianism. You have no German heretics among your gleanings. This confirms me in a belief I have held for some time. The only death for which the murderer could have had a motive was the death of Karen Schumann. The others are either wanton killings or are intended to throw the police off the track.'

'You must admit that all this heresy stuff points to the scholarly Edward.'

'It could also point to Mrs Schumann, who, even more

readily than Edward James, has the run of her late husband's theological library.'

'On the other hand, now that we've got as far as this, it looks so *obviously* like one or other of them that it *must* be somebody else.'

'Now that we've got as far as this, yes. But the murderer probably had no idea that we should interest ourselves by looking into these dates, so he or she took a calculated risk. I do not imagine that, left to themselves, Superintendent Phillips or Detective-Inspector Maisry would have troubled themselves about ancient and exploded heresies.'

'I still can't see how it helps us, anyway, to have found out all this.'

'I do not agree. We can use this knowledge, but must proceed with caution. Say nothing to anybody about it at present. It is not direct evidence of guilt, but it can be a formidable weapon if we can use it wisely. If I drop the right hints in the right direction, I may at least be able to prevent another death. The supply of heresies has not given out on you, I trust?'

'I don't know. I only looked up those in which we had an interest. I'll go back tomorrow and dig into a book on the history of the early church, if you like.'

Before she could do this, however, the fifth body had been found. It was lying face-downwards in one of the New Forest ponds, and the cause of death was the same as before. The news came through on the telephone at breakfast-time, just before Laura was ready to set off for Southampton.

CHAPTER FIVE

Full Fathom Five

'And first I tried an English lass, but she was
    fat and lazy . . .
Away, haul away, haul away, oh!
And then I tried an Irish lass who well-nigh
    drove me crazy . . .
Away, haul away, haul away, oh!'

(1)

'Yes, it's like the others,' said Gavin, 'except for one or two
points which might indicate that it's a copycat murder and
not one in the sequence. For one thing, my chaps and Phillips
have traced where she comes from. She's an Irish girl who
lived in Swansea, so the first difference is that she wasn't, in
the usual sense of the words, a foreigner. Then, second point,
she has no connection whatever with that comprehensive or any
other school. She wasn't one of the campers, either, and as
nobody on the site had ever seen her before, the police chaps
didn't at first know why she was in the neighbourhood. The
inference was that she was on holiday, or else, of course, that
she had taken a job around these parts, but they found out
all about it later.'

'Didn't any of the campers hear anything suspicious?' asked
Laura.

'Not a thing, so far as any of them can remember. The
police have checked on all of them very carefully, as you may
imagine, but I'm told there's nothing even remotely suspicious
about any of them. At this time of year the camping season
hasn't really got into its stride, so there are only five caravans
on the pitch, and as there's nothing much to do after dark
the people all turn in pretty early. Whoever dumped the body
– she'd been dead for some days when she was found – probably carried her some distance so as not to bring a car within

122

hearing of the campers. She was a well-built girl, so the chances are that her murderer was a man, although, of course, some women would be quite strong enough to kill her, dump her in a car and then drag her over the short turf to the edge of the pond where she was found. Only her head and one arm were in the water.'

'How did the police find out where she came from?' asked Dame Beatrice.

'They recovered her handbag from the water. It had been gutted, but the murderer had overlooked the fact that in a tiny pocket inside the otherwise empty notecase was the return half of a railway ticket to Swansea. After that, of course, it was a routine check, a long, boring sort of job, like most police work, but they also issued a description and her Welsh landlady recognised it and came along. Said the girl had answered an advertisement for a children's nurse, but it was only for a fortnight while the parents were on holiday. The pay was good, so the girl took her own holiday by exchanging dates with another typist in the same office, and hoped to combine business with pleasure, as it were.'

'So that accounts for the return ticket,' said Dame Beatrice. 'Had the landlady been shown the advertisement?'

'Yes. One clause in it struck her as peculiar, although not suspicious. It was that an application from a young woman of Irish extraction would be preferred to any other.'

'But the advertisement had been sent to a Swansea local paper?'

'Exactly.'

'What had the paper to say about it?'

'Nothing helpful. It had been paid for at their usual rates, there was no explanatory letter and the notice was to be displayed for a week unless it was cancelled earlier.'

'Did the paper file the application?'

'Oh, yes, and turned it up for us. It was typewritten and signed in ball-point T. H. Edon (Mrs). It bore the address of an empty bungalow near Ringwood, a place with one of those enormously long front gardens with a postbox on the front gate. The chaps have tried to find somebody who saw this postbox being rifled, but the bungalow is remotely situated, so the chances are that, if the murderer was careful, nobody saw anything of him.'

'The girl must have answered the advertisement and received a letter back.'

'Yes, she did, and showed it to the landlady. Again, the letter telling her to come along was typewritten, with the same signature, but, as I told you, everything in the handbag was missing except the return ticket, and all the ticket did was to save my chaps a bit of time, as the landlady assured them (and there's no reason to disbelieve her – she's a motherly soul and seems to have been quite fond of the girl) that she would have made enquiries at once if the girl had failed to return at the end of the fortnight and had not written to explain her prolonged absence.'

'So the fortnight was not up when the body was discovered?'

'It had eight days to run. The inference is that the murderer met the girl at Bournemouth and murdered her that same night. Well, you know what tremendous crowds get off the Bournemouth trains as soon as the holiday season starts. The chances are one in a thousand that anybody at the station remembers any particular traveller or notices who met her. There's always a rush for taxis, and any number of private cars are parked in the road outside. Of course, the chaps are still trying, but it's a forlorn hope that anybody will come forward with a useful bit of information, especially by this time.'

'Did the landlady remember what the girl was wearing when she left Swansea?'

'Oh, yes. She went to see her off. She was wearing exactly the same outfit as the one she had on when the body was found. That's why we are pretty sure she was murdered almost as soon as her killer met her.'

'What about her luggage?'

'She had only one suitcase, bought at Marks and Sparks, and it hasn't been traced. It may still be in the murderer's possession, of course, but the chances are that he dumped it somewhere else in the Forest. If so, it will be found sooner or later, but it won't help us, so far as I can see.'

'I suppose the newspaper which accepted the advertisement had not kept the advertiser's envelope?'

'Oh, no, they merely filed the application, which had this bogus address on it, so there's no help from the postmark. Even if we had it, it wouldn't tell us much. The chances are that the murderer posted it in Bournemouth or Southampton, both of which are probably miles from where he actually lives.'

'Well, something's got to be done,' said Laura. 'This can't be allowed to go on. Five murders in a row makes the police look pretty silly.'

'Was there a note attached to the body?' asked Dame Beatrice.

'Yes, I've seen it. What it said (in Roman capitals, like the others) was: *In Memoriam P.431*, which makes no more sense than the other messages. This one was fastened to the back of the girl's coat by a large safety-pin, so it had not been affected by the water and was plain for all to read.'

'Why should a girl of Irish extraction be preferred, I wonder?' said Laura. 'There ought to be a clue to the murderer in those probably pregnant words, and, if there is, I may be able to spot it, but *P.431* sounds like the page of a book . . .'

'A very long book, then. We thought of that ourselves, but it's like all these secret codes – easy enough to work out, once you know which book, but there's the rub. I'd think it meant dates if any of the dates made sense,' he went on, 'but what can you do with March 4th, 1901, for example?'

'Or, as some others might read it, April 3rd,' said Laura. 'Obviously the date of somebody's death, if that's the correct reading of the numerals, but it would take a lifetime to go through all the files, and, at that, the figures may not be dates at all. Mrs Croc. and I are of the opinion that they *are* dates, but . . .'

Gavin interrupted her.

'They're so wide apart, though. The first one – what was it?'

'In Memoriam 325.'

'That's right. Well, if we're reading the figures English fashion, that would be the third of Feb., 1905. The second one . . .'

'380 – which could be the third of August, 1900, if your hunch is right, and, of course, it may be. It's not as far-fetched as ours. Well, let's see. The next was 1155.'

'First of Jan., 1955 – half a century later, which seems, on the face of it, unlikely – or, of course, the eleventh of May, 1905, which, taken in conjunction with the other two, seems more sensible. But what do we do with the fourth bulletin, dated 1208?'

'We use your same reasoning process which, as I admit, could make more sense than ours . . .'

'I don't dispute it,' put in Gavin, grinning.

'Well, that would make it the first of Feb., 1908.'

'Oh, that won't do! If we use the same reasoning process, dear heart, the figures should be 198. What's the zero doing in there?'

'You're splitting hairs!'

'Maybe. Have you any ideas, Dame Beatrice?'

'Yes, but they are far-fetched and unlikely, as Laura has tried to point out.'

'So are these bizarre and seemingly motiveless murders. Another thing: if this dates thing we've hit on is going to work out at all, the murderer has waited a hell of a long time to get his revenge on these girls.'

'Oh, it could be a *vendetta*,' said Laura. 'Passed down from father to son. Why don't you begin with the death of the Italian maid, and work back and forth from there?'

'I'd rather hear what Dame B. has thought up.'

'I have not crystallised my ideas sufficiently to expose them to the cold air of argument and disbelief,' protested Dame Beatrice, 'but I will work upon them and test them and then you will probably laugh at them and resolve them into the state of liquifaction wherein, at present, they lie.'

(2)

'We've never had a case like this, have we?' said Laura, when her husband, who was on a flying visit, had returned to London. 'I mean, our murders usually come in single spies or, at the most, a twin-pack, but this time they've certainly come in battalions, haven't they? Look here, now that Gavin has left us, will you tell me how we can work out our hunch? I'd hate all my sweat about heresies and things to be wasted.'

'We must tackle our suspects. I wish Mr James would consent to see me.'

'Pity we can't make him. Can't we tell him we know something to his disadvantage, and *threaten* him either into coming to see us or having us go to his lodgings?'

'I fear not. Apart from the disinclination I have for using threats, Mr James, I fancy, is a cool and resourceful person who would refuse to be intimidated and would probably summon me for attempted blackmail, or something of that sort. Mrs Schumann, of course, is different.'

'There's no doubt in my mind, though – and the more I think about it, the more certain I am – that if we've got to choose between Edward James and Mrs Schumann as our murderer, James is the one. Mrs Schumann would never have worked out all that stuff about heresies and the different nationalities and so forth.'

'You underestimate the German capacity for thoroughness, but, unless another candidate appears on the scene, the choice must be between these two, with my personal conviction that Mrs Schumann is our murderer. Incidentally, do you feel equal to visiting the library once more and checking our latest figures?'

'If it's anything like the job I had in tracking down Priscillian, it will probably take me all day, but I'm willing to have a go, if only to prove Gavin wrong.'

'Before you go, perhaps we should clarify our thoughts. Now, in any case of murder, we need to know motive, means and opportunity. In the cases under review, we know, with any certainty, nothing but the means.'

'Agreed. So what?'

'What would you say is the primary approach by the police to a case of murder?'

'That's an easy one. They try to find out who, if anybody, gains (especially financially) by the death.'

'Exactly. Let us then approach the subject, bearing this intelligent gambit in mind.'

'I see what you mean, of course, but it's not going to help.'

'Why not?'

'Well, it might work in the case of Karen Schumann. We

think of three people who might benefit by her death, but, after that, we come to a full stop.'

'Elucidate.'

'Well, Karen seems to have won some money on Ernie . . .'

'Five thousand pounds.'

'Chicken-feed to the Rothschilds, but possibly a goodly sum to the Schumanns.'

'Proceed.'

'Right. If and when Karen died, three people, or any one or any two of them – we must preserve a broad outlook – could benefit from what she left. These people are her fiancé James, her mother, and her brother Otto.'

'Who claims that half the money belonged to him by right.'

'So, other things being equal, which they weren't, I'd suggest that Otto, to get his share of the cash, murdered his sister.'

'Which we know he could not have done.'

'If I were the police, I'd have a second, yes, a *forty-second* look at that alibi of his. He's just the type, I would have said, never to entertain scruples, and the second murder – the Spanish girl – keeps him right in the picture, you know.'

'Sad, but true. Well, now, Otto has murdered his sister. Unfortunately for him, all her money has been willed to her mother, as Mrs Schumann herself has told us.'

'She didn't mention the five thousand.'

'I wonder what Edward James thought of the arrangement that the death of his fiancée would benefit nobody but her mother?'

'Thought the will would be changed once they were married, don't you think?'

'Then the last thing he would want to do, surely, would be to eliminate his fiancée before they *were* married.'

'You mean *Pass, James, all's well*, do you?'

'Well, I feel that I have stated my conclusions already. Let us go further.'

'And fare worse? Right – if you think so. Let's consider the case of Otto Schumann in further detail. Now, it doesn't seem as though he can possibly have actually murdered his sister, but can he have murdered her by proxy?'

'My dear Laura!'

'Well, such things have been known. I don't want to refer to recent cases, but...'

'Very well. Otto Schumann could have prevailed upon a third person to kill his sister. The motive for his desire to take her life is clear and, to some minds, acceptable. And then?'

'Well, the police haven't found this substitute, and neither have we, but it doesn't prove his non-existence.'

'True. This brings us to the death of Maria Machrado.'

'Well, it still seems to me that Otto could have had a motive there, all right.'

'If Otto were like Edward James, I could agree with you, but, as I see it, they are men of widely different character.'

'The girl was pregnant.'

'Apparently it is impossible to show that Otto was responsible for that. She seems to have been a young woman of many lovers.'

'Still, he seems to have been the current issue.'

'You ignore the passage of time. Otto was probably on the high seas when the girl conceived. Are you suggesting that her pregnancy was also by proxy?'

'Don't press your advantage! I'm being serious. Apart from anything else, James couldn't have had anything against her, could he?'

'Not so far as we know. One cannot say more than that. He must have met her at Mrs Schumann's cottage, of course. We concluded that such was the case.'

'We know she was going to have a baby, and I still believe it was Otto's. You said he was probably on the high seas when she conceived, but it came out that they'd known one another quite a bit before she ever came to England, and he admits she travelled on his ship.'

'Granted. I agree, therefore, that the baby might have been Otto's.'

'Well, the Spaniards being what they are, her brothers would have killed him if ever it had come out. He murdered her to stop her telling them who the father was. What do you say to that?'

'Most plausible. Otto killed his sister by proxy, either be-

B

cause he expected that she would have mentioned him in her
will, or out of revenge because she refused to give him half
of the five thousand pounds which he claimed was his own;
then he killed Maria Machrado for the reason you have stated.
The trouble is to account for the other deaths, if all the murders
were committed by the same person. That is where I think the
case against Otto Schumann breaks up. We have found no
shadow of connection between him, the Italian maid Lucia,
Mrs Castle and now this Irish girl who came from Swansea.
Indeed, I think this last death exonerates Otto almost completely.'

'How do you mean?'

'Swansea is a port. His ship must sometimes have called
there. We could find that out.'

'You mean he could have got to know her there? Granted.
But he may have preferred to murder her somewhere else.'

'We had better find out whether she was pregnant, whether
by proxy or otherwise,' said Dame Beatrice.

'All right, all right!' said Laura, grinning. 'I still think Otto
stays in the picture. Well, tomorrow morning I renew my
studies of heresy. I shall be able to write a book on it by the
time I've finished. The odd thing about these heretics, you
know, is that they all seem to have been so well-meaning. They
were in advance of their time, that's all.'

'*Well* in advance of it, in some cases,' commented Dame
Beatrice, 'although even the most advanced of them have not
caught up with some of our modern theories concerning the
nature of the Deity. But let that pass. We are concerned with
an Irish heretic who had some connection with Wales.'

'I don't believe there ever were any Irish heretics, but we'll
see. If we really *do* get a tie-up, I shall consider our theory
proved, and we will go gunning for James and Mrs Schumann
in the biggest possible way.'

She returned on the following evening in high feather.

'There's no doubt Otto's out of it,' she said. 'He'd never go
to all this bother, I'm perfectly certain, but whether the answer
is James or Mrs Schumann I wouldn't care to say. The two of
them in collusion is the other answer, of course.'

'What have you unearthed this time?' asked Dame Beatrice.

'Enough to make your hunch a certainty. It *can't* be coincidence. You remember the P in front of the 431? Well, listen to this: it's all about a heretic named Pelagius. He was born in Britain and, although there's no certainty that he was either Irish or Welsh, there's a strong tradition that he was of Irish origin and settled in Wales. He was a student, not a priest, and he attacked some of the other heretics, notably the Arians and the Manichaeans, but he fell foul of Saint Jerome at Bethlehem after Saint Augustine had also objected to his opinions. Unfortunately for him, his followers seem to have perpetrated acts of violence, and in the year A.D. 418 the Emperor Honorias ordered him to be exiled, and Pope Zosimus, who had some sympathy with his views, (which rejected the doctrine of original sin, among other things), was persuaded to condemn him. The church by no means rejected him, however, and, although nobody knows for certain what happened to him, he wasn't executed, but is thought to have died in exile some two years later. But – this is the point – his opinions were finally ditched by the General Council of Ephesus in 431.'

'Well,' said Dame Beatrice, 'I am very much obliged to you for your researches. Unfortunately, it seems to me that these extraordinary murders could continue until the supply of heresies gives out. I imagine there are others?'

'Good gracious, yes! I got interested and looked up a book on the history of the early church. There were Docetism, Gnosticism (which came in three waves, all a bit different from one another, so far as I can make out), Macedonianism, Donatism, Manicheeism, not to mention downright paganism. This carries us up to about the year A.D. 500 and is probably not an exhaustive list, at that, and there were still the heresies of the Middle Ages to follow, not to worry about the Reformaion itself, and the teachings of Calvin and John Knox, and so forth.'

'Enough,' said Dame Beatrice, with her reptilian smile. 'We will now step in and put an end to these matters. I think we know enough to begin to make things very uncomfortable for our suspects.'

Fergus walked over to her and pushed his muzzle adoringly into her thin ribs. She laid a yellow claw on his head.

'As for you,' she remarked, 'you are undoubtedly a heretic in your own right, for whereas, by all the canons of decency and good taste, you should cleave unto Laura, who is your meat, drink and comfort, you prefer to pursue strange gods who do not even care very much about you.'

The dog sighed, lay down at her feet and thrust his head hard against her knee.

'How do you mean, you are going to begin making things very uncomfortable for our suspects? You'll be careful, won't you?' said Laura anxiously. 'Somebody who has committed five murders isn't going to worry much about a sixth.'

'Have no fears for me. I shall keep all my wits about me. I am suffering from a bad attack of conscience. You see, I have felt almost certain, from the time of the first death, that I knew who was responsible, and although, in view of the lack of concrete evidence, I do not see how it could have been done, I feel I ought to have been able to prevent four of these five deaths by denouncing the murderer of Karen Schumann.'

'We still don't know whether all the murders were done by the same person, don't forget.'

'I am certain that they were, and I shall now take the necessary steps.'

'Do I ask for details? You see, I'm responsible for your safety, and if you've really rolled your sleeves up and are going into action, it might be as well for me to be within hailing distance.'

'That evening, the evening of Karen Schumann's death,' said Dame Beatrice, 'when Fergus left you and went off across the common . . .'

'Yes?'

'It was misty and beginning to get dark?'

'Yes. I lost sight of Fergus in less than a hundred yards – in not more than fifty or sixty yards, perhaps.'

'That is what I wanted to be sure of, although I took it that such was the case.'

'If you're thinking of Mrs Schumann, I don't think she owns a bike.'

'That is my point. If the mist and the darkness made visibility a matter of less than a hundred yards, whoever enticed

Fergus away from you could have been on foot. If Mrs Schumann is the murderer, she would have blown her personal call on the dog-whistle, and the dog, who had been trained at her kennels to respond to it, would have obeyed the summons immediately. The visibility was such that you could not see her, for she could have been two hundred yards or more from where you stood, and she knew that, although the dog could hear the whistle, you could not. All she had to do, after that, was to walk the dog across the common as far as the woods, following the path which would still have shown up sufficiently in the darkness and which, doubtless, she knew well, lead him to the body and command him to stay. He obeyed this order, as we know, until I came along and countermanded it.'

'There are a lot of objections to this theory, you know.'

'I realise that. It is one of the reasons I had for not acting upon it earlier. You refer to the difficulty we should have in proving that she knew you were out with the dog that night, and that you would not return by the shorter and more obvious route. It is, indeed, a problem, as you infer.'

'I don't see how you'd ever be able to prove she was there on the common that night, and, if you can't prove that, your whole theory goes west.'

'We still have your evidence that the dog left you and was found more than seventeen hours later, standing guard over the body.'

'Granted. But the defence would make mincemeat of that sort of evidence.'

'They might not regard it as evidence at all. Evidence has to be capable of proof, even if the proof is only the credibility of the witness.'

'Nobody would dispute your credibility and I hope nobody would asperse mine, but what we've got at present to offer the prosecution is negligible.'

'Another thing I should like to know,' went on Dame Beatrice, 'is whether it is possible for a particular call on a dog-whistle to be taught to another person.'

'So you *do* think James is still in the picture!'

'We must leave, as you yourself have often said, no stone unturned.'

'Well, it wouldn't be very easy for anybody to teach another person how to whistle up a dog, because, of course, the pupil wouldn't be able to hear the call. Wonder whether you could do it by teaching him by means of a sort of Morse Code – you know, dashes for the long blasts and dots for the short ones.'

'It sounds possible. One could only judge of the success of such a scheme by its effect on the dog. Anyhow, whether he likes it or not, I am determined to obtain an interview with Mr James. This will best be accomplished by bringing Superintendent Phillips to bear on him.'

'Get him to the police station, do you mean? He'll beef a bit at that, won't he? Phillips has nothing on him so far.'

'Superintendent Phillips has always made him his first choice in the matter of Karen Schumann.'

'What approach will you make?'

'I shall give Superintendent Phillips the results of your researches at the library and indicate that they do much to suggest that either Mr James or Mrs Schumann is our murderer. That will fit with either his choice of murderer or my own.'

'He knows they're the only real suspects already, and won't my researches and the conclusions we've drawn from them seem to him a bit far-fetched, anyway? He'll regard them as a lot of ballyhoo, I shouldn't wonder.'

'With Mr James studying to become a Doctor of Divinity, and Mrs Schumann with her husband's theological library at her disposal?'

'But, you know, James had access to that library, and, anyway, I find it almost impossible to believe that these murders were committed by a woman.'

'But for the incident of Fergus and the (presumed) dog-whistle, so might I. I am beginning to wonder – no, as a matter of accuracy, the thought has been in my mind for some time – whether perhaps Mrs Schumann hoped to gain more than her daughter's small fortune by that daughter's death.'

'You don't mean . . . ?'

'Oh, yes, I do. She and James are much of an age, and she is a personable enough woman and at an age when women often behave in what might seem to others an irrational way.'

'Go off their heads for a bit, you mean? Yes, that's right

enough. What would she be – forty-five to fifty? But if the defence could prove that she wasn't responsible for her actions when these murders took place . . .'

'She would be sent to a mental hospital, which, at least, would be preferable to being sent to prison.'

'Do *you* think she's off her head?'

'I think she was sane enough when she planned and carried out her daughter's murder. After that, one cannot be sure, although I should be inclined to think that the murder of Maria Machrado could be explained in terms of expediency and therefore was the action of a sane and vicious woman.'

'And the other three?'

'Murder lives by what it feeds on, and mass murderers have a dangerous lust for power, are completely self-centred and, especially if they believe that they have thrown dust in the eyes of the police, inordinately conceited. In this case, besides, I think there is no doubt that the murders of Lucia, Mrs Castle and this Irish girl from Swansea, being motiveless from any rational point of view, were simply intended to lead the police away from any theories they might have formed concerning the motivated murders of Karen Schumann and Maria Machrado.'

'But we don't know what the motive was for the death of Maria Machrado, and, as for Mrs Schumann and James, I thought that, earlier on, she said she didn't care for him much.'

'A statement which, at present, I shall entirely disregard. But now to gain audience of Superintendent Phillips.'

(3)

'If you have further information for us, Dame Beatrice,' said Phillips, 'I wonder whether you'd mind if my colleague from Scotland Yard, Detective-Inspector Maisry, joined us?'

'By all means let us have him in, Inspector.'

Maisry had been allotted a room of his own, and, having been summoned by Phillips, suggested, in his gentle tones, that, as Dame Beatrice's evidence might require further study, a shorthand writer in the person of his detective-sergeant might be advisable. Dame Beatrice deprecated the use of the word 'evidence', since all she and Laura claimed to have discovered was an interesting but possibly valueless sidelight upon the cases under review.

'But let us have a shorthand writer, Detective-Inspector,' she said, 'because the importance (if any) of what I have to tell you is that I have one (I do not say *the*) explanation of the puzzling messages left upon the bodies. If my solution is the right one, it confirms my previous view that our suspects are but two.'

'And the two, Dame Beatrice?'

'Edward James and Karla Schumann.'

'You think we may dismiss Otto Schumann from our minds, then?'

'That is for you to decide when you have heard what I have to say.'

Maisry called in his sergeant.

'Shorthand – *verbatim*,' he said. 'Callum's speed is one hundred, Dame Beatrice, if that will suit you.'

'Admirably.' She took out her own notebook in which she had inscribed the results of Laura's researches. 'My findings are the result of my secretary's work in the public library and concern various heresies, so-called, which raised their thoughtful, learned and, occasionally, extremely popular voices against the teachings of the Church from the fourth to the thirteenth century. This is what Laura discovered.'

Maisry's eyebrows went up and he smiled, but he did not interrupt until the flow was ended. Then he said,

'Before we discuss what you have told us – and I agree that it is full of interesting possibilities – perhaps Callum will read back to us what he has written, pausing at all the proper names which, as a shorthand writer, he has, so far, contracted and also has spelt phonetically. We had better have the full longhand spelling, Callum, I think, in case we need to check this information against any later evidence which may come our way.'

This was done.

'I'll make a typed copy in triplicate, as usual, sir,' said Callum, a long, lean, dark-visaged man of Irish ancestry. 'Would you like it done at once?'

'Yes. I'll sound the buzzer if we need you in here again before Dame Beatrice leaves. And now,' he went on, when the door had closed behind the detective-sergeant, 'perhaps, Dame Beatrice, we could have your full analysis of these discoveries. How did you come to hit on this idea of the heresies in the first place?'

'It really began, I think, with a remark made by James (although he says he has no recollection of making it) to Karen Schumann. He seems to have called her "a misguided little Aryan". The more I thought this over, the more unlikely it seemed to me that he should have called her any such thing. Although she was of German parentage, she was, in all other respects, an Englishwoman, having been born, brought up and educated over here. Then I realised that the word could be spelt in two ways, and that, as it was used by James during the course of a theological discussion, the chances were greatly in favour of the second spelling, which indicates a follower of an heretical priest of Alexandria named Arius.

'I did not pursue this theory further at the time because it seemed, in itself, pointless, for I had made up my mind that the identity of Karen Schumann's murderer was sufficiently indicated by another factor.'

'You thought it was Mrs Schumann,' said Phillips, 'while the rest of us, including the Assistant Commissioner himself, plumped for Edward James.'

'And James is not altogether out of the picture even now,' said Dame Beatrice. 'I propose to attempt, with your permission and kind assistance, to banish him from it completely.'

'How do you suggest you do that?' enquired Maisry.

'By having him here at headquarters for official and, I hope, alarming questioning.'

'And you think this will exonerate him?'

'I am sanguine that it may.'

'Well, if you will brief us, we will put your questions to him. I hope you will agree to be present during the interview and will not hesitate to "chip in" if the interrogation is not to your liking or if you want him to clarify or expand upon any of his answers. I only hope we *can* eliminate him from our enquiries, but, personally, I think he's got a good deal of explaining to do, and, of course, in spite of what you've told us this morning, we're still keeping an eye on Otto Schumann for the murder of Maria Machrado. We've come to the conclusion that the first two killings were deliberate, and by two different hands, and that there's a joker in the pack who committed the other three.'

CHAPTER SIX

How Should I Your True-Love Know

'Oh, Tommy's gone! What shall I do?
Away down Hilo.
Find me a man to love me true –
Tom's gone to Hilo.'

---

(1)

James seemed a very different man from the cold and self-possessed schoolmaster whom Dame Beatrice had met in the headmaster's study at the comprehensive school. He was obviously ill-at-ease when she faced him again at the police station.

'So you have found a way to force me to see you,' he said sullenly. 'I thought you would.'

'No question of force, Mr James,' said Maisry in his smooth and gentle way, 'but we shall be very glad of your co-operation, and Dame Beatrice, like yourself, is here at our invitation. We thought that you might prefer to visit us here in a district where you are a stranger, rather than have us go to your lodgings or to the school.'

'Vastly considerate of you, I'm sure.'

'Irony will get us nowhere, sir.'

'Well, what do you want from me? Surely it's clear to you by now that the murderer of my fiancée is a madman with a lust to kill, and that her death was no more significant to you, so far as I can understand it, than the deaths of the rest of these unfortunate women. I can't think what help you think I can give you, and I protest, most strongly, about being dragged again into a case which you have not the wits to solve.'

The words, in themselves, were bold enough, but it was clear that they were nothing but bluster. The man looked ill and was afraid. Not only the psychiatrist but the two police officers were well aware of the fact.

'All we want from you, Mr James, is confirmation, or the reverse, of some dates,' said Maisry. 'We are relying upon your special knowledge, the result of your extensive reading and research.'

James, at this, expressed open alarm.

'What are you hinting at?' he asked. 'What dates? What special knowledge? I tell you I know nothing which will help you. Why are you hounding me?'

'My dear sir,' said Maisry, 'we should be in dead trouble if we hounded anybody. We simply need your help. Five women have been done to death. To be frank with you, we believe that we are trying to find three murderers, two of whom are sane and culpable, the third of whom is a madman. As it happens, Dame Beatrice has discovered what appears to be a tie-up between these persons, but, so far, unless you can suggest an explanation, this tie-up does not lead to anything except a blank wall.'

'You believe there are *three* murderers living in this area? That seems incredible,' said James. Dame Beatrice noted that his voice and his attitude had changed. He spoke with an air of interest and animation; his sullen demeanour and hangdog look had vanished; he was sitting up straight in his hard-backed chair and was leaning slightly forward as though anxious not to miss a word of what was being said.

'Well, sir, consider the facts,' went on Maisry. 'I need not recapitulate them now. That will come later, perhaps. It is these dates we are concerned with.'

'Yes? What dates?' The question, on the face of it, was innocent enough, but Dame Beatrice was conscious of a slight stiffening in the attitude of Superintendent Phillips. Maisry, however, remained urbane and undisturbed.

'It seems possible,' he said, 'that the numbers on the pieces of paper which we found attached to the bodies may have some significance as dates. Take the first one, for example. You remember what it was, I suppose?'

'I am not likely to forget it, but why should you suppose it was a date?' He looked directly at Dame Beatrice.

'I believe you also remember my asking you whether you could tell me any signficant dates in the fourth century A.D.' she said, 'or something to that effect. You gave me, I recollect, the dates of the reign of the emperor Julian the Apostate, of whom, I admit, I knew nothing but his name.'

'I remember that, of course, but the dates were not the same as the number found on – found on Karen. Do you mean that the other bodies . . . ?'

'Yes,' said Phillips, speaking for the first time during the interview. 'We've managed to keep it from the Press, but similar pieces of paper, not all with the same wording but all bearing a number, were found on the other bodies. We tried various solutions, and the idea that they might be dates occurred to Dame Beatrice as well as to ourselves, although our interpretation of them was not the same as hers.'

'By the way,' said Maisry, 'how did you know that a piece of paper was found on Miss Schumann's body?'

'Mrs Schumann told me. She saw it – was shown it, I believe – when she identified the body.'

'Oh, yes, of course. We asked her whether she could explain it, but she said she could not.'

'I see. Well, what do you expect me to do?'

'Suppose that Dame Beatrice is right, and that 325 refers to a date in the fourth century, what would it mean to you, as a scholar and a theologian?'

'I have no idea.'

'Come, come, sir! It is a definite date in church history. You must have come across it in your studies.'

'Come across it? Well, it's the date, near enough – some of those dates are approximate only, you know – of the condemnation of the heretic Arius by the Synod of Antioch.'

'And,' said Dame Beatrice, 'you once called your fiancée a misguided little Aryan or Arian.'

'So you told me before. I have no recollection of it.'

'It was during a discussion you had with her one afternoon after school hours. You were in the school library. The discussion was interrupted by the school secretary, who came to ask for the key to the library so that she could lock up and go home.'

'Oh, yes, I begin to remember. We had been debating the Divine Nature. Karen had access to her father's very considerable library and had a moderately good brain. It helped my studies to talk things over with her – clarified my ideas, fixed facts in my head, and so forth.'

'And did her mother ever discuss your work with you?' Dame Beatrice asked.

'Not often. Occasionally she would quote her late husband's opinions when Karen and I were talking, but whether her recollection of them was as complete as she claimed I could hardly say. Some of them sounded very unorthodox to me.'

'I wonder...' Dame Beatrice paused, as though doubtful of the propriety of her thoughts.

'Yes?'

'I wonder whether you were more attracted by her father's library than by Karen herself?'

To her surprise, James smiled.

'I knew, of course, that her father *had* such a library, but it was closed to me until some months after we became engaged,' he said. 'The room was kept locked in respect for his memory, so Mrs Schumann told me.'

'Indeed? What led her, then, to admit you to it, and to allow you the use of it, as I understand is now the case?'

'Oh, as to that – well, does it really matter?'

'If it did not, you would have no hesitation in answering my question. Let me put it in another way. It is true, is it not, that you have had the *full* use of that library only since your fiancée's death?'

'In a sense that is true. Before that, at Mrs Schumann's invitation, I used to make out lists of books which I wished to consult, and Karen would bring them to school on Mondays when she returned from the week-end spent with her mother.'

'While Miss Schumann was alive you spent only about one week-end in four with her at her mother's cottage?'

'About one in four, yes. I could not take any more time off from my studies. I needed my week-ends to visit public libraries in Southampton, London and elsewhere.'

'Yet, since Miss Schumann's death, you are far more frequently at the cottage.'

'Only owing to my having been given free access to the library there. We seem to be moving in circles.' His first sullenness and an air of apprehension were returning, Dame Beatrice noted. She decided upon shock tactics.

'What was Mrs Schumann's price,' she demanded, 'for allowing you the full use of her husband's valuable library?'

Caught off his guard, James blurted out the truth.

'My promise to marry her when Karen had been dead for a year and a day,' he said.

(2)

'You must have knocked him for six with that question,' said Laura, when she had received from Dame Beatrice a full account of the interview.

'It took him by surprise, as I had expected that it would. Then, like a great many reserved, self-contained and somewhat lonely people, once he had committed himself I heard a great deal more than I could have hoped for. It appears that, although Mrs Schumann did not openly pursue him during her daughter's engagement, she was not above innuendo.'

'As how? Disparity in age between James and Karen?'

'Mostly, yes, added to which she was inclined to stress the point that a mature man must expect to be cuckolded if he insisted upon marrying an immature girl.'

'She really went so far as to warn him that Karen was not likely to remain faithful to him after they were married?'

'She stated that her husband had several times strayed from the righteous but unenterprising path of marital fidelity, and reminded him that the son, Otto, was a young man of unstable character and vicious habits and that Karen was Otto's sister and her father's daughter. She seems to have contrived to render poor Edward James both insecure and unhappy.'

'I should jolly well think so, the wicked old puss!'

'When Karen was killed, she suggested that the inference must be that Karen had had a secret lover who had killed her because she refused to sacrifice her virtue to him. She pointed out that for three week-ends out of four Karen was free to do as she pleased and also stated that she seldom spent a Saturday night inside the cottage.'

'Good Lord!'

'Yes, indeed. Then, after Karen's funeral, she made James a definite offer – two, as a matter of fact, both very tempting to an ambitious man. In return for his promise of marriage she agreed to allow him unrestricted access to her late husband's library, and to give him, as a wedding portion, the five thousand pounds which her daughter had gained on a premium bond. She pointed out that, with its help, he could resign his teaching post for a couple of years and devote his whole time to study and research for his doctorate.'

'He didn't accept, of course.'

'Oh, yes, he did, but as the months passed, and these murders accumulated, he became more unhappy about the bargain he had made.'

'So *he* believes Mrs Schumann is the murderer, the same as you do!'

'I do not think he can quite bring himself to go so far as that, but I think his suspicions have been aroused strongly enough to make him averse to the projected marriage.'

'I wonder whether Mrs Schumann knows that?'

'He has gone to the length of telling her that he wants the murderer found before he is willing to enter into matrimony.'

'How did Mrs Schumann take that?'

'He did not say. He did give us another valuable bit of information, though. It confirmed what I had always suspected.'

'About what?'

'About Otto Schumann's statement that, after her landlady had shown her the door, Maria Machrado announced her intention of returning to Mrs Schumann's cottage. According to James, she did return there. Shortly afterwards her body was found in those bushes near Badbury Rings.'

'Of course, we know we can't really believe a word Otto says, but this confirmation from James means that, for once, Otto told the truth.'

'It also means that Karla Schumann is a liar. She declared that Machrado had never returned to the cottage.'

'Also, as we've already noted, she told us she didn't care

much about James. Well, well, well! Where do we go from here?'

'I think we must leave the police to decide that. I see nothing else for them to do except to begin their investigation all over again, in a sense.'

'With Mrs Schumann as the centre of it, you mean? Yes, but, if they're still thinking in terms of three murderers, not one, they're not going to make her the centre-piece, are they? It's a nuisance, though, that she thinks of us as her friends. I feel we've shopped her, in a way.'

'It is some time since she thought of us as her friends, if, indeed, that thought was ever in her mind. In any case, we may be fairly certain that she will learn from Edward James of his summons to the police station, and, even if he does not recount all the details of the interview, a guilty woman will reconstruct enough of it to realise that somebody has put the police on her track, and that the likeliest person to have done so is myself. In addition to that, a mind capable of planning and carrying out five deaths without, so far, leaving sufficient evidence to warrant her arrest, is also capable of working out the unenviable nature of the position in which she is now likely to find herself as a result of James's admissions and disclosures. In view of that fact, and at risk of sounding melodramatic, I require two promises from you.'

'Not to go about alone and unarmed, which is, as you will allow, quite ridiculous, because I am more than a match, physically, for Mrs Schumann.'

'Nevertheless, if I am to sleep at night and to be saved from gnawing anxiety by day . . .'

'Oh, all right, if you put it like that. What do you want me to do? – wear a dog-collar like Lord Peter Wimsey's Harriet in *Gaudy Night?* Anyway, what's the other promise?'

'I do not want Hamish here until this woman is dead, or gone, or in prison.'

'Dead? You think she might commit suicide?'

'I think it not unlikely.'

'Gavin could take Hamish straight from school to my people in Scotland, I suppose. They're always crazy to have him; I can't think why. Actually, feeling as we do about Mrs Schumann, I'd rather, myself, not have anything so vulnerable as a kid around the place until she's well away from it.'

'Good. My mind is made easy.'

'I wonder what Maisry's first move will be?'

This question was answered by Maisry himself some three days later. He arrived, after a telephone call, at four o'clock in the afternoon and gratefully accepted tea.

'Well,' he said, in his gentle voice. 'I have set the ball rolling by calling on Mrs Schumann and asking her to confirm or deny Mr James's assertions.'

'That he is contracted to marry her and is promised the sum of five thousand pounds for consenting to do so?'

'Yes. She denied both statements, of course, as I was quite certain she would. My object in confronting her with them was to ensure that, if you are right and she is our massmurderer, these indiscriminate killings will stop. They will, I have no doubt, if she is sane, and that is where *you* come in. As psychiatric adviser to the Home Office, you may be called upon to give an opinion as to her mental condition if she is convicted, but I should be very much obliged if you would give me your private views beforehand. You see, if there had been only the one death, that of Karen Schumann, I would say that, on the evidence of motive, we now have enough justification for her arrest. Unfortunately, there are four more deaths to be accounted for, and over those we are as much in the dark as ever we were. My theory that there is a mad person at work is still tenable, but whether Mrs Schumann is that person is open to doubt. Of course, I'm only a layman in these matters, but I must admit that she seems to me to be quite as sane as I am myself.'

'How did she take your visit?'

'Well, that's just the point. I took my sergeant with me, and asked her whether she objected to his taking down the interview in shorthand. She replied that she had nothing to conceal, and would be agreeable to his doing so, provided that, at the end, he read to her what he had written down. To this, naturally, I consented. I have brought with me the full typescript of what was said at the interview, if you would care to read it. It will convey much more to you, I think, than if I gave you an *extempore* report.'

'May I read it aloud, so that Laura can hear it? I shall wish to discuss it with her.'

'By all means. Here it is. Better still, I'll leave it with you. I have another copy, and so has Superintendent Phillips. They've put him on to another case for the time being – an armed robbery – so I'm working on my own at present, as it happens, but I wanted him to see the report, all the same.'

'Do you care to take more tea?'

'No, thank you. I've done splendidly. What wonderful cakes your cook makes!'

'I will tell him you said so. Henri appreciates compliments.'

'Ah, a French chef! That explains it. And the maid who carried in the tray and the cakestand?'

'French also, and, incidentally, Henri's wife. They have been with me for very many years. *French*!' repeated Dame Beatrice, when Maisry had taken his leave. 'I wonder!'

'You wonder what?' asked Laura, intrigued by something in her employer's tone.

'Ring the bell. You know, the last thing one sees, very often, is what is under one's nose. I am so much accustomed to Henri and Celestine that I have ceased to think of them as anything but my friends and servants. When the warning went round to foreigners to take certain precautions, I doubt very much whether Henri and Celestine were included. I myself said nothing to them. I regret to admit that it did not occur to me that Celestine might be in danger.'

'Neither did it to me. Perhaps Phillips said something to them, though.'

Summoned to the drawing-room, Celestine made for the tea-tray to remove it, but Dame Beatrice said,

'Not for a minute or two. Sit down.'

'In the presence of madame? But no, I stand.'

'Do as you're told.'

'Very well, madame.'

'You've heard all about these dreadful murders, of course. You and Henri have probably discussed them with George.'

'Only when we have sent Zena out of the kitchen, I assure

you, madame. Such matters are not for the ears of young girls.'

'I dare say she has been fully informed from other sources, but you have acted very properly. That, however, is not my point. You remember a Mrs Schumann who has visited here once or twice?'

'But perfectly, madame.'

'Has she ever made any sort of friendly approach to you?'

'Ah, yes. Once she invited me to take tea with her at her house.'

'But you did not go?'

'Certainly not, madame. For me, I do not like Germans, and I was most grateful, madame, for your graciousness in arranging that Zena, not I, should wait on Madame Schumann at table.'

'How did you get out of accepting her invitation?' asked Laura.

'Very simply, madame. The letter was pushed under the kitchen door after dark one night and was in very good French. I thought it was done that way to save payment for a stamp which, at fourpence, is very dear, but when I told Georges that the letter was an invitation from Mrs Schumann, he said that, if it had come through the post, you, Madame Gavin, would have seen the writing on the envelope, for it is my custom, as madame knows, to bring *all* the letters to madame, not looking to find out *how* they are addressed.'

'I don't suppose we should have known Mrs Schumann's handwriting,' said Dame Beatrice, 'but we might have recognised it as a Teutonic script, which would have come to much the same thing, I suppose. What else did George say?'

'That, if the letter could not be addressed openly, to come through the post, that the writer was what Georges, in an English idiom which I still cannot persuade him to interpret for me, says, is "Up to N.B.G." From this I gather that the action of Mrs Schumann in writing the letter was clandestine, and of this I do not approve.'

'So what did you do? – ignore the invitation?' asked Laura.

'But no, madame. Also, I had not the *bêtise* to write back – *by* post, *with* the stamp which costs fourpence – to say I do not eat with Germans. I wrote only that, as *domestique*, I do not find it suitable to visit on equal terms with those who have been the guests of Madame Lestrange Bradley, Dame of the British Empire, so called in the lists of honour.'

'You make it sound like a tournament or joust,' said Laura, 'but let that go.'

'Did you ever receive a warning from the police not to go about alone while this mass-murderer of women is still at large?' asked Dame Beatrice.

'But no, madame. It would not have been necessary. Never have I been without escort since the second of these assassinations. Seldom I need to shop, since, as is the careless English custom, goods are delivered to the house and are not marketed as in France, but, if I go out for any reason, it is never without the good Georges or with my husband. Also I forbid Zena to walk out, except with what she call her boy-friend, and he to come for her to the back door *always*, and not to make an assignation to meet her elsewhere.'

'Good,' said Dame Beatrice. 'You may clear away the tea-things.'

'So poor Mrs Castle may have been a third and not even a second choice of victim,' said Laura. 'Well, shall we get down to the book of words as supplied by Inspector Maisry? It should be full of interest.'

(3)

The 'book of words' was a straightforward catechism consisting simply of questions and answers.

Q. I wonder, Mrs Schumann, whether you would be willing to help us?

A. Always I help the police. Why not? What have I to fear?

Q. Would you object if my sergeant, who writes in short-hand, took down this conversation?

A. He will read it to me at the end, of course. If so, I do not object. I have nothing to fear.

Q. We recently had an interview with a Mr Edward James. He was your daughter's fiancé, was he not?

A. That, yes. Very sad for him, my Karen's death.

Q. No doubt. Did you think it might be less sad for him if, when the period of mourning was over, he married you?

A. He told you he had asked me to marry him?

Q. Not quite. Isn't it more accurate to say that you asked him to marry you?

A. No woman does that, except she is, perhaps, of royal blood.

Q. May I suggest to you that not only have we Mr James's word for this, but he says that you offered him certain inducements.

A. Inducements? I do not understand.

Q. Did you lead him to believe that, if he would consent to marry you, you would settle five thousand pounds upon him so that he could give up teaching for two years?

A. He would not wish to give up teaching. He and my Karen were teachers together, both at the same school.

Q. That is not what I wanted to know. He is studying for a higher degree, is he not?

A. *Ja, ja.* He is clever, intelligent, ambitious, hard-working.

Q. And very anxious to obtain the degree of Doctor of Divinity?

A. What has that to do with it? I have said he was ambitious.

Q. Yes. Would it not seem very attractive to him to be able to give up teaching for a while so that he could give all his time and energy to study and research?

A. Very likely so. I do not know.

Q. Do you deny that you proposed marriage to him?

A. What is that to you?

Q. Did you not often say that he was too old to make his marriage with your daughter a success?

A. I thought it might be so. Twenty years between their ages. It is a long time.

Q. I must stress this point, Mrs Schumann. Were you prepared to give Mr James five thousand pounds if and when he married you?

A. What means five thousand pounds to me? It belonged to my daughter, and now she is dead.

Q. Yes, but, until she died, you did not have the five thousand pounds, did you?

A. No, of course I did not. You are telling me that Edward – no, I will not believe it!

Q. Believe what, Mrs Schumann?

A. I will not believe that Edward killed my Karen!

Q. But why *should* Mr James kill her? If he married her he would still have the five thousand pounds, would he not?

A. You did not know Karen. So mercenary. No part of the five thousand pounds for *him*. But with me he knows that if he can persuade me to marry him, he has it, *ja*, he has it all. I am of generous nature. When I love, I give – just like to Karen's father. I give it all – love, youth, strength, money, to have the babies he want – everything.

Q. Do you suggest, then, that Edward James killed your daughter, knowing that he would get the five thousand pounds when he married you?

A. Me to suggest? Nothing! I say no more. You must think as you please. Myself, I stop thinking. It does no good to think. What is done is done. No use to grieve. No use to say, 'If, if only, if'. No. I continue my life like Spartan mothers. If you think Edward James killed my Karen for five thousand pounds, I say I do not agree. Edward is a good man. Any more I do not know.

'So she's prepared to throw James to the wolves if it comes to a question of having to save her own skin,' said Laura.

'There is more,' said Dame Beatrice. 'Detective-Inspector Maisry appears to have gone quite as far as he dared in questioning Mrs Schumann without cautioning her first. The document goes on: '

Q. I know you have satisfied Superintendent Phillips as to this, Mrs Schumann, but he was able to talk to you before my department was brought into the case. Will you tell me just how you spent the day on which Superintendent Phillips believes your daughter died?

A. I will tell you anything you wish to know, but you must not make traps for me with my words. I will tell you what I have already told the so kind Superintendent Phillips, also Dame Beatrice, always my friend. On the day before she died, my Karen telephones me to say there is a day's holiday for the school – two special half-days which the teachers decide to turn into one whole day – you understand? Karen asks shall she come home for the day. Edward – her fiancé, you know – wants to spend the day at his books, and the two girls who share a flat with Karen are to go out with their friends. I say no, not convenient to come, as I have an engagement at Ringwood and too late to alter it.

Q. And you went to Ringwood to fulfil this engagement? At what time would that have been?

A. I go to Ringwood in my car, taking my prize dog to give a service, and I get there – I do not know exactly, but it would have been – oh, I am desolate to think of it! – it would have been while my Karen was being done to death by this monster.

Q. Yes, but what time by the clock was this?

A. Oh, half-past eleven, perhaps. I do not know.

Q. Superintendent Phillips has been to see the people concerned. They say that you arrived with your dog at about a quarter past twelve.

A. No, no! Much earlier than that.

Q. I see. You suggested to Superintendent Phillips that your daughter must have left her flat very early in the morning to have arrived at the spot where her body was found, and to have been killed there at the time the doctors stated at the inquest, but I do not follow your reasoning. How long would you say it took your daughter to reach your cottage from her flat?

A. Twenty miles – let us say an hour, allowing for traffic. But my daughter did not come to the cottage that day. How could she, when she knows I have arranged to go out?

Q. Well, we have come to the conclusion that she *did* go to your cottage that morning, that she was killed there and her body taken to where it was found.

A. But why should you think that?

Q. The time factor leads us to think so. Your daughter finds out that the cottage will be empty during the late morning and the middle day. She arranges to meet somebody there. That somebody kills her. Now, at what time would you say you got home that afternoon?

A. I was invited to stay for lunch – this also I tell Karen over the telephone – and I leave at perhaps half-past two, a quarter to three, something like that. What does it matter, since, by that time, my Karen is dead?

Q. It matters to this extent: if your daughter was killed at the cottage, the murderer had plenty of time to move her body to where it was found. What do you say about that?

A. I have always believed – the police, they tell me nothing! – I have always believed that Karen had an assignation with someone in those woods, and that he killed her there.

Q. The ground was expertly and very minutely examined, and there was no sign of a struggle.

A. But she would have been taken by surprise. She would not have had a chance to struggle. The murderer came on her from behind and twisted the cord of the dog-whistle around her neck and made her unconscious, and then he – then he—

Q. Finished the job by manual strangulation. I still think she would have threshed about a bit, you know, wouldn't she?

A. Please, please! I do not like this picture!

Q. Neither do I. How do you account for the fact that the dog-whistle was round her neck at all?

A. The murderer put it there, like I am saying, to make her unconscious.

Q. I am trying to form another picture in my mind. She must have been on terms of some intimacy with her murderer if she allowed him to put a string round her neck. It sounds as though a playful situation had been contrived, of which he then took advantage.

A. You mean she had a lover, my little Karen?

Q. What does it look like to you?

A. But she was engaged to Edward!

Q. His alibi has never been proved, you know.

A. You think *Edward* killed her?

Q. I did not say that. Let us return to this dog-whistle. There seems to be no doubt that it was in response to it that Mrs Gavin's dog left Mrs Gavin's side and followed somebody across the common and into the woods where your daughter's body lay. Further, that whoever used the whistle knew the dog and commanded him to stay with the body. Now I want you, Mrs Schumann, to think very hard about this. I want to know – and here I do not believe that anybody except yourself can help us – I want to know the names of any persons whom the dog would have known and would have trusted to that extent.

A. There was nobody except Karen herself.

Q. Who must be ruled out for obvious reasons.

A. I think the dog was using instinct, not following a dog-whistle.

Q. Another point which I find extremely puzzling is this: how could the murderer have known that Mrs Gavin was exercising her dog that evening?

A. How should I know?

Q. How well do you know Mrs Gavin?

A. You think *she* killed my Karen and led the dog to the spot, so she can pretend to find the dog and the body next day? Well, she is so big and so strong, of course ...

Q. Yes, it's a thought, that. I must see what Mrs Gavin has to say about it. Can you think of any reason, though, why she should wish to kill your daughter?

A. Oh, yes, that I know.

Q. Indeed? What reason?

A. Karen desires to take the dog back again.

Q. Really?

A. *Ja.* Mrs Gavin – Karen tells me this, but, of course, I do not repeat it until you force it from me – Mrs Gavin has her son in mind. It is for him that the dog is purchased. So she says she cannot part with the dog and disappoint the boy. I think they meet and argue. I see it all, now you say the killing was done at my cottage. Karen finds I shall not be there, so she makes this appointment to meet Mrs Gavin and talk things over, but there is argument, and Mrs Gavin, so much bigger and stronger than my Karen, throws the string of the dog-whistle round Karen's neck and pulls it tight – in bad temper, you know, not perhaps intending to kill. But Karen falls unconscious and Mrs Gavin is so frightened she strangles her, so my Karen cannot live to tell of the attack.

Q. Well, thank you, Mrs Schumann. You have certainly given me something to think about. And you have had this in mind all along?

A. Not all along, no, but I think it is the truth.

Q. Then how do you account for the other four deaths?

A. Only the death of my Karen concern me. I am sorry for the others, but I do not care all that much, and I still think Otto, who is a very bad boy, killed Maria Machrado because he get her with child and she demands to be married.

'And, of course, she could be right about that, you know,' commented Laura to Dame Beatrice. 'I wouldn't put it past him and, of course, he *is* her son and she *did* kill her daughter. Karen went to the cottage that morning, had a bust-up with her mother about James, and that was the end of Karen. Then Mrs Schumann hid the body, probably in an empty dog-house, went off to Ringwood, came back in the afternoon and took the body to the woods. Then she must have come along here and followed me to the post-office and round the village. She knew I'd have to take Fergus for a run at some time before nightfall. All she had to do was hang about long enough. She'd have seen me leave the post-office, then she cut back to the common, went along that path, whistled up Fergus, and – Bob's your uncle! She simply had to walk him across to the woods and leave him on guard. She knew I wouldn't be able either to hear her whistle him up or to spot her in the mist and the darkness.'

'She also knew that you would not rest until you had found him, and that, in finding him, you would also find the body and have to report it. Her suggestion that you are the murderer arose directly from this interview with Detective-Inspector Maisry and was made on the spur of the moment. He must have given her a fright for her to have invented so far-fetched a theory.'

(4)

'For the record only, Mrs Gavin,' said Maisry, when, two days later, he visited the Stone House, 'can you cast your mind back and remember how you spent the day on which Miss Schumann was killed?

'I'll have to work backwards,' said Laura, 'from the time I took Fergus down to the post-office. I left this house at about a quarter-past four, or maybe a bit earlier, because I wanted to catch the quarter-to-five post. Before that, I had been writing the letter I was going to send. That would have taken me possibly twenty minutes.'

'Takes us back roughly to between a quarter to four and four o'clock. Let's say a quarter to four.'

'We finished lunch at two. We have it most days at a quarter past one, so as to get a long morning.'

'And that day, so far as you remember, was no exception?'

'It was no exception,' said Dame Beatrice. 'Our habits are regular, unless there is some special reason for altering them, and on that day there would have been none, since the murders, which lately have sometimes thrown the times out of joint, had not been committed.'

'Right. So we are back to a quarter past one.'

'From ten o'clock until I went to wash my hands before lunch, I was dealing with Dame Beatrice's correspondence and typing a couple of chapters of her new book,' went on Laura.

'You confirm that, Dame Beatrice?'

'Certainly. I was with Laura the whole time. I spend little time on housekeeping duties, for Henri does his own ordering of food and Celestine looks after everything else, with the help of a young girl who lives in and has her own regular routine of duties.'

'Oh, well, that disposes of Mrs Schumann's unlikely theory that Mrs Gavin murdered her daughter. To my mind, there is no doubt about what *really* happened, but, unfortunately, so far I have no proof on which I should be justified in arresting and charging the good lady. My next move will be to go over all the ground again in the case of Maria Machrado. Otto Schumann's ship docks at Poole this afternoon and I shall be there to meet it. I wonder whether you would care to accompany me, Dame Beatrice? – in your official capacity, of course. I shall get him along to the station and you might like to examine him there. I also shall have a few things to say to him and, between us, we may get at the truth, so far as he knows it.'

Otto was at his jauntiest and appeared not in the least perturbed when Maisry boarded the ship and extracted him therefrom to the annoyance of his captain and the interest of the first officer.

'Glad you don't belong to the uniformed branch,' Otto said chattily, when he was in Maisry's car. 'Bad for the morale of the crew to see the second officer being carted off to the jug. I suppose it *is* to the jug, isn't it? You know, like the last time, when you had to let me go because you knew you'd boobed.'

'Just to the station itself, to answer a few questions,' said Maisry gently. 'You can refuse, of course, or you can ask to have your lawyer present.'

'Mean to say you haven't put the bracelets on your mass-murderer? Bad, you know, Detective-Inspector! A lot of slackness somewhere.'

'Just as you say,' said Maisry unemotionally. 'I've got Dame Beatrice Lestrange Bradley at the station. She wants to talk to you about psychiatry. You'll find her very interesting and, if I may offer a word of advice, I wouldn't try to be too clever, if I were you. She probably eats a couple of young lads like you as a snack between meals.'

'Glad you cautioned me. Where's the bit about "be taken down and may be used in evidence", though?'

Maisry did not reply and a little of Otto's ebullience appeared to leave him, for he said nothing more until they reached headquarters and he was taken into the office which Phillips had put at Maisry's disposal. There, having mentioned that the colour of the walls clashed with the colour of his eyes, he sobered down again, took the chair which was offered him and looked at Dame Beatrice with an innocent, enquiring expression. She said,

'Good afternoon, Mr Schumann. Would you mind doing a word test for me?'

'You say "bird" and I say "wench" – that kind of thing?'

'Talking of "that kind of thing", we now know that you were correct about one thing you told us about Maria Machrado.'

'Only in *one* thing? Surely that's understating it? I could tell you a bookful about that Spanish doll, and it would all be true.'

'But possibly not useful. After you had parted from her, she *did* go back to your mother's cottage. That is where we believe she was murdered.'

'Oh? What gave you that idea?'

'It fits with what we know of the other murders,' said Maisry, 'so it would be a good idea if you told us your story of the quarrel you had with her.'

'Look here, when I told the other dick – what's his name? – Phillips, that Maria said she was going back to my mother's cottage, I told him a shiner. Why would she go back there? My mother hated the sight of her, and she knew it. The best she could hope for there was to be shown the door.'

'And the worst, that she would be murdered,' said Maisry. 'Now, Mr Schumann, I am not cautioning you yet, but in fairness I must emphasize that you do not have to answer my next question. Who, besides yourself, could have known that Maria Machrado intended to go back to the cottage?'

Otto stared at his fingers. They were thick, long and strong. He flexed them and then, turning both hands over, he studied the golden hairs on the backs of them.

'I dunno,' he said at last.

'Will you give us an account, as full a one as you can manage, of the last time you saw Miss Machrado alive?'

'Look, I've done all this before! Remember? You had nothing on me at all, and you had to let me go. You can't arrest a man twice for the same offence!'

'You can't *try* a man twice for the same offence. There is

a difference. I advise you to help us, not to try to lay us a stymie. I will admit to you that we did not proceed against you that last time because we were convinced then that all the murders were committed by the same person. Now we are not nearly so sure. We know who killed your sister. We know it was not you. But it is up to you to convince us that neither did you kill Miss Machrado. No . . .' for Otto had begun to bluster . . . 'that kind of attitude won't help you. Just sit there and do a bit of quiet thinking. You're in a spot, my boy, and don't you lose sight of that fact. You're known to have been running around with the girl, you're known to have had a quarrel with her at which blows were exchanged, and you're known to have a violent temper. Furthermore, it seems as though you, and you only, knew that she intended to return to your mother's cottage and demand shelter.'

'Demand? A fine position she was in to demand anything!'

'Her demand would be based upon the fact that she was carrying your child.'

'You can't prove that!'

'I think we should have little difficulty in getting a jury to believe it.'

'I see.' He was silent. All the bounce had gone out of him. It was an extremely dejected boy who sat there, staring down again at his large hands.

'Tell me,' said Dame Beatrice, 'when you have answered, or decided not to answer, Detective-Inspector Maisry, all that you remember about your father.'

'My father? What's he got to do with it? He's been dead five years.'

'I know that. What was your relationship with him?'

'Not too good. Karen was his pick. She shared his interests, such as they were.'

'How do you mean – such as they were?'

'Oh, religion and all that. He never made any money, you know. We lived on my mother and the dogs. I used to rile the old man by looking up things against the Faith and arguing with him.'

'What kind of things?'

'Oh, it was all in his books. People back in the Dark Ages

who challenged the Church with ideas that weren't in the book of rules.'

'And you deliberately studied these ideas with the intention of annoying your father?'

'Oh, yes, and it always worked. I enjoyed baiting the old man.'

'What was your mother's attitude?'

'I don't think she had one. She never attempted to argue or interfere. It was Karen who did that. My mother just used to sit and knit and listen. She never took any part. I think she thought father ought to have kept on his job as a schoolmaster – he taught when he first came over here – but he threw it up just to do reading and studying. He said he was going to write a book, and he did send a couple of chapters to a publisher, I believe, but they came back, so I don't think he tried any more. He said that posterity would do him justice. Anyway, I got sick of it at home and went to sea, and having, as I told you, a pretty good brain, I've got on. I shall have my own ship by the time I'm thirty.'

'Not if you half-kill the crew, you won't,' said Maisry, gently and with a slight smile. 'Well, now, let's get back to Miss Machrado.'

'Oh, Christ! I didn't kill her, and I don't know who did.'

'You say you have a good brain, and I do not dispute it,' said Dame Beatrice. 'Have you also a good memory?'

'You need a good memory in my job. Do you know what a second officer's duties are? But then, why should you?'

'Why, indeed, since they do not affect me or my question. If your memory is a good one, I wonder whether you can remember any of the subjects about which you used to tease your father?'

'One or two. Three, in fact, because he clouted me on the ear once, when I'd already got earache, although, mind you, I don't think he knew that.'

'Yes? What were these three?'

'One was about a chap named Priscillian. He claimed that the local bishops were too fond of luxury and converted some of them to his ideas. He was also in favour of some birds

called Gnostics, who, as far as I can make out, derived somehow or other from the Jews. Anyhow, I was chiefly interested
in Priscillian because he was condemned for sorcery, a subject
in which I've always been interested.'

'His dates?'

'Dates? Oh, I've never bothered with dates. Pretty early on,
I believe, but I couldn't really say.'

'And the other two?'

'Oh, a fellow called Arnold. They hanged him and burnt
the body and chucked it into the River Tiber. The other one –
the one when I had earache – was Pelagius. He interested me
because his followers became violent and did all sorts of
things that weren't exactly what you'd call Christian.'

'Your tastes, then, even as a young boy, ran in the direction
of necromancy, cruelty and violence.'

'Oh, well, hang it all, you know what boys of fourteen
and fifteen are like!'

'I think I interrupted Detective-Inspector Maisry, who was
asking you to return to the subject of Maria Machrado.'

'I've told him all I know about her.'

'Tell us again,' said Maisry, 'and I'd prefer the story
straight, if you don't mind.' So far as essentials went, it was
the story he had told before. He had met Maria Machrado
in Bilbao, she had subsequently come to Southampton on his
ship, they had been intimate, he had introduced her to his
mother as a paying guest at week-ends and during college vacations. His object, he admitted, was so that the intimacy might
continue.

'Now tell us about this last quarrel,' said Maisry.

'You're trying to trap me.'

'On the contrary,' said Dame Beatrice, 'we are almost convinced by your story, so far. You have gone a long way towards proving to us that you are innocent of murder.'

He looked at her with suspicion in his gaze, Maisry with
slight surprise in his.

'Well, all right, then,' said Otto, 'if that's the way you want
it, but it was only the usual sort of row that springs
up between the likes of her and the likes of me, you
know.'

F

'Right,' said Maisry. 'The truth, the whole truth and nothing but the truth will help you, so any embroidery or airy persiflage is *out*.'

'I can take a hint. I don't know about you, but I really believe the Dame is willing to see me in the clear. Here goes, then. I met Maria at my mother's a couple of week-ends – I expect mother told you. Then I stayed with her at her digs – I expect you remember hearing about that, too. I spent all I could afford, but she wanted more, and when I told her she couldn't have it she got sore with me and threatened to tell my mother that she was going to have my baby. Of course, I laughed, who wouldn't? As though my mother would give a damn, I said, whose baby she was going to have. At that she fished out a knife and went for me like a mad thing. Well, you don't get to be second officer on our kind of ship without knowing how to handle blokes with knives, so I side-stepped and then smacked my hand hard down on her knife-wrist and, of course, she had to let go the knife. It fell on the floor and I kicked it under a chair and smacked her face.

'She was yelling blue murder by this time, and I didn't want her landlady phoning up the police and giving me in charge for assault, so I slung my hook p.d.q. That didn't do for Maria. She followed me out and all down the street, shouting curses and insults in Spanish and bringing quite a few of the citizens to their front doors. At last I got her into an alley and took hold of her and told her what I'd do to her if she didn't shut up.

'She turned quiet at that, and began to cry. She said she was sure her landlady wouldn't have her back, so what was she to do, and where could she go? I said, "Well, you threatened to go to my mother. Why don't you just do that? You can say what you like about me. She'll believe you, whatever it is, and I believe she'll take you in until you can find fresh digs for next term." Then I gave her a five-pound note I couldn't really spare, and put her on the train for Lymington. I knew she could thumb a lift from there if she switched on the old charm.'

'But a lift would not take her to an out-of-the-way spot like your mother's cottage,' said Dame Beatrice.

'It was the best I could do, and I didn't think she deserved even that much.'

'Did you ever hear from her or see her again?'

'No. The next thing was the dicks pulling me in for murdering her. I reckon she got fresh with some lorry-driver or car-owner, and he had what he wanted and then did for her and ditched her. She wasn't found so far away from one of the roads to Dorchester, you know. Quite a lot of stuff goes to the south-west that way.'

'Of course,' said Maisry, 'you've no alibi for the time of her death – nothing that would convince a jury.'

'Then why did you let me go, after you arrested me? You knew you had nothing on me, and you've got nothing on me this time, either.'

'We are not arresting you this time,' said Maisry.

'Back to square one,' he added to Dame Beatrice when Otto had gone. 'What did you make of our likely lad this time?'

'Nothing that I had not made of him before. I think we ought to have another talk with Edward James.'

'If Maria Machrado *did* go back to Mrs Schumann's cottage, the inference, considering what we suspect about that lady, is pretty clear. The trouble will be to prove that she *did* go back there. Personally, I should doubt it. She must have known what kind of reception she would get after the deception she'd practised, and all that sort of thing.'

'I pin my hopes on Mr James. He may have been at the cottage when she turned up, if she *did* turn up.'

'Yes, that's a thought. Right. We'll sort him out.'

(5)

This time James was not required to go to the police station.

'We know where we stand,' said Maisry. 'There are only two bits of information we want from him. Even with those we shan't have enough to secure a conviction, but now we're certain as to means and motive, it's only a question of patience plus spadework before we know opportunity. Once we can show all three we'll be justified in making an arrest and, after that, it's up to the prosecution. I couldn't, at first, see why you questioned Schumann about his father, and I'm not sure I grasp the point now.'

'A father's relationship with his children is always important, I think, particularly with his sons. I did not know, when I began, exactly how Otto would react, but it was immediately apparent that his answers, from our point of view, were important. The relationship does not seem to have been a happy one. I imagine that the father was bigoted, narrow-minded and selfish, and that his attitude towards the boy was humourless and unkind. Otto expressed his resentment and intolerance of this attitude by annoying his father in a way which, to a religious although bigoted man, must have been particularly galling.'

'In other words, he delighted in taking the micky out of papa in the most irritating way he could think up. Apart from indicating that he'd inherited a streak of cruelty, I didn't see where this got us, though, and I was very much surprised (although I tried not to show it) when you told him that he was practically in the clear. After all, if there was one thing which his evidence showed, it was that, as a boy, he was perfectly familiar with these heresies which seem to be part of the plot and, as a man, he certainly remembered a good deal about them.'

'Yes, that is my point. I mean, that is why I practically exonerated him. I think a guilty man would have left out Priscillian and given us Arius, of whom he most certainly would have heard, since Arianism was easily one of the longest-lasting, and, except for Protestantism, which is, to all intents and purposes, now widely acceptable and respected, by far the most important of the heresies.'

'I see your drift. Arius connects with his sister, whom we know with absolute certainty he could not have murdered...'

'Whereas Priscillian connects with the Spanish girl, whom he most certainly could.'

'Yes, it's a point, but to you it seems a stronger one than it does to me. I wouldn't put it past him to bluff matters out. He's a slippery young customer.'

'No, he is a boaster and a liar. I doubt whether he has the strength of character to bluff his way out of anything.'

'You think he was telling us the truth this time, though, do you?'

'I think we know enough from other sources to be reasonably sure that he was. The most important piece of information which he gave us we cannot check at present – indeed, I doubt whether we shall ever be able to check it sufficiently to be able to make court evidence out of it, but it is psychologically so satisfying that I propose to accept it without question.'

'You have me fogged. I haven't the slightest idea what you're getting at.'

'Really? Did you not obtain a mental picture of the family? The father studying and making notes for this book he is going to write, but which never comes to anything? The daughter possibly helping him by looking up his references? The impudent aggravating son looking up material with which to harass, embarrass and interrupt his father? And the mother, that smooth-skinned, fresh-faced, silent German housewife and dog-breeder, resentful of her necessity to be the breadwinner and of her husband's selfish determination to devote himself to work which does not bring in a penny, sitting there knitting, listening, not interfering, merely drinking in all that is said, all that is quoted, and storing it away in that solid, methodical German memory of hers?'

'But it was her daughter who was killed, not her husband.'

'It was her daughter who was killed, yes, but I wonder – this is mere idle speculation, and perhaps you would do well to take no notice of it – but I wonder what we should find if Pastor Schumann's body were exhumed?'

'Good Lord!' exclaimed Maisry. 'You don't surely mean to suggest . . . ?'

'No, no, it was a passing thought, and she would have had no motive unless . . .'

'Unless what?'

'Unless Edward James was known to the family before Pastor Schumann died. We have been given to understand that Schumann was a schoolmaster and then gave up this work in order to write a book. What could be more likely than that he and James met as fellow-teachers? Even if they were not at the same school, there are inter-staff meetings for various purposes, teachers' unions and the like, at which they could have got to know one another. After all, they had this common interest in theology, the one for his book, the other for his degree.'

'*Well*!' said Maisry. 'You *have* given me something to think about! You mean she wanted James so much that she was prepared to murder first her husband and then her daughter in order to get him?'

'I have little doubt of it, so now for Mr James.'

James was interviewed at the Stone House, which, previously, he had declined to visit. His attitude was abject and defeatist. The maid shewed him into the library where Maisry and Dame Beatrice were waiting to receive him, and his first words were:

'Well, I've accepted your invitation rather than be called to the police station again, and, if you are charging me, I can only assert my complete innocence.'

'I am not charging you, Mr James,' said Maisry, 'neither have I the smallest intention of doing so unless some entirely fresh evidence turns up which appears to point towards you, but I assure you that I consider this is utterly unlikely. You are here – and thank you for coming – because we think there are just one or two small points which you may be able to clear up for us.'

'Yes, I see, but I can't think what they are. I am absolutely certain I've told you every single thing I know.'

CHAPTER SEVEN

He is Dead and Gone Lady

'Tommy's gone! What shall I do?
Away down Hilo!
Oh, Tommy's gone, and I'll go too –
Tom's gone to Hilo.'

---

(1)

'First,' said Maisry, 'we would like you to tell us the full story of your acquaintance with the Schumann family. Did you know them, or any of them, before Miss Schumann joined the staff at your school?'

'Oh, yes. The father, Heinrich Schumann, who was a Lutheran pastor in his own country, fled from Germany with his wife soon after Hitler came into power. I had not long left college and was in my first teaching post at an independent school in Bournemouth, and Schumann, seeing no prospect of continuing his own profession, took a post at my school as French and German master.'

'The same subjects as his daughter taught.'

'Yes, they were both excellent linguists and Schumann took to me because I could speak German and, of course, had as my main interest, even at that time, those theological studies which were his own delight. He was ten or twelve years older than myself, but that made his society the more enjoyable, as I have never been altogether at ease with my contemporaries.

'After a time he took to inviting me to his home for weekends. He and his wife had a flat in Poole at that time, and, as I have always lived in lodgings since I left college, it made a very pleasant change for me, as you may well imagine.'

'Mrs Schumann was not breeding dogs at that time, then?'

'Oh, no. She often talked of it – she had done a little in that line in Germany – but, of course, living in a flat in a large and busy town, there was no scope for it.'

'How did the couple get on? There were no children at that time, I take it.'

'No, the twins, Karen and Otto, came much later. I am no judge of how couples get on, unless they quarrel, in which case' – he gave his hearers a wry smile – 'I suppose one would have to say that they *don't* get on. I never heard a word exchanged between them which would indicate anything but a reasonably satisfactory relationship, but, all the same, I received an impression that they were not fully compatible.'

'In other words,' suggested Dame Beatrice, 'Mrs Schumann found her life and her husband extremely dull.'

'Well, one felt rather sorry for her, in a way. The flat was a small one, just three rooms, including the kitchen, and the only other thing was a tiny bathroom, so I don't think she had enough to keep her occupied.'

'So you never stayed the week-end?'

'Oh, yes, indeed I did. They were very kind about that. They used to make me up a camp bed in the living-room and I used to go to lunch with them on Saturdays, sleep there on Saturday night and leave again on Sunday evening after church. We attended church together on Sunday mornings, too, Schumann and I. Mrs Schumann – Karla, as I was soon asked to call her – cooked the dinner and came to church with us in the evening.'

'Surely not a Lutheran church?'

'No, a Presbyterian one. I would have preferred Church of England myself, but it seemed unmannerly to suggest that, so I accompanied them to their chosen place of worship.'

'And how did you spend the rest of the week-end?'

'On Saturday afternoons, if it was fine, we walked. Like many Germans, the Schumanns were great walkers. We would take the train to Brockenhurst and spend the day in the New Forest, or go to Lymington and cross over to the Isle of Wight, and then walk our legs off, while Heinrich and I talked theology.'

'And Mrs Schumann?'

'Oh, I imagine she listened. At any rate, I do not remember that she ever joined in the discussions. At five o'clock or thereabouts, when we found a suitable spot, we would have a picnic tea. Both of them carried rucksacks and at first I felt it incumbent upon me to attempt to relieve Karla of hers, but

she always refused and Heinrich supported her, saying that I
was their guest and must carry nothing. I will not pretend
that I was sorry. I have a weak back and a tendency to
sciatica, neither of which was helpful in carrying a heavy pack.
In fact, the walks themselves were almost more than I could
manage.'

'Were the Schumanns naturalised at this time?' asked
Maisry.

'Not for a couple of years, but the news from Germany was
such that they were convinced war was inevitable and, knowing
this, I suggested that, as they had fled the country and had
no intention of ever going back, naturalisation might save them
a good deal of trouble later on. They took my advice, and
Heinrich was drafted into the Pioneer Corps when war broke
out.'

'With his intellectual background he could not have been
pleased about that,' commented Dame Beatrice.

'Well, he received quite good treatment, I believe,' said
James, 'and, when the air-raids began in earnest, I think anybody with a German name and speaking with a German accent,
might have had a difficult time if he'd still been living in a
place near Southampton, which suffered terrible damage and
loss of life during the war. Karla, of course, retreated to the
country and was not molested or annoyed in any way.'

'But, until the war interrupted your friendship with them,
you saw the Schumanns frequently and stayed many week-
ends at their flat?'

'Yes, I knew them intimately from 1935 until 1939, but then
came a change in our relationship.'

'Oh, before the war began?'

'Yes, indeed. Two things happened. Just before the war, as
you may or may not know, the staffs of schools were instructed
to issue gas-masks to the children, but to take care to stress
the fact that this was a precautionary measure only, and that
it was in the highest degree unlikely that they would ever need
to be used, as, indeed, they never were. Well, Heinrich,
probably with the best of intentions, was rash and irrespon-
sible enough to tell his form – he was form-master of a group
of twelve-year-olds, boys and girls – that the masks would be

quite useless if the new and deadly poison gases which the Germans had secretly invented and perfected since the 1914 war should ever be used by an invading German army.'

'With the result that some of the youngsters went home and spread alarm and despondency, I suppose,' said Maisry.

'Exactly. Parents, especially the parents of some of the little girls, bombarded the headmaster with tales of broken nights, of children screaming in nightmare or refusing to go to bed, etc. etc. until Schumann was severely censured by the headmaster, and the long and short of it was that he lost his job, and really one can scarcely be surprised. Of course, he was, in many ways, a singularly obtuse man, like so many Germans.'

'I wonder what possessed him?' said Maisry. 'It seems such an idiotic thing to have said to a pack of youngsters.'

'An attack of conscience. He had to tell the truth, as he saw it,' said Dame Beatrice. 'I am quite sure he did not realise the harm he was doing. So that is why he gave up teaching! His son told us that he had done so, but did not give us the reason.'

'I doubt whether Otto knew it. His father would not have told him, and his mother was so incensed when Heinrich lost his job that she would never have made the slightest excuse for him, I'm sure. To her, he had simply been given the sack for incompetence.'

'You mentioned a second reason for a break in your friendship with the Schumanns,' said Dame Beatrice.

'Yes, well, that had nothing to do with the war.' He paused. 'It's not a subject I care to discuss,' he said. To give him time, Dame Beatrice asked,

'And how did *you* get on during the war?'

'I saw how things would go, so I changed my job. Our boys and girls were sent home as soon as school reassembled in the September of 1939. Most of them, in fact, had been sent to reputedly safer areas by their parents and did not return to the school at all. The headmaster had been going to retire at Christmas, in any case, and had sold the school buildings and our small playing field on advantageous terms to an hotel company, so we on the staff had been looking about us during the summer holiday and it seemed to me that my wisest plan would be to try for a post in a state school. Not only would this offer me better security in the form of a retirement pension, but I reasoned that teaching under the state scheme would have to become a reserved occupation, at least for a time, and would defer my being drafted into one of the armed services.'

'And did it?' asked Maisry, in order to keep James talking, since he had not, so far, received any useful information from him.

'For a time, yes. I obtained the post of history and religious knowledge specialist at a school in West London and was there during the worst of the air-raids. It was a strange time. At first, when the alarm sounded, we used to get the children into shelter and have community singing and all that sort of thing, but as time went on we carried on with normal lessons. When at last I got my call-up papers I was rejected on medical grounds – nothing serious – flat feet and defective eyesight, as a matter of fact, but it meant that I had the good fortune to remain a civilian.'

'And did you keep up a correspondence with the Schumanns during the war?' asked Dame Beatrice.

'Oh, yes – well, I sent my London address to Mrs Schumann – but we did not write very often, just enough, I suppose, to keep in touch. Then, in 1943, Karen and Otto were born, and I suppose she was kept pretty busy looking after them and going to the clinic for their orange juice and cod liver oil or whatever, because for the next few years we scarcely corresponded at all. In fact, it got down to an exchange of cards at Christmas, and that was about the extent of it.'

'But you picked up the threads later?' suggested Dame Beatrice.

'Oh, yes. Ten years ago, when the plan for comprehensive schools was getting under way, I applied for the post I now hold. I have never cared over-much for London and was glad to return to my old haunts.'

'And this brings us to your second point,' said Dame Beatrice. James dropped his eyes and fidgeted with his fingers. They were long, white and well-manicured.

'I suppose it does,' he said. 'Oh, well, having said so much, I may as well give you the rest, although it shows nobody up in a particularly good light.'

'It is connected, of course, with the virtual cessation of correspondence between yourself and the Schumanns.'

'That is correct. Briefly – and you will understand that even the recollection of it is embarrassing to me – all I can tell you is that before the twins were born and while her husband was in the Pioneer Corps and away from home, Karla, in the plainest possible terms, made a certain suggestion to me. I was, of course, quite horrified, and she withdrew it immediately, pleading that she was lonely, that the war frightened her, that she needed support and comfort, and that she regretted making an advance which was unwelcome to me.

'I pointed out that I had never given her the slightest reason for thinking that it could be otherwise, and she begged me, in the most abject and heartfelt way, not to allow her ill-judged suggestion to make any difference to our long friendship, but, as you will understand, things could never be the same again between us, and, as gradually as I could, not wishing either to be unkind to her or to arouse any suspicion in Heinrich's mind that Karla was not as chaste as he would have wished, I almost ceased to correspond with them and I gave up going to see her unless I heard from Heinrich that he would be at home.

'When he was demobilised, and when having the twin children, I felt, would have altered Karla's feelings towards me, I picked up the acquaintanceship again. During the war there was little to do but read, so I had embarked upon a further course of study in theology, and it occurred to me that I might try for my doctorate in divinity. I will be frank about my motives in taking up with the Schumanns again. Not only had they been the closest friends I had, but I needed to pick Heinrich's brains and borrow books from his library.'

'Had you borrowed from his library before that?'

'No, never. He had shown me his books, but there had never been any suggestion on the part of either of us that I should borrow them. When I did approach the matter, I found that he was a bibliophile of the type which cannot bear others to handle his collection, so I was obliged to rely upon public libraries and my own purchases for the books I needed. I could understand his attitude and sympathise with it, and I remained his friend up to the day of his death.'

'Did that come as a shock to you?' asked Dame Beatrice.

'Not a shock. I felt grief, of course, and a sense of loss, but he had been ailing with some sort of internal trouble for some time, and complained of pain and had attacks of vomiting. He had been under the doctor for some months, in fact, before he died.'

'By that time I suppose the twins were more or less grown up,' said Dame Beatrice.

'Yes, they would have been nineteen years old at least. Karen was at the University and intended to teach, and Otto, always an undisciplined, very unsatisfactory boy, had gone to sea at the age of sixteen. Karen had attached herself to me at an early age and I regarded her, until she came out of college, as a privileged younger sister, and, indeed, I have never regarded her in any other way.'

'Yet you became engaged to her,' said Maisry.

'I knew she would accept me if I asked her, and I asked her to safeguard myself, as I thought, from Karla, who, after her husband's death, importuned me again. However, when Karen obtained a post in the same school as myself, which, it seems, was what she had set her heart on, Karla's attitude changed. It was she who suggested that I should not come to the cottage more often than about one week-end in four, urging me to work hard for my doctorate and not allow Karen, who was a gay, fun-loving girl, to cause me to dissipate my time, and she also said that Karen was too flighty and unsettled to make a good wife at that time, but that teaching, and living away from home except at week-ends and during school holidays, would quieten and develop her.

'By this time I was so much engrossed in my studies as to feel that this was very sensible advice, so I settled down to what we both realised would be a long engagement and my life became peaceful and satisfying until this dreadful thing happened to Karen.'

'Now,' said Maisry, 'you must have done a lot of thinking

about that. Have you any idea in your mind as to the identity of the murderer?'

'The only idea to come into my mind won't bear thinking about, and that is all I am going to say, particularly as I haven't a shred of proof. Besides, the other four murders make nonsense of my idea, anyway.'

'Yes, the other four murders,' said Dame Beatrice. 'You must have met one of those unfortunate girls.'

'Yes,' said James, eyeing her steadily, 'I did. Twice, at Karla's cottage, I met the Spanish young lady.'

'Who was of a very lively and forthcoming disposition.'

'Yes.'

'Will you not go a little further?'

'The second time I met her at Karla's she turned very playful and sat on my knee. Oh, not by invitation, I assure you! She also kissed me and suggested returning with me to my flat. That, I fancy, was because she had been turned out of her own. At least, so Karla told me when I said good night and she saw me off in my hired car.'

'I see. Was Mrs Schumann a witness of what one might term the goings-on?' asked Maisry.

'Oh, yes. The young woman was quite shameless. Karla took it extremely well. She merely said, "One day, Maria, you will go too far", to which the hussy replied, "But already I go too far. I am to have a niño. Did you not know? One cannot go farther than that." Upon this Karla said, quite good-naturedly, "Oh, go and get the supper. You will have to spend the night here, I suppose," and added, when the girl had gone into the kitchen, "I have to put up with her. She got the baby by Otto." Then the next thing I heard about Maria was that she was dead.'

'In fact, that she *had* gone too far,' said Maisry.

(2)

'Well, we can be pretty sure of ourselves, I think,' he went on, when James had gone off in the car which seemed to be on perpetual hire to him. 'Motive, means and opportunity seem to be established in the first two cases, and I think we should aim now at the fifth, for I am extremely doubtful whether we shall ever satisfy ourselves, except by inference, about numbers three and four. Five is a different matter, and may prove to be our strongest card. Once we can prove a connection between Mrs Schumann and this Irish girl who lived in Swansea, I think our case is complete, unless she's got a very good explanation indeed. I wonder whether there's any way of getting her fingerprints verified? The letter which I asked the Swansea newspaper to let me have must be fingerprinted all right – it's on that glossy note-paper which takes prints very well, although we haven't tested it yet.'

'And their duplicate ought to be on a note beneath this very Stone House roof, but I doubt whether it has been retained,' said Dame Beatrice. 'Mrs Schumann wrote this note to my French maid and it was delivered by hand by being pushed underneath the kitchen door.'

'Why should she write—? Oh, to your *French* maid!'

'Exactly.'

'Well, let's hope she did keep it, although I agree it's rather unlikely. What was the note about?'

'It was an invitation to take tea at the cottage.'

'Good Lord! Of course your maid did not go, otherwise I don't think you would still have her with you. But what a risk for Mrs Schumann to take! If your maid was known to have gone to the cottage and later turned out to have been strangled, we should have had an open and shut case!'

'I am sorry to disappoint you, but I confess that I would rather have Celestine than any number of open and shut cases. But let us find out whether she has indeed kept the letter. Of course, it will be smothered in finger-prints by this time. Not only Celestine herself, but her husband Henri and my chauffeur George are certain to have handled it.'

'The same holds good about the letter asking for the advertisement to be inserted in the Swansea newspaper, but that won't fox the boys at the Yard. If Mrs Schumann's prints are there, they'll find them, and if they're on both letters I should say we've got her, and when we've got her I'll have the husband's body exhumed and we'll find out exactly what he died of. If he had these internal pains and vomited and so forth, it sounds quite a bit like arsenic, administered over a long period of time – several months, according to James, wasn't it?'

'Of course, even if you find the same prints on both letters, you will still have to prove that they were made by Mrs Schumann.'

'We'll find some way of getting round that one, Dame Beatrice, never you fear. May we have your maid in now?'

Celestine, who usually received visits to Dame Beatrice by the police with a metaphorically arched back and claws at the ready, succumbed at once to Maisry's gentleness and charm. No, she was desolated, but what did one do with old letters except throw them away? She had not dreamed that the note was important, although she deprecated the lack of taste in the writer to invite her, the servant of madame, to take tea with one of madame's friends.

'Acquaintances,' amended Dame Beatrice. Celestine accepted the correction with a toss of the head and replied that perhaps 'guest at the table' would be an accurate description. Dame Beatrice accepted this, said it was a pity that the note had been thrown away, but that, of course, nobody had known it would have importance for the police, and dismissed her.

'Pity,' said Maisry, 'but one couldn't have expected anything else. Oh, well, we shall have to find another line of country if we want to proceed in the direction of Swansea.' He had risen to go when there came a respectful tap on the door.

'That sounds like George,' said Dame Beatrice. 'The indoor servants do not knock.'

It was indeed the chauffeur although, as it was his afternoon off, he was not in uniform but was wearing a grey suit of respectable cut and a rather natty light-blue shirt with an orange-coloured tie.

'Excuse me, madam,' he said, 'but I'm told you would be requiring the note which Mrs Schumann sent to Madame Lemaître. I have it here.' He produced it from behind his back and offered it to Dame Beatrice.

'Celestine told us she had thrown it away,' said Dame Beatrice, taking the envelope and handing it to Maisry.

'There not being a fire in the kitchen owing to clement weather at the time, madam, Madame Lemaître tossed it into the small rubbish bin with the lid which can be manipulated by a pressure from the foot. Having my own ideas about the letter, I offered to empty the little receptacle into the dustbin instead of Zena going out in the dusk with it, her being nervous about these murders, and, out of sight of the kitchen window, I abstracted the letter and have retained it.'

'Wonderful, George, but why?'

'It struck me as a rather peculiar letter, madam, for a lady who had sat at your table to write to one of your domestic staff.'

'How right you are, George, as always. This letter is going to prove helpful to Detective-Inspector Maisry.'

'Mighty helpful,' said Maisry. 'Now we really can get cracking,' he added, when George had gone. 'I'm sorry your Chief Constable has tied Phillips up with another case. He'd be interested in this fingerprint business. It may give us some concrete evidence at last, and we could certainly do with some. Of course, if it goes blue on us we may have to go back to my idea that we are looking for more than one murderer.'

'But you no longer think there are three?'

'Oh, no. I've washed young Schumann right out of it. James is the nigger in the woodpile. There's no doubt left in my mind that Mrs Schumann killed her daughter in order to get him, and did for Maria Machrado before she could vamp him – not that I should have said there was any fear of that!'

'Oh, I am sure there was not.'

'The trouble about this fingerprint business,' went on Maisry, more as though he were talking to himself than to Dame Beatrice, 'is the fact that these are on paper. I'm not a fingerprint expert – that's for the backroom boys in the forensic laboratory – but I do know enough to realise that whether we have any luck or not depends very largely on the absorbent properties of the paper she used. She was cagey enough not to use the same kind for both letters. This one is on a white unlined sheet. The one in our previous possession, the one she sent to the newspaper, is also on unlined paper, but the colour is light blue and the sheet is a different size. That, in itself, won't matter a bit, so long as the prints correspond, but, at this lapse of time, we'll be lucky to get any identifiable prints

G

on either document, and, anyway, one is of no use without the other.'

'You mean that paper, being an absorbent material...'

'Exactly. Everybody's fingers perspire to a certain extent, and, after a time, the damp from those fingers impregnates the paper and makes the prints useless from the point of view of identification. If this has happened on these letters, cold iodine fumes may be the answer. Anyway, now we know who she is, we'll nobble her one way or another.'

'I'm doubtful whether Mrs Schumann will have left finger-prints on those letters, anyway,' said Laura, when she and her employer were discussing Maisry's visit. 'If *I'd* been in her place, I should have rested my hand on blotting-paper when I wrote to the newspaper, and then put on thin gloves before I folded the letter and stuck it in the envelope. As for the letter to Celestine, it wouldn't matter how many of her prints were on that. She signed it in her own name, and there's never been any query as to where it came from. So long as the same prints are not on both letters, she's as safe as houses.'

'Houses have been known to be undermined,' said Dame Beatrice, 'but I confess that my faith in the fingerprint clue is less strong than it was.'

There was no fingerprint clue. There were no fingerprints except those of the office staff at Swansea on the letter whose advertisement the unfortunate Irish girl had answered, and of the advertiser's reply to her there had never been any sign, for, except for the half of the return ticket to Swansea which at first had seemed a valuable piece of evidence, her sodden handbag had been found empty. Police, assisted by willing helpers from among the campers who had been staying in the vicinity of the pond in which the victim had been found, dis-covered the girl's suitcase about a mile and a half from the body. It had been hidden at the entrance to a culvert which bridged a stream.

The girl's landlady in Swansea identified its contents as having been those of her lodger, but nothing was found which could provide a pointer to the killer. The letter which, pre-sumably, had caused the girl to travel to Hampshire, must have been in the handbag and was never found.

(3)

'Well,' said Maisry, reporting the failure of his mission to the Chief Constable, who had been dining with Dame Beatrice, 'I'm afraid there's nothing for it but the exhumation. We're not likely to get her on any other charge, so far as I can see.'

'I don't like exhumations,' said the Chief Constable, 'but if you and Dame Beatrice are sure of your facts, we certainly can't allow this maniac to go on indiscriminately murdering innocent girls and women.'

'Indiscriminately is not quite the right word,' said Dame Beatrice. 'She *does* discriminate. Her victims have to become part of a pattern. As to her being a maniac, that will have to be decided later.'

'Well, you can't say that her behaviour is normal, my dear Beatrice.'

'Neither was that of Florence Nightingale, Elizabeth Fry and Joan of Arc – not that I am making any real comparisons, of course.'

'I should hope not, indeed! '

'My point is that abnormal behaviour, which, I take it, means beyond that which would generally be expected, seemingly beyond the scope of the general run of women – is not necessarily an indication of insanity. In any case, I doubt very much whether Mrs Schumann is insane in the legal sense. I am perfectly certain that she knew what she was doing when she did it, and that she knew that it was wrong.'

'If she murdered her husband, though, that would not conform to the pattern to which you referred. Whatever happened to him, he certainly was not garrotted and then strangled. The doctor would have noticed it' – he smiled ironically – 'if that had been the case. Besides, all the other victims have been women. It doesn't add up.'

'Oh, I think it might. Herr Schumann was killed to leave the way for her to marry James.'

'But James preferred the daughter,' said the Chief Constable.

'Yes, but he only became engaged to her in order to choke the mother off, it seems,' said Maisry. 'Putting two and two

together, as Dame Beatrice and I have done, there could have
been no commitment to the daughter until James realised that,
in spite of his expressed distaste for her advances, Mrs Schumann was still determined to pursue him. We believe that she
continued with this campaign, even after he had announced his
engagement to the daughter, and I personally think – and Dame
Beatrice upholds my opinion – that on the day of Karen Schumann's death there was a show-down between her and her
mother, and Mrs Schumann, long the toad under the harrow in
what, to her, must have been a depressing household, went
berserk and murdered her daughter. She half-strangled her in
the cord of the dog-whistle and then (in a panic, most likely)
finished the job off.'

'Then, you mean, she set about diverting suspicion from herself by moving the body and leaving the message which was
found on it? I see.'

'There was no fake about the message,' said Maisry. 'She'd
been told by her daughter that James had once called her a
misguided little Arian. She told Dame Beatrice so, in order
to direct suspicion towards James for daring to prefer her
daughter to herself. At least, that's the way it looks.'

'It sounds quite feasible, I suppose.'

'Everything else follows from it. Machrado seems to have
been, well, a trifle kittenish with James in Mrs Schumann's
presence, and that led directly to her death. Again, the note
left on the body was intended to incriminate James. "Hell
hath no fury", you know, sir.'

'Quite. But, of course, Phillips strongly suspected James at
first, you know. You are certain, I suppose, that he is cleared?
You see, even if we get permission to exhume Herr Schumann's
body – and that may not be easy – it seems to me there is
nothing to prove that, *if* Schumann was murdered, and ten
to one you'll find no indication of that, you know, James isn't
just as likely to have done it as the widow. You seem, if I
may say so, to have swallowed his story hook, line and
sinker, but there's no more proof that he *didn't* commit all
these murders as that Mrs Schumann *did*. What do you say
to that?' He looked at Dame Beatrice. She replied:

'There is one point – I will not call it proof – which indicates that James was not responsible. Once we had traced the source of the messages – that is to say, once we had worked on the connection between the nationalities of the victims and the heresies implicit in the numerals which formed part of the messages – it became so unlikely that James would have given such a pointer to himself that my own always very slight suspicions of him vanished.'

'The murderer, whether it was Mrs Schumann or not, could hardly have thought it likely that you would trace any connection between the dates on the messages and the heresies with which they were connected.'

'It took us some time to trace the connection, of course, but time was on the murderer's side in the sense that, the greater the number of deaths she could bring about, the greater the chances became that we should come to the conclusions which, in the end, we *did* come to, and that those conclusions would automatically implicate James because of his studies in theology.'

'I still can't see why they don't,' said the Chief Constable discontentedly. 'Well, if you're both set on having Schumann's body disinterred, we'd better get on with it. You'll have to back me up, Beatrice, you know, if the powers that be are going to allow us to do it.'

'As to why they do not implicate Edward James,' said Dame Beatrice, 'there is the almost unassailable evidence of the dog-whistle which lured away Laura's wolf-hound and led him to find the body of Karen Schumann.'

'Be that as it may,' said the Chief Constable, 'I propose to leave no stone unturned before we actually get to the stage of approaching the Home Secretary for an exhumation order. As I see it, we ought to get in touch with the doctor who issued the death certificate, and ask him a question or two, before we do anything so drastic as desecrating a grave. I don't care for the idea of that at all. There is no connection whatever between murdering a man by poison and strangling several young women. We shall need safer ground to tread on than we've got at present before we proceed to extremes.'

'Very well, sir,' said Maisry. 'It is always a good idea to take precautions. The only trouble is that in taking precautions we're also taking up time. We don't want another young woman to be murdered.'

'Quite, quite. So you'd better get cracking, what?'

(4)

The doctor was not pleased.

'But, my dear chap,' he said to Maisry, 'if there had been the least thought in my mind that there was anything suspicious in Schumann's dying like that, I should have been on to you fellows at once.'

'Yes, of course,' said Maisry. 'Still, you would have had to be *very* certain before you came to us, wouldn't you?'

'Well, one has to think of one's other patients, you know. I mean, I myself am absolutely convinced, as I was at the time, that Schumann's death was a perfectly natural one, given the circumstances of his illness, although I'll admit I had not expected him to succumb to it like that, but, for the sake of argument, suppose I'd refused to issue a certificate and had called for an inquest, and then, when all the proceedings were over, nothing out of the ordinary had been found wrong with the poor chap, what do you suppose would have been the effect on my other patients and, particularly, on their relatives? Nobody is going to trust a doctor whose aim and object seems to be to suspect that the family corpses have been poisoned! If it will help to clarify the thing in your mind, I can lend you the case-notes, always remembering, if you'll forgive my mentioning it, that they are highly confidential.'

'I'd prefer a résumé of them, if you don't mind, sir,' said Maisry, taking out his notebook, 'because, although I'll bear in mind that they are of a confidential nature, I'll need to discuss them with the Chief Constable and with Dame Beatrice, and there are things my own notes can tell me better than a verbatim report, which, as we have your permission, sir, is also being taken.' He nodded towards the corner of the room where his shorthand-writing sergeant was busy.

'I see. Oh, well, then, half a minute.' The doctor rang the bell for his receptionist. 'Hope you needn't keep me too long. I've evening surgery at half-past six and a confinement lying in wait over at Burley. Oh, Miss Warner, will you look up *Schumann, Heinrich Otto,* and bring it in here?'

The case-notes were perfectly straightforward. Heinrich Schumann had suffered for two years from gastric trouble and had brought with him from his previous doctor, now retired from practice, a history of this illness which dated from 1939, the year, Dame Beatrice noted, in which Schumann had lost his job. So far, so good. It was not at all unlikely that the shock and, as he must have seen it, the unfairness of his dismissal from his school, would have brought on an anxiety neurosis with its physical complement of an ulcerated stomach.

'I don't see anything in this which would justify me in asking for an exhumation order,' said Maisry unhappily. 'The illness seems to have taken a normal course, doesn't it?'

'So far as was known, yes. Would you care to ask what use veterinary surgeons make of something they call butter of antimony?' suggested Dame Beatrice.

'Antimony? You still think Schumann was poisoned, then?'

'There have been similar cases. Proof, admittedly, is difficult, but there is a remarkable similarity between the course of Schumann's illness and that of a certain Mrs Ann Smith, who came to Liverpool from Devonshire and lived on Merseyside with various relatives and a man named Winslow who acted as manager of some rooms above the shop and restaurant. These rooms were let to members of the family and to other lodgers. To summarize the story, it is only necessary to say that, after a comparatively short time, Mrs Smith's sister's husband, a certain Mr Townsend, and two of his sons, died.

'After this, the man Winslow seems to have acquired some sort of ascendency over Mrs Smith, so that, in the end, she was persuaded to leave the stock and goodwill of her business to him. Previously, when she first became ill, she had given him written authority to withdraw money from her Savings Bank. Other attempts on his part to possess himself of what she owned were disallowed, however. Now the similarity between her case and that of Heinrich Schumann is this: both were known to have been suffering from stomach ulcers. Neither, however, should have suffered such deterioration in health as to die of the illness so soon. In the case of Mrs

Smith it was found that somebody – the evidence, although strongly presumptive against him, was not sufficient to convict Winslow – had been administering small doses of antimony to her over a period of time, and so had hastened, if he had not actually caused, her death.

'Further, the poisoner Pritchard also used antimony to ensure the deaths of his wife and his mother-in-law, and Chapman, otherwise known as Klosowski, murdered three women by administering tartarised antimony, again over a period of time.

'Now it is clear to me that Heinrich Schumann's doctor did not expect him to die when he did. The treatment shown in these case-notes was the correct one for an ulcerated stomach such as the doctor describes, and it is clear that the patient responded satisfactorily to it until a few months before his death. All the same, the doctor had no suspicion that anything untoward was going on, but, bearing in mind the two cases I have cited, I think we will proceed with the exhumation. If nothing is found, so well and good, although not for my reputation, but if we find traces of antimony, then there will be a *prima facie* case, I think, against Mrs Schumann.'

'If there *is* antimony in Schumann's body, you think it was administered in the form of a purge for dogs, then?'

'Well, Mrs Schumann is not a qualified veterinary surgeon, of course, but, no doubt, as a breeder of dogs, she has learned ways of avoiding the expense of calling on professional assistance. I shall be interested to see the body when it is disinterred.'

'Its state of preservation, you mean, Dame Beatrice?'

'Yes. In spite of the fact that Chapman's first wife had been dead for five years when the body was exhumed from a common grave, it was in an excellent state of preservation. So were the remains of the second wife, after two years.'

'Schumann has been dead just over five years,' said Maisry. 'I think I'll be rather interested to see the body, too, but I do hope you're right, otherwise it'll be the back of the Chief Constable's hand to me, to borrow an expression from our cousins in Eire. I wonder when Phillips will be back on the job with me? He'd like to be in on the findings, if there's going to be an autopsy.'

CHAPTER EIGHT

Come Away, Come Away, Death

'He's dead as a rat on the store-room floor . . .
Oh, we say so, oh, we hope so!
He's dead as a rat on the store-room floor.
He won't never come back to us no more . . .
Oh, poor old Joe!'

---

(1)

'Antimony in all the parts examined,' said Maisry, 'and the body so well preserved, even after more than five years, that you can hardly believe it. It seems ridiculous that we can't pin the girls' deaths on her, but we shall question her about poor Schumann, and James will be questioned, too, of course, although she's obviously the one who could have got hold of the poison, even if James administered or helped to administer it.'

'Does James have to be brought into it?' asked Laura.

'I only said we should question him, Mrs Gavin. In fact, we're going to get his story first, before we tackle Mrs Schumann.'

'I don't believe he's guilty and, if he's brought to trial, it will ruin his career, you know.'

'We wouldn't want that, if he's innocent, of course, and he can have a solicitor present at the interview, as I expect he knows.'

James declined to do this.

'I don't know why you think I can help you,' he said. 'On the other hand, I have nothing to hide.'

'You say that you were not surprised when Heinrich Schumann died.'

'Why should I have been? People as ill as he was do die ultimately, some sooner and some later.'

'Are you surprised to hear that his death was brought about by poison?'

185

'By poison? You mean he committed suicide?'

'No, we think he was murdered.'

'Murdered? Oh, that's fantastic!'

'Antimony is not a suicide's poison, Mr James, and the particular form of it, *liquor antimonii chloride*, which we think was used in this case, is even more unpleasant to take than tartar emetic, *antimony potassium tartrate*. No, Mr James, it wasn't suicide. The antimony was given to Heinrich Schumann in small doses over a period of time without his knowledge or consent, and, in the end, it killed him.'

'He suffered from extreme sickness and diarrhoea, with severe abdominal pains, and was under constant supervision and treatment by the doctor. Surely, if he was being slowly poisoned, the doctor would have realised it?' said James.

'The use of antimony by murderers is extremely rare, and, as is the case with arsenic, the symptoms are similar to those of other illnesses. For instance, in the case of Chapman (real name Klosowski) his first wife was said to have died of tuberculosis, the second of intestinal obstruction coupled with the same symptoms as you yourself witnessed in the case of Schumann, and the third woman (he wasn't married to her) was thought to have died of tuberculous peritonitis. There was every excuse for Schumann's doctor to overlook the possibility that he was being poisoned, although a smarter man might have suspected it, I suppose.'

'But – antimony! Wouldn't you have to sign a book before a chemist would let you have stuff like that?'

'There is a substance used by veterinary surgeons known as antimony butter.'

'I don't question that, but I am not a vet.'

'No, but Mrs Schumann was a breeder of dogs.'

'You mean she might have had a legitimate use for this stuff? What is that to me? I know nothing about dogs. I don't even like them.'

'Do you deny that you knew Mrs Schumann had this compound in her cottage?'

'Most certainly I deny it. I took no interest in her work with her animals. It was her husband who was my friend.

Our interests were identical, and I was extremely sorry when he became ill and subsequently died. I missed his companionship and I found his mind stimulated mine. He was a very great loss to me.'

'Yes,' said Maisry. 'Did he raise any objection when you became engaged to his daughter?'

'I was not engaged to her during his life-time.'

'Because you knew he would object?'

'No. She was too young, that is all.'

'Did you know that your school secretary, Mrs Clancy, had an Italian maid?'

The sudden change of questioning, part of Maisry's technique, did not appear to disconcert James. Looking slightly surprised, but in no way put out, he replied,

'But I thought the woman had been murdered.'

'Please answer my question, Mr James.'

'Oh, I see, yes. I suppose everybody on the staff knew about her. The women gossip and chat about their small concerns all day long, and Mrs Clancy always took the break-time tea with us.'

'Did you ever talk about her servant to anyone?'

'Not that I remember. I wasn't interested.'

'You don't remember mentioning her to Mrs Schumann?'

'Oh, that!'

'What, Mr James?'

'Why, Mrs Schumann was always very anxious to sell her puppies, of course. It was her livelihood, so occasionally she would ask me whether there was anybody new on the staff and, if there was, she would want to know whether they would like to buy a dog – a clumber spaniel if it was to be a pet, or a wolfhound if they wanted something to frighten away tramps or burglars or people selling things at the door.'

'And you obliged by passing on the message?'

'I? Oh, no. I wasn't her errand boy. Karen used to make the enquiries for her, I believe.'

'Ah, yes, of course. Mrs Clancy had had the Italian maid for some time before Miss Schumann's death.'

'As a matter of fact, now I come to think of it, I remember that Karen did approach Mrs Clancy about buying a dog, because the bungalow she lived in was so isolated, but Mrs Clancy said she was never alone in the place.'

'And when Mrs Castle came on to the school staff, did you mention her to Mrs Schumann?'

'No.'

'Then how did they come to be acquainted?'

'I had no idea that they were acquainted. That is news to me. I was not aware that they had ever met. All I know is that Mrs Schumann said to me that she supposed the school would have to find someone to fill Karen's place, as, of course, was obvious. We could not, at a comprehensive school, do without a teacher of modern languages.'

'Did the two young ladies who lodged with Miss Schumann and, later, with Mrs Castle, have any connection with Mrs Schumann?'

'I believe Karen sometimes asked them to Saturday tea at the cottage, if you call *that* having a connection.'

'But you know of no connection between Mrs Castle and Mrs Schumann?'

'You are putting a very strange and unpalatable idea into my head, Inspector.'

'Surely not,' said Maisry, in his gentle voice. 'I think the strange and unpalatable idea has been in your head for some time, Mr James.'

(2)

It was arranged that Phillips should make the arrest. A warrant was obtained and he drove over to Mrs Schumann's cottage to discharge it, only to find the place empty. He first knocked several times, and then hammered on the door. As these actions provoked no response, he peered in at each window in turn. Everything was tidy and in place. He found a ladder in an outhouse and climbed it to look in at the bedroom windows, but there was nobody at home. He came again in the afternoon and at six o'clock on the following morning. Still unable to gain admittance by fair means, he broke a window and climbed into the kitchen. From here he made a tour and a search of the whole cottage. The absence of any article of clothing and of any form of luggage indicated that the occupant had flown. The barking of the dogs made him think of feeding them, but there was nothing to be found but a quantity of dog-biscuit, so he gave them that and some water and let them out into the yard for exercise.

There were only five of them, a clumber spaniel bitch, two dogs of the same breed, and a wolfhound dog and bitch. There was at first no sign of any puppies, but, strolling around while the dogs were loose in their paddock, he came upon a small pond, and what had happened to the puppies was obvious. He raked out the little bodies and buried them, then he went back to the paddock and shut the dogs up again in their new and expensive quarters.

'I don't know what we can do about them,' he said to Dame Beatrice and Laura. 'We've put a dragnet out for Mrs Schumann, of course. I suppose James tipped her off that we were on her trail. It's a nuisance, but we're bound to find her sooner or later. The fact that she's taken all her clothes doesn't make it look as though she's contemplating taking her own life. We shall continue to watch the cottage, of course, but I think it's a case of locking the stable door after the horse has been stolen. The car is still there, but I'm surprised, though, at her leaving the dogs like that, although I suppose she couldn't have taken five of them with her.'

'They'd have been rather a give-away, apart from anything else,' said Laura. 'It's beastly about the puppies, but if she hadn't drowned them they might have starved, which would have been even worse.'

'Or the dogs, if nobody fed them, might have eaten them,' said Phillips.

'Well, I'll feed the dogs,' said Laura. 'I'll drive over every day. It can only be once a day, but they'll manage if I make it a substantial meal, I think.'

'You'll look out for yourself, then, Mrs Gavin, won't you? If she *should* turn up again, she'll likely be a very dangerous customer.' Phillips looked at Dame Beatrice, but she said nothing. 'You'll take Fergus with you, I hope.'

'Hardly!' said Laura. 'Considering that she lured him away from me after her daughter's death, he isn't likely to take my part against her.'

'We will both feed the dogs,' said Dame Beatrice suddenly. 'Fergus cultivates my friendship and I think he might ally himself with me, even against his former owner.'

'The thing is,' said Laura, 'will he ally himself with the other dogs, or will they go for him? If we keep him with us we run the risk of having him mauled, and if we shut him in the car he's no use to us as a guard.'

'Then we will leave him at home,' said Dame Beatrice. 'It is in the highest degree unlikely that Mrs Schumann will return to the cottage if she has decamped with all her personal effects, and, even if she does, I think Laura and I, between us, can manage her.'

'Well, as I say, we shall keep watch on the cottage,' said Phillips, 'so you should be all right. If you're willing to feed the poor beasts, that's fine.'

(3)

The drag-net put out by the police for Mrs Schumann met at first with no success. Her description was circulated to all police stations and to ports and airfields, but either she had gone to ground successfully in England or she had made a clean getaway to West Germany, where she was known to have a sister.

'We've sent a description to Interpol,' said Maisry, 'and we've arrested James as an accessory after the fact, because, unless he tipped her off, it's very odd that she should have slipped through our fingers like this. All the same, to hunt for a woman who must bear a resemblance to about half the West German housewives and who has the name Schumann, well, it's probably like looking for a man over here who is wearing a raincoat and a trilby and whose name is Thompson or even Smith.'

'We know she has a sister in Germany because she came over here to stay a week or two. I expect the son, Otto Schumann, knows the address,' said Dame Beatrice. Otto, whose ship put into Southampton at the end of the following week, denied all knowledge of his aunt's address.

'I believe she did stay with my mother for a week or so,' he said. 'But I was at sea at the time and I've never even met my German relatives and haven't the vaguest notion where they live, except that it must be in West Germany, because, if they were East Germans, I don't suppose my aunt would have been allowed to come over here.'

As it was impossible to prove whether or not he did know his aunt's address, his statement had to be accepted and the search for Mrs Schumann went on. The police watched the cottage for a full month and then, feeling that this was a waste of man-power, they called off the precaution and Laura and Dame Beatrice, briefed to report any suspicious occurrence, continued to feed the dogs every day.

This went on until Hamish, Laura's son, was due to come home from school for his summer holiday. Laura, while fully appreciating that the teachers needed this break, felt, as she herself expressed it, sick and faint at the thought of having her son for the best part of nine weeks. As she had sent him to her parents for the Easter recess, she felt that something different must be done for him in the summer. A fortnight of the time would be accounted for by a school camp in the Dolomites, but that still left more than six weeks, two before the Continental holiday and four and a half after it was over, to be passed in some way or ways which would keep a lively boy from boredom and, consequently, out of mischief.

Gavin, at his son's urgent request, picked Hamish up at school on breaking-up day.

'For there's not much point in having a father who is an Assistant Commissioner at Scotland Yard if the chaps don't get a good few looks at him, and quite often you can't get along for school things – the sports and so on – like other fathers,' wrote Hamish. 'Can you come in a police car and have a policeman driver who will open the car door for you and give a crashing great salute when you get out? Canby's father is a brigadier, but he only comes in a perfectly ordinary Bentley and not even a chauffeur to drive it, so if you *can* come in style it will be marvellous, and be no end of a credit to me.'

Gavin, however, turned up in a 'perfectly ordinary' Humber, self-driven and without a single uniformed constable on the horizon, and, having made arrangements to have the pony transferred from the riding-stables, where it was kept during term-time, to the Stone House, Wandles Parva, he drove his son home and stayed the night.

The news that Laura and Dame Beatrice were feeding five dogs, apart from Fergus and his now firmly-established pet, the Yorkshire terrier presented to him by his headmaster's wife at Easter, reconciled Hamish to his father's failure to provide pomp and circumstance, and he immediately offered to take the task of feeding Mrs Schumann's dogs off their hands. To this Laura could not agree, neither was she prepared to disclose her reason for not accepting the proposal. She hedged by saying that she had become very much attached to Mrs Schumann's dogs, but that he might accompany her each day if he so wished.

'But where *is* Mrs Schumann?' he asked.

'Away from home for a bit,' Laura replied. She did not add that, but for this fact, she would not have allowed Hamish to stay at the Stone House.

'Oh, gone on holiday, you mean,' said Hamish, accepting the situation as he saw it. 'How long will she be away?'

'We don't know. She doesn't know, either.' This was the truth, so far as it went, for she would be away, presumably, until the police found her. 'By the way, I don't want you to go riding alone during these holidays.'

'Why ever not, mamma? I shall be all right.'

'All the same, I'd rather you didn't.' Wherever Mrs Schumann was, there was no excuse for failing to take precautions. 'I'm in, well, rather a nervous state, and I should worry all the time.'

Hamish gazed at her with respect and awe.

'I say, you're not going to have a *baby*, are you?' he demanded.

'Stranger things than that have happened,' said Laura.

'Oh, then, *of course* you must have your own way! And in *everything*! Does my father know?'

'I haven't told him yet.'

'Does Mrs Dame know?'

'I haven't told her yet, either – well, not definitely.'

'Then do you mean that I'm actually the first person – *the very first* – to be told? Oh, mamma, how absolutely *great*! But why haven't you told people?'

'Because I can't be absolutely sure until I've seen the doctor again.'

'But, mamma, it's wizard! Do you want a boy or a girl?'

'I don't much mind. Which do *you* want?'

'I don't really mind, either. I say! I shall be old enough to be its uncle, shan't I?'

After this, there were no arguments about his not being allowed to go riding in the Forest on his own. The pony was put out to grass, and any riding which Hamish did was in the field attached to the Stone House grounds. Every day, after tea, he and Laura, accompanied by Dame Beatrice, Fergus and Lindy Lou, drove over to Mrs Schumann's cottage to give her dogs food and fresh water, the huge wolfhound and the tiny terrier remaining in the car with Dame Beatrice while Laura and Hamish carried out their errand of mercy.

The climax to all this came in the middle of the following week. The three had left the Stone House at just after a quarter past five, and as the car drew up outside the cottage Dame Beatrice said,

'I think I saw a large dog go into the woods about half a mile back. It looked, from the glimpse I had of it, remarkably like Fergus. I suppose, after they had had their run yesterday, the five dogs were safely fastened up again?'

'Oh, yes, they were,' said Hamish, who was on the back seat with Fergus and Lindy Lou. 'We both tried the doors. We always do. It wouldn't be at all the thing to let Mrs Schumann's dogs roam loose when she's trusted us to look after them.'

The polite fiction that Laura and Dame Beatrice had arranged with Mrs Schumann to feed and exercise the dogs while she was away from home had, of course, been allowed to stand.

'And they couldn't possibly get out on their own,' said Laura. 'It must have been someone else's dog you spotted.' She and her son left the car, carrying the food they had brought with them. Since Phillips had broken the kitchen window there was no difficulty in obtaining a supply of drinking-water for the dogs. Hamish climbed into the kitchen as usual and had unbolted the back door preparatory to emerging with an enamel pitcher filled with water from the scullery tap when he heard a shout and a horrid snarling noise.

He emerged to see his mother flat on her back outside the shed where the two wolfhounds were housed and, standing over her with all his hackles up, was an enormous, unkempt, cross-bred dog.

'Oh, mamma!' he cried, in fright and dire dismay.

'Don't come any nearer,' said Laura, calmly. 'He won't attack unless I try to put up a fight. Go back to the car as steadily and confidently as you can, and ask Mrs Croc. to get help. Don't hurry. Above all, don't run.'

Hamish did exactly as he was told, although his heart was thumping until it made him feel sick. He reached the car and said, in a voice which came out in a curious croaking tone,

'A big ugly dog has flown at my mother and knocked her down. He's standing over her with his teeth bared, and he's snarling like anything. She says he won't hurt her so long as she keeps still. She says will you go for help. Oh, Mrs Dame, dear, what on earth shall we do? Would Fergus tackle him?'

'I have no idea, and I do not think we will risk it,' said Dame Beatrice. She produced from a capacious skirt pocket a small, elegant, but sinister revolver. 'You had better stay here with the dogs. They may be alarmed when they hear the shot.' Her real reason was that she did not want the child to see the other dog killed.

(4)

'Well,' said Laura, 'that was quite an experience.' She switched on the engine and drove with apparent composure along the woodland track and on to the road which led ultimately to the Stone House.

'What happened exactly?' asked Dame Beatrice.

'Why, I went to open the wolfhounds' shed, as usual, but the door stuck, so I gave it a bit of a kick. It flew open, and, instead of Sean and Maire, a beastly great lurcher jumped straight out at me, full tilt, caught me off balance and ditched me. I realised that my only chance was to lie quite still and hope for the best. I didn't know you had your little gat with you. What a bit of luck!'

'Oh, I expect Mrs Dame always carries it in the Forest,' said Hamish, speaking airily to cover the fact that he had had a terrible fright. 'I don't know why, but I have a feeling that she does.'

'Oh, yes, there's been some rumour of a mad bitch roaming loose,' said his mother. 'That's why I said I was nervous about your riding in the Forest this holiday.'

'Oh? *Not* the other, then?'

'Well, I don't think *that*, in itself, would make me nervous, but it wouldn't be much fun having *that*, if anything happened to *you*, would it?'

'Of course, there is only one conclusion to be drawn from today's episode,' said Dame Beatrice, when Hamish had gone to bed.

'That there *is* a mad bitch loose in the Forest. Yes, I know,' said Laura, 'but if she's been in the Forest all this time – let's see – it must be the best part of six weeks – where on earth can she have been hiding? I mean, the police have combed the country for her.'

'I do not think, (and I base my idea on the dog which, unfortunately, I had to destroy), I really do not think that she has been at any great distance from her cottage. She has been overlooked, in fact, because she was so near to it.'

'But she'd have to eat. Surely, with her description circulated as widely as it has been, somebody would have spotted her and given her away, *wherever* she's been hiding?'

'I can think of an explanation and I have just passed it on to Detective-Inspector Maisry over the telephone. He has announced his intention of discussing it with Superintendent Phillips. I think it possible that she may have been staying at a gipsy encampment. There are still gipsies in the Forest and they are the last people to mix themselves up with the police. Indeed, I am not at all sure that they read the newspapers or listen to the radio.'

Laura looked perplexed.

'Gipsy encampment?' she said. 'How do you make that out? She's the complete German housewife – clean, neat, tidy, house-proud. She'd never cast in her lot with the gipsies, surely? And, anyway, would they have her?'

'She may have shown them goodwill at some time, or, perhaps more likely, her husband did.'

'Allowed them to camp on some land belonging to the cottage, you mean? Well, that's possible, I suppose, but we've no knowledge that it was so, so where does your idea come from? Is it a shot in the dark?'

'Not altogether. The dog I killed was a lurcher, a type of animal, my reading informs me, which is widely used by poachers, and gipsies, in country districts, are inveterate poachers.'

'Where on earth did you read about lurchers, and relate them to poachers and gipsies?'

'My dear Laura! "A Pharaoh with his wagons coming jolt and creak and strain." '

'Oh, *Roundabouts and Swings*! "And keep that lurcher on the road, the gamekeepers are out!" ' Of course! Simple, when you come to think of it, but I must admit I didn't. Well, now, are the police still holding on to Edward James? It's a bit much, if all he did was to tell Mrs Schumann that he had been interviewed again by the police. You can't call *that* being an accessory after the fact! '

'So the magistrates thought. The Bench declined to commit him. They dismissed the case.'

'Good. By the way, I take it that we are going over to the cottage again to leave food for the dogs? I mean, if they've been turned loose, they'll come back to where they're accustomed to being fed.'

'Yes. I left the doors of the sheds wide open so that they could get to their bedding if they wished to do so, and you, I noticed, left them the food we had brought. A pity I had to shoot the other dog, but I felt that there was no alternative.'

'Yes, I was sorry about that, too – very sorry. Afer all, he was only doing his job as he saw it, I suppose.'

'A magnanimous observation on your part.'

'I suppose it *was* Mrs Schumann who shut him up there and let the other dogs loose?'

'Nobody else would have left such a booby-trap for us. I

hope the police have buried the poor thing. And now I do not wish to pry, but did I gather from something Hamish said—?'

'Yes, you did. I *think* it's so, but I have to see a doctor to get my diagnosis confirmed. I wasn't going to tell anybody until I was certain, but something I said seems to have caused Hamish to do an inspired bit of guessing. I wonder how soon the police will get hold of Mrs Schumann now that we can be pretty certain she's somewhere in the neighbourhood? You know, dreadful creature though she is, I hate to think of her being hunted down.'

Something in her voice made Fergus lift his noble head from its resting-place on Dame Beatrice's left instep. He rose, walked sedately across to Lindy Lou's basket, picked up the tiny creature – she was about the size of a small cat – and carried her by the scruff of her neck over to Laura. He deposited her in Laura's lap and, with great dignity, resumed his former position.

Lindy Lou climbed rapidly up Laura, gave her a swift lick on the cheek, walked round the back of her neck, descended by way of her right arm and, settling down on her lap with a sigh of pleasure, turned round twice and went to sleep.

'*Dogs!*' said Dame Beatrice suddenly. Laura, her hand almost covering Lindy Lou's small body, looked across at her employer and grinned.

'In the plural,' she said, indicating Fergus and Lindy Lou. 'One Irish wolfhound, one Yorkshire terrier. Saint Patrick converted the Irish, and Saint Hilda had a nunnery-cum-monastery at Whitby. Neither of these saints, however, was a heretic, so what, exactly, are you getting at?'

'I was not thinking in terms of Irish wolfhounds and Yorkshire terriers. Clumber spaniels, I think, might be very much nearer the mark. I must go and see Miss O'Reilly and Miss Tompkins. I wonder where they are living now?'

'Oh, the two girls who shared digs first with Karen Schumann and then with Mrs Castle? What on earth have they to do with clumber spaniels?'

'Time will show. Ring up Superintendent Phillips. If they have moved from Mrs Castle's house, he will have their present address. Better still, ask him whether he can spare the time to come and see me.'

(5)

'It's another link in the chain, ma'am,' said Phillips. 'Acting on your suggestion, we asked the two young ladies whether Mrs Castle had received any letters on Whit Saturday. She had. Miss O'Reilly collected the post, as she usually did, and sorted it out. She *thinks* there were two letters for Mrs Castle, and she *knows* there was one. She noticed it particularly, and remembers it, because it had been re-addressed from the school and was marked, *Please forward*. I then asked them whether Mrs Castle had ever mentioned to them that she thought of buying a dog, and Miss Tompkins said she certainly had, and added that she herself had said, "If an Irish wolfhound or a clumber spaniel would do, I know the very place. A girl we used to dig with, her mother breeds dogs, and Karen was always handing out sales talk in the staffroom and telling us that the dogs were pedigree animals, but that there would be a special price to members of the staff." '

'If the letter was addressed to Mrs Castle at the school, why did it need to be forwarded?' asked Dame Beatrice.

'I asked Miss Tompkins and Miss O'Reilly that. They said that the afternoon post reached the school at round about four o'clock, but that on the eve of a holiday the school breaks up at half-past three and everyone hurries away.'

'Then the fact that the sender of the letter asked for it to be forwarded may have significance.'

'Exactly, ma'am. It certainly must have come from somebody who knew the ways of the school.'

'I suppose Mrs Castle made no mention to the other two of what was in the letter?'

'No, it seems she didn't.'

'Well, when you find Mrs Schumann, Superintendent, ask her whether Mrs Castle wanted to buy an Irish wolfhound or a clumber spaniel.'

'That ought to shake her,' said Laura, when Phillips had gone. 'If she's guilty, that is.'

'Somebody was guilty of shutting up that savage dog, knowing that it would fly at the first intruder, and that the intruder would be either you or Hamish, or, possibly, myself,' said Dame Beatrice drily.

'You mean that Mrs Schumann has been keeping watch on us, and knew we fed the dogs?'

'It seems likely. Of course, we cannot be sure.'

'When they find her, I wonder which charge they'll prefer?'

'They will charge her with the murder of her husband, and Edward James will be called as a witness for the prosecution.'

'I don't envy him. He's had a pretty rough deal all along, unless he's as guilty as she is, and that is something which now, even at this stage, I can't believe, and you never have believed it, have you? Incidentally, why should she want to set that dog on us? Just a bit of bloody-mindedness, do you suppose?'

'It is difficult to think of any rational explanation, certainly, but, as we have good cause to suspect, Mrs Schumann is not a particularly rational woman.'

(6)

On the following morning Laura telephoned her husband. Maisry and Phillips had wasted no time, but by the time they reached the encampment the gipsies had gone, leaving the usual unlovely tokens of their sojourn. They were soon followed up, but Mrs Schumann was not with them and they refused to admit that she had ever sought their help.

Gavin came down to the Stone House, having decided to persuade his wife and Dame Beatrice to leave it and to stay in Kensington until Mrs Schumann had been apprehended.

'I'm taking Hamish back with me, anyway,' he said, 'and if you're going to have a baby, you're coming, too. Dame B. must please herself what she does, of course, but if my advice is asked I suggest that she joins us. I don't like the sound of this savage dog episode. The woman must realise that she's in for bad trouble and is out for her revenge and is reckless as to how she brings it about. These murders were obviously the work of a totally unbalanced person, and, in my opinion, her brain has now gone completely over the border and she is no longer responsible for her actions.'

'Take Laura and Hamish to London, by all means,' said Dame Beatrice, 'but my place is here. If we do – and we shall – track down this wretched creature, I shall be needed.'

'To certify her?' asked Laura. Dame Beatrice did not reply. 'Anyway, if you stay, I stay. I'm not going to leave you here alone.'

'I shall not be alone. There are four other people, two of them men, in the house, and, if you feel anxious about me, I will ask Superintendent Phillips to make this house his head-quarters while the search for Mrs Schumann goes on.'

'Will you really? Is that a promise?'

'If it will make you happier, yes, it is.'

'That's that, then,' said Gavin, greatly relieved, for he had occasionally experienced his wife's obstinate moods where Dame Beatrice was concerned. 'We'll push off tomorrow morning, if Laura can get the packing done today.'

At ten that evening he took Laura to bed, leaving Dame Beatrice to her notes and to the fourth chapter of a book she was preparing for publication. When Gavin was in London, Laura occupied a room next to that of her employer, but when Gavin stayed at the Stone House, he and his wife had a much larger room in another wing. Thus they were too far from the scene of her operations to hear Dame Beatrice leave her room at just before midnight and slip out of the house by a side door.

Forewarned, George had driven the car some distance down the road while the family and Dame Beatrice were at dinner, so that the sound of his driving it off so late at night conveyed nothing to Laura, half-asleep in her husband's arms, nor to Gavin, holding her close, nor to Hamish, fast asleep in the room next-door to theirs.

'Pull up well away from the cottage, George,' said Dame Beatrice. 'I am pretty sure she is there.'

'Then I will do myself the honour to accompany you, madam. Is she likely to be armed?'

'I think not. Accompany me, if you feel you must, but remain silent and invisible unless or until it is obvious that I need assistance. Indeed, it may be as well to have a witness to any conversation I may have with Mrs Schumann.'

'Have you your little gun, madam?'

'Yes, but I shall not use it against a woman.'

'Wouldn't hurt to let her know you've got it, madam.'

'If it proves necessary, I will take your advice.' They drove for the rest of the way in silence until Dame Beatrice said, 'About here, I should think, George'. George pulled up the car and handed her out. Then he followed her through a wicket gate and across the paddock where the dogs were let out for exercise. As they entered the long, untidy garden the dogs from their sheds near the cottage door set up a loud barking. 'So the animals are re-housed,' she remarked. 'Their noise should wake Mrs Schumann if she is asleep.'

This proved to be the case. As the two approached the back door of the cottage a bedroom window was opened and Mrs Schumann's voice was heard admonishing the dogs. Dame Beatrice said, loudly and clearly,

'Come down and open the door.'

'You!' cried Mrs Schumann. 'Go away! I wish nobody!'

'Did Mrs Castle come here to buy a wolfhound?' Dame Beatrice enquired.

'Go away! I set the dogs on you!'

'You set one dog on us, and it is dead.'

'You threaten me?'

'Or did Mrs Castle prefer a clumber spaniel?'

'You know it all, then?' said Mrs Schumann in an altered voice. 'Are you alone?'

'I am not accompanied by the police.'

'*Ach*, your police! Fools, all of them! Five of these silly girls I kill, and your police do nothing! I spit at your police!'

'I know you killed five women. What made you kill your husband?'

A stream of curses, in German, was the only answer to this question. Dame Beatrice waited for the screaming profanity to come to an end. Then she said,

'I have come to take you back home with me. In the morning you will be arrested and charged.'

Mrs Schumann laughed, an unpleasant sound.

'*Nein, nein!*' she shouted. '*That* for you and your police!

You think I shall come down? You think I shall walk into prison? Yes, then! I come down! I loose my dogs at you! They see you, they smell you, they kill you! You cannot see them to shoot them! Even if you shoot one, the others tear you in pieces before you shoot them all!'

'Come down, and let us see,' said Dame Beatrice.

'She means it, madam,' murmured George. 'We wouldn't stand much chance if she sicked all five of them on to us.'

The window was shut and a light went up in the room. George clutched the spanner he had brought from the car, and waited grimly beside his employer. The barking of the dogs had ceased at the sound of their owner's voice. Dame Beatrice walked over to the door of the shed which housed the two wolfhounds and spoke to them gently and softly in her beautiful voice. Then, before George realised what she was doing, she unlatched the shed.

'Meat!' she said. 'Come along.' It was the keyword which she and Laura had always used when they fed the dogs during the weeks that Mrs Schumann had been away from home. They followed her to the car, George and his spanner following close behind. He opened the door of the car and Dame Beatrice took a torch from her pocket and shone it on the meat she had taken from the back seat. She tossed it, wrapped in newspaper, on the ground. 'That will keep them happy for a bit,' she said. 'Come, George.'

They retraced their steps, carefully shutting the wicket gate behind them, and returned to the cottage. As they reached it, the back door was opened and Mrs Schumann stood there, framed against the light. In her hand she held a dog-whip. Dame Beatrice touched George's arm and they slipped behind a rhododendron bush. Apparently Mrs Schumann heard the slight sound.

'So – run!' she shouted. 'My dogs will soon catch you!'

(7)

'So she came along without trouble?' said Maisry. 'I can hardly believe it. She's been like a mad thing since you brought her here.'

'I think that, by this time, she probably *is* a mad thing,' said Dame Beatrice.

'Be a Broadmoor H.M.P. case, I suppose?'

'She was sane enough when she killed her husband and, in the legal sense, she is sane enough now to stand trial for murder.'

'How did you manage to get her here?'

'I think she was completely staggered when she opened the wolfhounds' pen and found that the dogs were gone. We took the opportunity of seizing her while her astonishment left her transfixed. She had no chance to resist. I held her left wrist and George her right and I think he twisted it to make her drop the dog-whip. I expect I could have managed her by myself, but it made matters easier and our progress back to the car decidedly more decorous, with him to help me.'

'What about the wolfhounds?'

'I called to them and they came, having finished the meat, so George kicked the wicket gate to behind them, and, although Mrs Schumann addressed them, they did not jump it. I must go over and see to them and the spaniels when you have done with me here. By the way, she made, in a boastful spirit, a full confession of her crimes while we were bringing her here in the car, but I doubt whether she will be equally obliging now that she is in the hands of the police. By her crimes, I mean the murders of the five women. Of her husband's death she said nothing.'

'Well, that's what she'll be charged with, because that's the one where our evidence is strongest. We shall put the doctor in the box and he will admit that the death was unexpected. Then, of course, we can trace the poison to her and James will testify to her proposals to him. She'll be asked, too, to explain her flight from her cottage and why she spent those weeks in a gipsy camp. What made you so sure she'd gone back to her home, by the way?'

'I thought she would need a roof over her head when the gipsies moved on and refused to take her with them.'

'You think they turned her out? She certainly wasn't in their camp when we went there. I think they must have had their suspicions of her, you know, when she bought that lurcher, and didn't want to get themselves tangled up with us. I still can't see why she took the risk of going back to her cottage, though. I should have thought she'd have attempted to get over to her relatives in Germany.'

'She may have decided that, after her attempt to set that dog on Laura, we should be too wary to go to the cottage again to feed the dogs.'

'She abandoned them quite callously when she went to live with the gipsies.'

'Ah, but she may have believed that, when it was discovered that she had left her home, the police would see that the dogs were cared for.'

'Well, so we should have done, had not you and Mrs Gavin offered to feed them. Did you – I mean, was there some feeling in your mind that she would come back to see how they were getting on?'

'I did not think she would leave the district without making certain that they would not starve. I think it must have broken her heart to drown those puppies.'

'Well, that's something to her credit. We shall bring her in front of the magistrates, and she will reserve her defence, I suppose. I wonder what it will be? Our case against her is reasonably strong, I feel, but it's going to be very difficult to prove that she actually administered the poison to her husband. I wish, really, that we could have got her on one of the stranglings. I thought we stood a chance with the Swansea case, but it went blue on us over those fingerprints.'

(8)

The defence was that Heinrich Schumann, depressed by the pain and inconvenience he had suffered from his illness, had decided to make an end of himself and had committed suicide. The defending counsel pressed the doctor hard, and he was compelled to admit that, until he had been informed of the result of the autopsy after the body had been disinterred, he had been fully convinced that the patient's death had been due to natural causes. Cross-examined as to the attitude of Mrs

Schumann to her husband's illness, he stated that it had always seemed to him sympathetic and kind.

Edward James was called for the prosecution, but, whether intentionally or not, made a bad witness and was cross-examined ruthlessly by the defence.

'Did the prisoner at any time tell you that she wished to be rid of her husband?'

'Not in so many words, no.'

'What made you think she wanted to marry you?'

'She said so.'

'In so many words?'

'Not exactly.'

'Did she say, "I want to marry you" – were those words used?'

'No. She said she loved me.'

'But not that she wanted to marry you?'

'That was implied.'

'But you were engaged to her daughter, were you not?'

'Not at the time of her husband's death.'

'Did she consent to your engagement to her daughter?'

'I suppose so.'

'Well, did she or didn't she?'

'She did not like it much.'

'How do you know?'

'She told me that her daughter would be unfaithful to me.'

'Then didn't that imply that she supposed the marriage would take place? You could not marry her *and* her daughter.' And so on and so forth, until James's replies came dangerously near self-contradiction.

'The jury don't like Edward James,' said Laura. 'I've got a feeling we are on the eve of an acquittal. Pity they didn't charge her with Karen Schumann's death. That dog-whistle evidence is foolproof.'

'I doubt whether it would have convinced a jury. In the present case,' said Dame Beatrice, 'the jury will have to believe that Heinrich Schumann died of poison, but the defence have probably succeeded in convincing them that the poison was self-administered. They have established that Heinrich must have known that "butter of antimony" was kept in the cottage as medicine for the dogs, and the doctor's evidence showed that Heinrich, although often very ill, was not always confined to bed.'

'In other words, if he really intended to swallow the stuff, he not only knew where it was kept but was able to get hold of it and help himself to a fatal dose. On the other hand, the doctor agreed that it was filthy stuff to take, and is a corrosive poison,' said Laura.

'Heinrich may not have been aware of those facts.'

'What happens if she is acquitted?'

'There is little to be gained by anticipating the verdict of the jury.'

There was no acquittal. The jury were out for less than an hour and the verdict of *Guilty* was unanimous. The summing-up by the judge had been fair and impartial and leaned, if anything, towards the case for the defence, so that the verdict was received by the knowledgeable with a good deal of comment and surprise.

It was some weeks later that an explanation came to light. Dame Beatrice was at a dinner-party given by her son, the eminent Q.C. Sir Ferdinand Lestrange, and found herself at table seated next to the man who had led for the prosecution. The talk between them led Dame Beatrice to ask which of his many cases he had been most surprised to win. He replied, without hesitation,

'Oh, Regina *v*. Schumann.'

'I was in court for that. She did do it, you know,' said Dame Beatrice.

'Yes, but I didn't believe we'd convinced the jury, and, actually, we couldn't have done – not on the evidence. The summing-up was fair enough, but I felt it went against us. The most I hoped for was a disagreement sufficient to make another trial necessary, and I didn't think we'd get any fresh material, at that.'

'Did you know what the foreman's profession was?'

'Yes. The defence knew it, too, and made no objection. In fact, they may have thought it an advantage to them, rather than the reverse. He was a vet.'

'Yes,' said Dame Beatrice. 'I was at Crufts last week. My

secretary was exhibiting her son's wolfhound and his Yorkshire terrier. I ran into this man and, of course, recognised him, and we talked about the trial. I asked him why the jury had convicted Mrs Schumann against the weight of the evidence. He said that he told them that the taking of antimony in any form was so unpleasant that no would-be suicide would have taken more than one dose of it, and that the medical evidence made it clear that small doses had been administered over a period of time. We ourselves had noted the same point, of course, but he appears to have insisted on elaborating it. What is more, he claimed that Mrs Schumann, because of her profession, would have known her husband was taking it, whether she had administered it or not, and therefore was certainly an accessory before the fact.

'His final argument had nothing to do with the case at all. He said, "Anyway, she killed her daughter, so we ought to get her for that".'

'Whatever made him think so? I remember reading something about it in the paper, now that you mention it,' said the barrister, 'but there was never any suggestion . . .'

'Mrs Schumann's photograph was published at the time of her daughter's death, and he recognised her when she stood in the dock. It appears that he had followed up the series of stranglings very closely, chiefly because of a sob-stuff article which had appeared in the press, giving a most moving account of the dog which had mounted guard over the daughter's body. Something about the story made him suspicious, he told me.

' "I traced the dog's history," he said. "You can always do that with these pedigree things. It was a very young dog and couldn't have been more than half-trained. It was reported that the body must have been dead for some hours when the dog found it, so it didn't find it on its own. It was taken there."

' "But not necessarily by Mrs Schumann," I argued. I was interested to hear what he would say to that.

' "Oh, I'm sure of it," he said. "The dead girl couldn't have whistled him up, and his new owner had only had him a few months, certainly not long enough to make him forget one call and learn another."

' "But that doesn't prove that Mrs Schumann killed her daughter," I said, anxious to pursue the argument.

' "Doesn't it?" he retorted. "Not if the daughter was in her way? Mrs Schumann wanted to marry that clot James, who was called for the prosecution and made such a mess of it!"

'I said that that was beside the point. Mrs Schumann had been tried for the murder of her husband, not for that of her daughter.'

' "Yes," he said, "but I don't like the name Schumann. They played him at my wedding, and I divorced my wife two years later. Anyway, that business of the dog-whistle damns her. The dog wouldn't have left his owner like that, unless he had recognised the call. Mrs Schumann had bred him – I found that out, of course – and the rest follows."

'I reminded him that the dead husband and dead daughter had also been called Schumann.

' "That's right," he said, "and if we hadn't abolished the law about hanging, this beauty would have been near enough dead, too, by now." I thought it better not to remind him that Otto was still alive.'

'Very odd, the way juries go about the business,' said the barrister. 'Very interesting, too.'

'There will be no appeal, I take it,' said Dame Beatrice. 'The defence can hardly claim that the jury was misdirected.'

MORE VINTAGE MURDER MYSTERIES

EDMUND CRISPIN

Buried for Pleasure
The Case of the Gilded Fly
Holy Disorders
Love Lies Bleeding
The Moving Toyshop
Swan Song

A. A. MILNE

The Red House Mystery

GLADYS MITCHELL

Speedy Death
The Mystery of a Butcher's Shop
The Longer Bodies
The Saltmarsh Murders
Death and the Opera
The Devil at Saxon Wall
Dead Men's Morris
Come Away, Death
St Peter's Finger
Brazen Tongue
Hangman's Curfew
When Last I Died
Laurels Are Poison
Here Comes a Chopper
Death and the Maiden
Tom Brown's Body
Groaning Spinney
The Devil's Elbow
The Echoing Strangers
Watson's Choice
The Twenty-Third Man
Spotted Hemlock
My Bones Will Keep
Three Quick and Five Dead
Dance to Your Daddy
A Hearse on May-Day
Late, Late in the Evening
Fault in the Structure
Nest of Vipers

MARGERY ALLINGHAM

Mystery Mile
Police at the Funeral
Sweet Danger
Flowers for the Judge
The Case of the Late Pig
The Fashion in Shrouds
Traitor's Purse
Coroner's Pidgin
More Work for the Undertaker
The Tiger in the Smoke
The Beckoning Lady
Hide My Eyes
The China Governess
The Mind Readers
Cargo of Eagles

E. F. BENSON

The Blotting Book
The Luck of the Vails

NICHOLAS BLAKE

A Question of Proof
Thou Shell of Death
There's Trouble Brewing
The Beast Must Die
The Smiler With the Knife
Malice in Wonderland
The Case of the Abominable Snowman
Minute for Murder
Head of a Traveller
The Dreadful Hollow
The Whisper in the Gloom
End of Chapter
The Widow's Cruise
The Worm of Death
The Sad Variety
The Morning After Death